I0581925

# Pigeon Falls

A NOVEL

## JEFF ELZINGA

WATER'S EDGE PRESS
TUCSON, AZ

Printed in the United States of America

Water's Edge Press LLC
Tucson, AZ
watersedgepress.com

ISBN: 978-1-952526-21-3
Library of Congress Control Number: 2024950452

Cover art and interior image by Reece Colberg
Epigraph is from the *Citizen Kane* screenplay ("Third Revised Final Draft") by Herman J. Mankiewicz and Orson Welles, in the public domain.

A WATER'S EDGE PRESS FIRST EDITION

For Chloe, Calvin, Ryan, Isabelle, and Eli
(when you're older)

It's no trick to make a lot of money…
if all you want… is to make a lot of money.

—Mr. Bernstein, *Citizen Kane*

# Contents

# Part One

## *Driftless*

## Thursday, October 31

Driving across the central plain of Wisconsin I pass dozens of old family farmsteads, many struggling to survive. On one side of the road a solitary tractor rusts in an unplowed field, its worn tires locked in what was. Across the way, a corporate mega-farm spreads out like a new college campus, its shiny roofs pointed towards what will be. Change in the heartland covers corn cribs like morning dew. It hangs from branches of dead ash like the memory of an abandoned dream. For the small farm families who've already given up, the tell-tale signs of surrender are easy to read: *For Sale, Auction, Foreclosure.*

High above US 10 and approaching the town of Fairview, a wedge of Canada geese is pointed south. The calendar says we're deep into autumn, yet my radio keeps boasting that Wisconsin is enjoying its longest second summer on record. Sometimes, it takes the behavior of other animals for us humans to understand what the sun's declining arc towards winter is trying to tell us. While summer warmth might still linger in the air in late October, the reality of winter is just around the corner. Watching the large flock of geese pass above me on their southward journey, I wonder what it would be like to travel up above everything like that, on an airy route that isn't defined by lane markers or gravel shoulders, where rest stops aren't pinned on a digital map.

Birds travel with fewer burdens than we do. They envision no vast intentional design upon the earth. They don't worry over the future of small farms or wonder who will repair the ancient barns crying out to be saved. Birds assign no greater purpose to life than to live for the day. And a bird's eye view, high above the countryside, recognizes neither symmetry nor disorder below, only random geometrical shapes reveled in myriad colors... which in Wisconsin in late fall, with farm fields at rest and forests in full autumn splendor, always spark red and gold.

As I leave US 10 at the Fairview exit and roll into this smallish city in Wisconsin's heartland, uncertainty slips in through my open window with the scent of burning leaves. I've come to Fairview not to worry over lost farmland or to watch migrating birds flying south, but because I've been fighting stomach pain since early summer. Fairview is home to the Fairview Clinic, a highly regarded medical facility.

This impressive fortress of grand buildings soon looms ahead of me. It's a complex larger than expected, rising out of a quiet neighborhood of older homes, and a destination all its own. The clinic's ample parking lots are coded in pastel colors. Each is laid out at the front of the renowned facility like a giant slice of asphalt pie. Taken together, the slices look like a seductive rainbow

Inside Building 7, I'm handed a stack of forms to fill in, details about insurance, next-of-kin, work history, lifestyle, diet. I'm weighed and measured, then led to an examination room, where a flock of medical staff in crisp white coats awaits me – three GI specialists, two medical students, one dietician, and a nurse practitioner. I sit half-naked on an orange plastic chair and thank everyone for giving me an appointment on short notice. Then, it's time to tell the story of me and my family.

Our history is no different from others', I say, good chapters and bad, lives lived and lost. "Yes, I'm divorced," I confess, "almost twenty years now." It's a memory from a lifetime ago that sometimes seems like only yesterday.

I then mention my mother, who died of lung cancer when I was twelve. My sister, a breast cancer survivor, whose life is racked with worry but still tumor free. And there's my father, his body and mind in decline after eighty durable years, who day after day still tempts fate with half a pack of Camels. I say to the crowded room, "My father claims he's never been sick a day in his life."

"Good genes," one specialist applauds with a knowing smile.

My father is a jokester, I admit, though the smoking part is true.

The nurse practitioner guides our conversation back onto a more serious track, remarking, "As for your mother and sister, cancer can be hereditary, you know. It's good at finding family weaknesses."

"Is that what you think I have?" I ask her, suddenly growing more anxious. "Cancer?"

A canyon-sized silence distances me from the medical team, until its leader, Dr. Welton, assures me, "That's not it at all, Tom. Let's not get ahead of ourselves. We have a lot of tests to run. What's bothering you could be anything."

Their diagnostic questions come like bricks laid carefully one atop another and meant to construct a patient profile or *platform*, as someone says. The dietician asks what I eat and drink. The female medical student asks the single question allowed her, "Mr. Bishop, what are your medications?" And Dr. Welton wants to know more about my mother.

The medical masonry goes on.

"Describe your bowel movements," says the nurse practitioner, as the interview rolls into its second half hour. Both medical students meticulously fill their over-stuffed notebooks. Finally, I'm asked about employment.

"I'm a surveyor," I say, proudly. "My company builds platforms too, the concrete kind that wind turbines stand on."

An hour into my interview, the team takes a short break. When they return, they have me sit on a table. Dr. Welton asks, "On a scale of one to ten, how bad is the pain?"

"Six," I say and explain it's not a hurt that keeps me from working, just a reminder that something's not right.

"Show us," he says. I make a line from below my rib cage to my groin. They have me lie flat, and everyone takes a turn pressing fingers into my abdomen. "On your CT scan from Rockford," says Dr. Welton, "there's shadowing around your intestines, but I can't feel anything unusual. We'll take some tissue samples while you're here." He consults a paper in front of him. "I see you've lost fourteen pounds since September."

"I always lose weight at the end of our work season. What do you *think* I've got, Doc?"

Dr. Welton calmly lists a number of possibilities and then says, "I understand you won't be back tomorrow to review your test results. You know, we can be here as early as eight." I tell them it won't work, that I can't return until next week. I apologize and explain that my job starts at dawn tomorrow, in a small town called Pigeon Falls, an hour from the clinic.

"Our company is pressed for time on this one," I add, as my hand reaches across my stomach to where the pressure has expanded. "We're taking advantage of the nice weather."

"That's fine, Tom. It's not a problem. We'll see you in a week."

The team files out of the room, and for the rest of the morning I'm x-rayed and scanned. Medical staff fill tubes with blood and measure my breathing, eyesight, and hearing. In the afternoon, a camera on a long cable is threaded down my throat, another one hunts from the other end. I ask the imaging technicians what they see, but they just shrug and smile. No one has anything official to report.

Exiting late afternoon through a maze of lively hallways, I'm greeted with passing bursts of "Howdy! Hello! Hi!" along with "Happy Halloween!" but these volleys of kindness elude me. My imagination has had all day to fester among the many possibilities Dr. Welton mentioned. Stomach ulcer, colitis, diverticulitis, Crohn's disease, pancreatitis, cancer, hernia, and other ailments I fail to recall.

The afternoon sun over Fairview is low and weak as I zig-zag out of town. Long shadows have crept across sidewalks and are bumping against curbs. Driving at dusk, with its shifting patterns of light and dark, has always been a challenge for me. Now, after an uncertain day at the clinic, I feel even more tentative behind the wheel. I still have an hour to go to reach Pigeon Falls, where our crew is assembling, but I'm having a tough time staying focused on the road.

Only a mile from the clinic, I pull to the side and turn on my radio. I find a station playing songs that my worries can get lost in, platinum hits from the '80s, '90s, and today. I roll down my window and find comfort in the warm in-coming air. Soon, I'm merging onto US 10 and back up to speed, the town of Fairview nothing but a hazy outline in my rearview mirror.

You might think with all the driving I've done over the years, much of it at night, I'd be tired of being on the road, that I'd want to stay put in a steady room somewhere, a quiet place closer to home, with a desk or workbench. Yet, the opposite is true. For the past fifteen years, the road has never grown old. There's always the feeling of freedom that comes from being behind a steering wheel, the anticipation of what lies ahead, the excitement of meeting new people and watching the landscape change. I enjoy spotting the latest models of cars and trucks passing by and look forward to sharing the ride with an ice cream or a cold drink.

But this afternoon, none of those joys appeal to me. I don't feel like traveling. I don't feel like meeting new people. I'm not sure what I'm feeling.

**Thirty minutes** from the clinic, I stop in Hillman, a crossroads colony with four gas stations guarding a cloud of stoplights. I wait with other vehicles for the light to change, as a parade of school busses crosses in front of us. School has just let out, which seems late in the day. I watch the swaying pods submerge left and right into the countryside, disappearing like an aging fleet of yellow submarines.

Minutes later, I trade the highway for a narrower county road. With the sun touching treetops now, the cloudless sky turns from sapphire to turquoise, with a darkening brush of cobalt blue expanding behind me in the east. The harvest in Wisconsin has already ended, so all that's left in the farm fields are tilled soil and the occasional pitch of withering cornstalks waiting to dry. At a fork in the road, I turn right, where the White Claw River comes in close along the gravel shoulder. Across the road, a scrum of heifers huddles in a pen of rusted wire, and down a ways, a *Going-Out-of-Business* sign has been tacked to a post where a single quarter horse stands in a corral built for twenty.

To my delight, I spot a large bird that's highlighted in beams of golden sunshine, a magnificent creature traveling at my speed and parallel to my path on the road. I recognize its white head, gold beak, and wide span of wings. Seems like my coworkers see bald eagles every month, but this is the first one I've spotted in years. The enormous bird descends and veers in close to my truck. It keeps pace with me for a quarter mile, gliding only twenty feet above the ground. Where the flat land recedes and a spread of almond hills looking soft and smooth like dove feathers rises in front of me, I look over and the majestic bird has disappeared.

The White Claw River returns on my right and soon an old steel bridge carries me across the water. The White Claw is shallow and barely moving. Downstream, white boulders crowd its riverbed. Upstream, the bank is wide and muddy and boulder free, but overgrown with cattails and strewn with fallen trees. A few miles farther on, an entire tribe of dead ash pose naked on a hilltop, their stringy branches gray and lifeless. I too am drifting into the unknown, so I turn up the volume on my radio.

The road I'm traveling enters a narrow passageway of white pines. On either side of me, the trees are tall and lean and bunched so close together that I can see only a dozen feet into their dark assembly. The sweet scent of pine reminds me of Christmas, less than two months away. For another mile, the shadows crossing the highway budge the lane ahead. Only at certain bends in the road do the last amber rays of sunlight spill over the pavement.

I'm comfortably engaged in music when I come to an unincorporated settlement named Cody. No change in speed limit has been posted, so I only brake as needed around a sharp curve. Another catchy song comes on the station, and I sing along. A mile later, a sign announces I'm entering Apple Grove, the crab apple capital of the world.

I slow to jogging speed because a police car is sitting in the parking lane ahead, its roof bar firing shots of red and blue warning. I brake to a stop, my pickup becoming fifth in a line of vehicles waiting to move on. We're paused in the commercial district of Apple Grove, two blocks of flimsy clapboard store fronts with square roofs and brick chimneys. It's a century-old scene plucked from a time capsule buried long ago.

I watch a policewoman bend towards a brood of young trick-or-treaters, shepherding the kids from one curbside to the other. I'd forgotten today was Halloween. Grabbed by the wind, the kids' plastic sacks stir like puffed-out sails on a sloop and pull the children to the opposite curb. Two ghosts, a unicorn, one princess, a skeleton, and Frankenstein's monster – it's a band of candy pirates with nothing but treasure on their minds. Off to my right, a man is mowing grass in the diminishing light. With the weather as warm as it's been, the grass is still green and in need of a trim.

Our string of vehicles waiting to move on has reached nine. Another swirl of costumes and candy sacks queues to cross. The policewoman continues to hold the rest of us back. In small Midwestern towns like this one, pedestrians still trump vehicles, especially if it's kids on the street. Once the last child has reached the far sidewalk, the officer straightens to adult height and briskly waves us on our way.

**With the** crab apple capital behind me a dozen miles and the sun having set, evening air blowing in my window turns cool and sends me a shiver, a sobering reminder that autumn never lasts forever.

I roll up my window and start thinking about the job ahead. I work for Midwest Stable Platforms, a construction company headquartered in Davenport, Iowa. We're concrete specialists. We build the underground foundations that anchor wind turbines to the earth, those tall spindly brigades of white acrobats you've seen cartwheeling across the landscape of rural America.

MSP is a small company and the most satisfying place I've ever worked, a place where everyone knows everyone else and most of us get along. Even better, MSP provides a lifestyle that suits me. I've remained single since my wife left me nearly twenty years ago, so the nomad routine of traveling between projects, living out of a suitcase, and bedding down in motels suits me perfectly. Best of all, I'm only responsible for my own happiness.

At MSP, every crew member knows what the company expects from them. Although we all share the same tasks of setting rebar and shoveling concrete, we also have our own individual specialties, some unique skill or talent each of us contributes. One person on every crew handles wiring, another pipe fitting, another fine surface finishing. My specialty is surveying, what's called *shooting grade*. After I quit college and a major in urban planning, I hooked up with a tech school where I earned an associate degree in land surveying, a decision I've never regretted.

Because we work with a special high-density concrete that won't harden correctly if daytime temperatures fall below 45°, our construction season only runs from April to October. We can't start work until after the spring thaw, and we must finish our last job in autumn before the first hard freeze. Normally, our work year is over before Halloween, but this fall has been unseasonably warm, and more warm weather is predicted over the next week. That's why our front office in Davenport accepted one additional project this year, a single platform job in Wisconsin, near the town of Pigeon Falls. My crew was chosen to build it.

**After leaving** Apple Grove I maneuvered through several minor dips in the road that have now given way to larger swells. I'm entering a part of Wisconsin with a unique geological history. It's called the *Driftless Area*, an angular topography of ridges and valleys that went untouched during the last Ice Age, the era when glaciers pushed down from Canada and plowed across much of what is now the Upper Midwest.

Fifteen thousand years ago, when those ancient walls of ice started melting, the sandy clay sediment they carried, or *drift* as we call it now, was left behind. But not in the Driftless Area. No sediment was left behind around here, because the original push of glacial ice bypassed this region. In this part of western Wisconsin, you will find *coulees* instead of flatland covered in drift. Coulees are what they call the many untouched ridges and valleys of soft limestone bedrock that were formed here a million years *before* the last Ice Age.

**Darkness has** already blanketed the landscape when I drive over a viaduct spanning Interstate 94 and its restless din of evening traffic. I slow through the hamlet of Brewster, only a few old houses crouching in the glow of one dim streetlight. Between two of the homes, I glimpse a woman standing alone along a line of picket fence. She is hunched over a burn barrel, her slight features caught in a haze of white smoke and the tawny glow of the escaping flames.

She's struggling to contain an armful of disorganized papers. Worn out recipes? Past due bills? Old love letters? All the while, her free hand deposits another tranche of the papers into the lively fire. Tiny gold sparks rush high into the pitch-black sky and are quickly consumed by darkness. I watch the woman rebalancing her load, but I'm already out of town before she gives her next offering to the fire.

A few miles farther west, when I enter the village of Pigeon

Falls, my dashboard clock reads 6:05 p.m. During my fifteen years with MSP, I've stayed in scores of cities and towns across the Upper Midwest. All of their motels, restaurants, and shops carried the same bland commercial look and are nothing more to me now than a medley of nearly forgotten memories. But on first glance, Pigeon Falls is a bit of a surprise. From the moment I enter the village, something here feels different from those other places that I've passed through, something that won't be as easily forgotten.

Maybe it's because this is the smallest town our crew has ever stayed in. It takes me only a minute to drive from one end of the village to the other. Along the way, I pass two churches, two taverns, and a few dozen homes with lawns that are leaf-swept and tidy. There's no grocery store in town or gas station. No school or hospital, but there are a few small businesses: a tool shop, a metal fabricator, and an auto detailer.

The volunteer fire department's two-bay home looks new and stands behind an old post office barely the size of a one-car garage. Streets are narrow and calm in Pigeon Falls, and the village projects a deep-rooted safeness that only comes from neighbors caring about one another.

I'm surprised that none of the village's charm has been repurposed for tourists, as often happens with quaintness like this. Pigeon Falls has no art galleries, no fudge shops, no stores selling Christmas ornaments year-round. Instead, the town appears to be a refuge for working class families, an unspoiled haven to come home to.

It's a place where families assemble at the end of the day for a shared dinner, and weekend fun is a grassy ballpark on the edge of town with an adjoining playground and a log cabin shelter for cookouts.

Up ahead, I spot a middle-aged man wearing only a white tee-shirt, dark pajama bottoms, and beige slippers. He's walking towards a large recycling bin that's open at the curb. As I pass by, he pours a wastebasket of assorted empty liquor and beer bottles into the container, and the prolonged crashing of glass, as the discards hit rock bottom, helps me readjust my impossibly perfect perception of this place.

**I find** the Horseshoe Inn and park across the street. This is where we're staying. The large old building is a combination hotel, bar, and restaurant. The exterior façade is made of brick and white shiplap, original to the early 1900s, though much of the exterior looks recently renovated. Tall picture windows with black metal frames have been added on either side of a new double-wide front door. According to the Inn's website, the second floor was used as a family residence until the building was sold ten years ago and remodeled into seven upstairs guest rooms, each with private bath. The second floor is reached by an outdoor staircase on the building's parking lot side.

A bar and restaurant occupy the first floor, serving breakfast, lunch, and dinner. Overall, the Inn looks classier than where we typically stay. We could have booked rooms at one of the cheaper chain motels in the city of Eau Claire, 30 miles to the north, but because time is so important on this project, the Horseshoe Inn was chosen so we could get ourselves to and from the jobsite as swiftly as possible.

Lively music coming from inside the Inn pulls me out of my truck and up the front steps. As I enter, I notice a tall waitress with a frizzy crown of bleached blonde hair standing with her back to me at the bar. She spins around on the sound of me opening the door, and her eyes lock on mine. My entrance has startled her. It's as if she was expecting me to be someone else, someone she doesn't want to see. Her chestnut eyes are anxious, fearful even.

When she realizes I'm not that person she's expecting, her expression brightens. Her eyes even begin to sparkle, and she smiles with maybe the most beautiful smile I've ever seen, all glistening teeth and perfect lips. It's been ages since I've seen a look this kindly, the face of unconditional goodwill. As I close the door behind me, the blonde woman calls to me above layers of overlapping music and conversation.

"Welcome to the Shoe!" she says.

This cheerful young waitress is dressed in the spirit of the holiday, wearing a white smock and orange apron over black leggings. On her head is a black headband holding a 2-D cut-out of a cheerful pumpkin, a sort of Halloween tiara. The word *Candace* is spelled out in black cursive on a white plastic name tag pinned to her blouse. Candace, I now realize, is even younger than I thought when I first spotted her, only on the near side of twenty something.

As she glides away from the bar and out into the crowded dining room, Candace balances in one hand a tray holding glass mugs and a pitcher of beer. She smiles at me a second time, and I think I notice that one of her front teeth is whiter than the rest, but she's off into the room before I can be sure.

I unzip my jacket and scan the crowded space. Patrons occupy a dozen red leather bar stools to my right. One old crow in an engineer's hat is nursing a shot and a beer. Next to him is perched another senior citizen pecking at a bowl of candy corn. Between them atop the bar sits an orange pumpkin the size of a basketball. Inside, a yellow flame flickers behind triangular eyes and a warm grin. Country music plays from the ceiling.

Only one bartender, a bald muscular man in a Batman tee-shirt and Zorro mask, is standing behind the shiny countertop, bar towel in hand. He nods as I pass, and I return the favor.

I've lost sight of the young waitress, Candace, and continue looking for my crew, finally spotting the men at a table in the back. Skinny Martin and Warren King sit facing me with their backs against a wall. A teenager I don't know is seated between them. Warren waves me in.

Buck Taylor and Manny Herrera are sitting across from Warren with their backs to me. They turn to glance in my direction and then raise an arm in welcome. At the head of the table is Carson Mayhew, though not because of any table hierarchy. Carson is texting, as usual, and likes having elbow room for his work, but he looks up from his screen long enough to give me a friendly salute. I know everyone, of course, except the kid.

"The tests took longer than I thought," I say and apologize for being the last one to arrive. I sit at the only open seat at the table, the one opposite Carson.

"We only settled in a minute ago, Tom," Warren says and hands me a room key. "They checked us through. You're in number five."

As I'm arranging my coat over my chair, Candace arrives and hands out menus.

"So… this is the one you're expecting?" she says and then turns towards me. "I'm glad you finally got here." There's that disarming smile of hers again. "Your friends are desperately thirsty but insisted on waiting for you."

Candace takes drink orders. I ask for a glass of milk, which gives her pause, but she carries on. When she comes to the teenager, however, it's a full stop.

"I have to card you," she says to the kid and then looks to Skinny Martin, as if the senior person at the table is father to us all. "Is he twenty-one?" she asks Skinny.

"I'll have an orange soda," says the kid.

"I'm not either," Candace laughs. It's a fun-loving hoot she brings, a response that comes not in the disrespectful manner one might imagine. Our waitress isn't making fun of the kid. Just the opposite, she's reaching out. "Orange Fanta's my favorite," she tells him. "Sunkist is okay, too. But the bad news is we don't have either. I can do you a 7 Up or a Coke. Ginger ale if you're daring enough."

As I watch our waitress and the teenager interact, I can see now that they're nearly the same age, and though I'm certain they don't know each other, they're already acting like they've been friends for a while, communicating in a language I no longer understand, the language of young people.

"Let's go for it," the kid says. "I'll have a ginger ale."

"One dangerous ginger ale." Candace's pen scratches across her notepad. "If you're here tomorrow, I'll make sure we have some Fanta."

She steps back to favor the rest of us.

"The special tonight was Nana's Pot Roast," Candace says, pointing at Skinny's menu, "but we sold out. Everything else on the menu is excellent. I'll give you a minute." I watch her walk away.

Warren motions in my direction, while saying to the kid, "Eddie, this is Tom Bishop, our surveyor."

"Tommy B, a gentler soul and a nicer surveyor you'll never meet," Skinny interjects. "In all our years together, never heard one goddamn swear word leave Tommy B's lips."

"Hell, no," chimes in Buck.

I reach out to shake the kid's hand. His almond skin is lighter than Warren's much darker tone. He has a strong grip, always a good sign in a young person.

"Pleased to meet you, Eddie," I say. "You from around here?"

"No, I live in Chicago," he says. "I've never been to Wisconsin, 'til today."

Before I can ask more, Warren claps his hands, which is something Warren does whenever he has news or an important point to make.

"My bad, Tom," Warren says. "Eddie came with me. Before you got here, I was explaining how Eddie and I met."

So, for my benefit, Warren restarts his story. He says he was in Indianapolis the past three days helping his siblings move their parents into an assisted living space. Warren left Indiana early this morning and on the southside of Chicago stopped for gas. As he was getting back on I-90, he sees Eddie standing on the on-ramp, thumb out, with a duffle bag slumped at his feet. Warren pulls over and offers the kid a ride. Warren soon learns that Eddie graduated high school in May and his dream is to see California. He was hitch-hiking to Los Angeles when Warren offered him a ride.

"You're on your way to California?" Carson says, looking up from his touch screen. "You got family out there?"

Eddie shakes his head and says he's never been anywhere outside Chicago, until today. "I promised my mom if she let me travel a few months, I'd come back and go to community college, like my brother."

"Your mother let you go alone?" I ask.

Eddie answers, but the noise of the crowded room swallows his words. "Yeah, she let me go on my own," he says, louder the second time. I'm thinking, not all parents would make that choice, but maybe Eddie's mother is a wise woman. Better to send your son with a blessing than to try preventing the inevitable and run the bigger risk of losing him altogether.

"No one hitch-hikes anymore," Carson warns. "You know, it's dangerous?"

A look of embarrassment flushes Eddie's face. I get the impression he doesn't know how risky it is hitching a ride today.

"Your mother, she didn't know you'd be hitch-hiking, did she?" Skinny says. Eddie shakes his head, sheepishly. "You're lucky Warren came along."

"Skinny's right," says Manny. "Bad shit happens on the roads nowadays."

And on those low notes Warren's story continues.

Eddie planned to go west by train. The idea to hitch-hike came to him only this morning. He thought thumbing rides could save him money, so he gave himself one hour to get picked up. If no one stopped, he'd continue to Union Station as originally planned and then go west on Amtrak. "He was on the ramp barely a minute when I spotted him," Warren says. "After we got to talking, he said he was curious how wind towers are built, so I offered him a job. I know Eddie can use the money, and with Jimmy Gilligan in jail we can use an extra hand."

"Especially with Jimmy gone," Buck says with a nod.

Jimmy Gilligan has been part of our crew the past three years and our foreman the last two. He's a master at pouring concrete, maybe the best in the business, particularly at the end of the season like now, when the weather gets cold. But Jimmy Gilligan was arrested on a DUI last weekend and put in jail. We all thought his problems with alcohol were behind him. He'd been sober his entire three years with us and was faithfully attending AA meetings while we were on the road. None of us saw a relapse coming.

"Why isn't Jimmy out on bail?" Carson asks.

"The car he hit had kids in it," Warren says. "Even if they let him out, I don't think he could leave Iowa. Anyway, he needs some time now to get himself back on track."

**Well liked**, organized, and upbeat, Warren King is MSP's office manager. The son of a pastor and the church's choir director, Warren was born a diplomat. His DNA skill set is not only something a struggling country could appreciate but one a construction business can profit from. Warren is late thirties, married, and the father to two girls. His round dark face is half hidden by a neatly trimmed beard. Though normally behind a desk in Davenport, he's been named our foreman for this project, in Jimmy Gilligan's absence.

Warren grew up in Davenport and started at MSP right out of high school, filing papers and making photocopies. When the company needed someone to learn a new software program, Warren volunteered. When they needed more crew electricians, Warren took night classes. It was during his time on the road as an electrician that Warren solidified his reputation for hard work, integrity, and team play. Everyone at MSP likes Warren and trusts him. He's the youngest member of the company's leadership team, and some call him the future of Stable Platforms.

**Manny asks,** "Eddie you ever work construction before?"

Eddie shakes his head. "In high school," Eddie says, "I was night manager at the dollar store."

Manny says, "Night manager… that's something."

I easily detect the hesitation within Manny's response and give Eddie a closer look myself. Building the foundation for a wind turbine is difficult work, definitely not a job for everyone. Although Eddie is seated, I can tell he's shorter than anyone else at the table. And his body isn't ripped from high school sports or weight training.

"You play on any teams in school?" I ask.

"JV soccer, but I didn't get in much."

My mind is already questioning if Eddie will be up to the demands of working with concrete, not so much with how to turn a trowel or handle a float, but more about how he'll manage the back-breaking weight of lifting fresh mix and its finger-numbing cold. My co-workers are eyeing Eddie as well.

Candace returns with a tray of beverages, and she places the correct bottle or glass in front of whoever ordered it, never once looking at her notebook or asking us for help. Seven drinks in all, each in its rightful place. It's an amazing feat. I've watched plenty of restaurant staff try to distribute orders by memory. Some workers, especially the youngest ones, will oftentimes make a mistake or need help if more than three or four items are involved. Candace's memory is flawless.

As I watch her move around the table, something else about this young woman grabs my attention, something familiar in how she bends and reaches and turns. I ponder this mystery for a moment but can't figure out what the solution is.

"I phoned Eddie's mom and got her approval for him to join us for the week," Warren says. "The front office is on board too. HR needed some...."

I lose track of what Warren is saying. My concentration is still attached to our waitress. I realize the sparkle of her smile is made more striking by her high cheekbones and noticeable overbite. She's an attractive young lady, but it isn't a sensual connection I'm feeling, though that reaction might have been likely if I weren't twice her age. What I'm feeling is more inspiration than invitation. When Candace reaches down and places my drink in front of me, I'm convinced it will be the best glass of milk I've ever tasted.

"We're going to be here all week, my dear," Skinny says to Candace and then points. "Your name tag says *Candace*. Do you want us to call you *Candace* or *Candy*?"

Although Skinny asked the question she answers looking at Eddie, who's returning her gaze. "Candace, please," she says. "Not Candy. My family name is Cane, with a *C*. As far back as I can remember, I was *Candy Cane*." She scrunches her face. "I hated it. Why do parents give their kids dumb names like that?"

Skinny nods, as if he knows everything there is to know about the unwanted attention that she's been feeling all these years. "*Candace* it is," he declares.

I watch Candace leave us, my eyes following her as she moves across the dining room like the fair heroine in a summer play, smoothly navigating a stage cluttered with prop tables and chairs. When she gets to the bar, she reaches for a mug to fill with beer. Her slim arms move as if they're floating on air. I'm finding myself unable to take my eyes off Candace, and I don't know why. Is it something about her posture, her figure, that toothy smile? I keep watching as Skinny leans in close.

"She's a keeper," he whispers.

"Moves with poise," I whisper back.

"It comes naturally in that one," Skinny says. "You can't teach it."

Warren is still talking. "With Jimmy not here," he's saying, "I'm putting Manny in charge of finishing." Skinny and Buck give two thumbs up.

Carson has put down his phone. "What do you want Eddie to do?" he asks.

"We'll need Eddie for a little bit of everything," Warren says. "He'll learn as we go."

Skinny asks Eddie if Warren has told him about our crew's working rules.

"There's only two," Eddie replies, eagerly. "One is, always lend a hand. And two… no talking about religion or politics."

"Good job, son," Skinny says. "You follow those rules to the letter, and you'll get along well with all of us."

*Team chemistry.* Skinny Martin knows it. Indeed, we all do. Skinny, Buck, Carson, Manny, and me, we've been a team traveling the Upper Midwest together for five years now, and as I mentioned, Jimmy Gilligan had been with us for three, until last weekend. Our two-rule creed is intended to prevent arguing, bullying, jabbing one another with a put down, acting selfishly, or anything else that gets in the way of our working effectively as a team. Help one another and don't talk politics or religion.

Because of those two rules, there's been no drama among our crew for five years, no unnecessary conflict, no big problems. That's a rarity in any workplace, and that's especially true in the trades. All of which is to say that Skinny and the rest of us don't want a newcomer messing things up. If Eddie sticks to those two rules, everything will be fine.

"Did Warren explain how hard the work is?" Manny asks.

"He said a lot of lifting and shoveling."

"And we'll be working ten-hour days on this project," Carson says. "With no days off. This platform needs to go up before it's too cold."

Eddie has turned silent and is looking at his hands, and I can tell he's re-assessing what he's gotten himself into. "Now, you've scared him," Skinny says, and I agree. From Eddie's expression, I wonder if maybe Warren didn't go into all the details with him about how strenuous the labor would be.

Eddie then looks up. "I can do it," he says with a sudden burst of confidence, and I wonder if he's trying more to convince us or himself.

"You sure?" Skinny asks. "It's okay to change your mind."

"I'm sure."

"Then, welcome aboard!" Skinny raises his bottle of beer. "We appreciate the help." Eddie raises his ginger ale, and they clink glass, two lifelong chums born in the last minute and with only forty years separating them in age.

Manny says, "We've been wondering how it went at the hospital, Tom."

"They tell you what you got?" Buck adds.

My co-workers are aware of my health issues. It's because of them that I was visiting Fairview Clinic today. Once my diet changed to soup and milkshakes this past summer, they convinced me to see my family doctor, who referred me to the Fairview specialists. "I won't get any test results until next week," I say and turn towards Warren. "If we're not finished up here by Friday, I'll need to take a few hours at the end of the week and drive back to the clinic."

"Not a problem," Warren says. "I think we'll be done here, but if we're not, take whatever time you need. We'll be okay."


*All for one and one for all.* That's MSP's business model in a nutshell. I've worked at enough mediocre companies to know what makes for a good one. Midwest Stable Platforms is a good one. It's family-owned, and that family cares as much about its employees as it does its bottom line, an exception in the industry today. I've seen all kinds of tricks that other companies play in the trades, messing with their employees' pay and benefits. I've also seen how quickly companies can turn on a worker if that person has a family situation that requires time away from the job. Any absence costs a company money. It's as simple as that.

Employers always tout their competitive wages, good benefits, opportunities for advancement, and friendly environment. From the outside looking in, most businesses seem like great places to work. The reality is that only a handful are. My first few years in the trades, after finishing tech school, I made four changes in employment, and each time I was never laid off or fired. My departures were all my own choosing. I left those jobs because I was disgusted by how the companies cut corners to increase profits, how hardship was always carried on the backs of employees, how the workers were never right.

Then I found MSP, a business that takes care of its people. MSP expects a lot from us, but we also expect a lot from the company, and they've always come through. That's why I've stuck with them now for fifteen years.

**As we're** chatting around the table, Candace and another waitress arrive with our food. Manny has just told us his wife left for Texas this morning to be with her parents. Rita is eight months pregnant with their first child. Both Manny and Rita are Dreamers who came to the U.S. from Mexico as children. Manny has been with MSP for eight years, since right out of high school.

"If that baby comes and you need to go, you go," Warren tells him.

"She'll be okay for now," Manny says.

I tell the crew I saw an eagle flying next to my truck on my way from the clinic. Buck says he saw thousands of geese heading south along the Mississippi River, on his drive up from Iowa. "The sky was full of them," he says, "like the fighters in *Armageddon*."

Buck is single, a common condition in jobs where a lot of over-the-road traveling is required. He announces that once we're done in Pigeon Falls, he's heading to the mountains of Montana to hunt elk for a week with his brother. Then, he's off to the Gulf Coast, either Louisiana or Mississippi. A lot of money can be made over winter, repairing homes damaged by tornadoes the previous summer.

"You still don't have enough to buy a new truck?" I ask.

"I'm almost there," Buck replies.

"Yesterday, I bought a boat online," Skinny tells us.

"Sight unseen?" Carson asks.

"I got photos and a video. I'll pick it up in the Ozarks when we're done."

Skinny is fifty-six, also single and never married, and currently without a partner. He winters in Key West and has been with MSP since the company opened, twenty-some years ago.

"What about you, Carson?" Warren asks, not wanting to leave anyone out. "Any plans for vacation?"

Carson looks up from his screen and shrugs. "Depends how this goes," he says, indicating his phone. Since I arrived at the table, Carson's been texting another woman he met online. Carson is always one click away from the beginning of a beautiful relationship. Like me, Carson is divorced and has no children. During our interactions around the table, I've also been watching Eddie and his eyes, as they jump from voice to voice, story to story. I'm sure our traveling culture is revealing a new world to him, a world that's light years removed from the life he's familiar with.

"Boss, what's up with our new client?" Skinny then asks Warren. "Don't they know they're gambling with the weather?" I've been wondering the same since Friday, when our front office told us that we could have one more project if we wanted it, a last-minute job pushed forward from the spring schedule. It'd only last an extra week, we were told, and it would pay very well.

"Our client's not a utility," Warren says. "He's a private party."

The rest of us exchange curious glances. "He's a farmer, and if we do this job now, MSP gets five more platforms from him in spring."

Carson takes a moment away from texting to look up. "You're saying, some guy's putting up a commercial wind farm for himself?"

"No, he'll be selling his electricity to the local grid," Warren explains. "But he's a private investor, not a utility." We take a moment to chew on this information. Then, Warren continues.

"His name's Burnell Sandberg. I met him in Davenport last week when he signed a revised contract. Mr. Sandberg got a lot of funding from Washington for this project. He said he's been working on getting his wind farm off the ground for a couple of years now, and his money came through earlier than he expected. The guy's really motivated, and with all the warm weather they've been having up here, he decided not to wait until spring, but start building now."

Skinny is shaking his head even before Warren finishes his explanation. "Something's not right with this picture," Skinny says.

"What do you mean?" Warren replies. "It's a normal commercial contract."

"Not that," Skinny says. "First, it's doing a project last minute and right before winter. That's risky enough, but then there's the money he's paying us. We'll be making a lot more than we should. What private investor throws money around like that?"

"He's a motivated guy," Warren says. "He wants his first tower online by Christmas."

"Yeah, well, the hourly he's paying is crazy."

To Skinny's point, while we all make different wages based on our seniority and responsibilities, this project has bumped up our wage-scale by a ton. With overtime, we will more than double our normal pay.

"All I know is that Mr. Sandberg wants to get started now, no matter the cost."

"Let him overpay us," Buck says. "I need a new truck."

"*¿Está loco?* We could get snow next week," Manny says. "What then?"

"The forecast still looks good," Warren says.

"I agree with Manny," says Carson. "This guy's either crazy or stupid."

"Maybe, maybe not," Skinny says. "I've got a feeling the guy knows that old saying, *Money talks and bullshit walks.* None of us would've come up here at the end of the season for normal wages."

Candace returns to our table. "How's the food?" she asks. Everyone nods appreciation or says something to that effect. "If you're around Saturday night, our special is spaghetti and ribs, all you can eat."

"Tantalizing combination," says Skinny, and I wonder if he's being facetious, because for me the thought of marrying pasta sauce and barbecue only reminds me of my stomach problems.

"People come from La Crosse and Eau Claire," she says. "Just to let you know."

Candace takes another drink order. After she leaves, Carson asks, "Anyone notice her wrist?" All of us noticed the mottled purple and yellow cuff on an arm that was silently screaming *manhandling*.

"She has good skin," Skinny says. "She'll bounce back."

Candace returns with more glassware and points out her parents sitting at the front of the dining room. The couple appear to be early sixties, average-looking, quiet folk. She tells us she's the last of their seven kids, many years younger than her nearest sibling. "I have to keep reminding them I'm one of theirs," she whispers, half in a laugh and half like an unsolved mystery, leaving me with the impression that there are important pieces in her family puzzle that we don't know.


**After dinner** and with suitcase in hand, I ascend the outdoor staircase to the second floor and notice, to my surprise, that a harvest moon is rising over the quaint roof line of Pigeon Falls. This lush lunar sphere is full and copper colored, so I stop on the landing to watch it floating there just above the horizon, suspended somewhere between heaven and earth. Seeing a super-sized moon like this is not a common occurrence, they happen only a few times a year. Tonight, this one is reminding me of my ex-wife, Paige.

When Paige and I were first married, more than twenty years ago, we would walk together after dinner, threading our way through the quiet streets and open spaces in the small town where we lived. Large colorful moons such as harvest moons, strawberry moons, and frost moons are visible only a few times a year, so for us to spot one was always a special occasion. Paige and I knew that the unusual size of these rare moons was merely an optical illusion, a phenomenon caused by solar angles and bending light. We knew that the moon wasn't any larger than normal or that much closer to Earth. It just looked that way.

Even though these distinctive sightings only lasted the hour it took for the moon to separate from the horizon, each one seemed to us like an event frozen in time, a magical show put on for our enjoyment alone. We even acted as if we were part of the performance, and our dialogue always followed the same script.

"Seems close enough to touch," Paige would say as she drew in close, reaching an arm around my waist.

"Something that beautiful can't be real," I'd answer and rest my arm across her shoulder.

"The color is so… *delicious*." Her other hand moves across my abdomen.

"Extraordinarily delicious." My mouth lowers to meet hers.

My scenes with Paige were performed a long time ago, yet little about them is forgotten, even today. Looking at this harvest moon rising over Pigeon Falls tonight, I'm also reminded that all marriages begin with great expectations. Ours was no exception. Even though half of all marriages end in divorce, I was sure that

Paige and I would stay together forever. Truth is, our marriage lasted only three years. And I never noticed the warning signs that it was wearing out.

Paige and I never argued. We suffered no infidelity or jealousy. No one got bruised or felt afraid. By all accounts, we cared about one another. Paige was a good person, with a big heart. I held no complaints. Then one day, she announced she's leaving. The words *I want a divorce* came with so little emotion in her voice that she could have been telling me she was on her way to the market, which I guess she was. Her message, however, landed in our small living room with the force of a bomb, and in that single explosive sentence, my life as I knew it had ended.

"Why?" I whispered, which is probably always the first question.

"I'm not having fun anymore," she said.

"What can I do to fix it?"

"It's not fixable, Thomas. It's too late for that." Paige had already anticipated every question I would ask and figured out every answer. She compared our marriage to an airplane that tries to take off yet never makes it airborne. For years she had wanted to fly, she told me, she had even prayed to fly, but our marriage never gathered enough speed to lift us off the ground, at least not enough to lift us both. "You're a good man," she assured me a couple days after her announcement, "but you're a planner, Thomas. Everything's the future with you. I'm tired of waiting for life to happen. I want to live now."

At another point, I asked, "Is there someone else?"

"Not yet," she replied, and the image of her with someone else, then or in the future, hurt as much as anything else. She said she'd been unhappy for more than a year, that I just never noticed. I asked her, *how do you notice something you cannot see?* I promised her I'd do anything to get her to reconsider, but her mind was made up.

"No, I need to do this now," she said, "before more time is lost."

Paige packed her things and a week later was living in Chicago. From there she drifted to New York and finally settled in Florida. First, she worked in the hotel business and then in real estate. After a few years I lost track of her. I searched online but never found any trace again. I even thought of driving to her hometown and talking to her parents, but I never did.

It's been twenty years since our split, and I've been on my own the entire time. I have no idea where Paige is now or who she's with. Looking back, though, I understand that she was right. I always was a planner, always researching and making lists, prepping to do something yet rarely doing it. How many trips had I mapped out for Paige and me that we never took? How many times had I diagramed an addition or remodel to our house that we never started? How many nights had we talked about going to a movie or a club but stayed at home because I was tired from work?

Too many, of course.

Some people are meant to find only one companion in their lifetime. If that person dies or moves on, there's no substitute or next chapter waiting to take their place. I'm one of those one-timers. After our house sold, I lived in a fog of loneliness and uncertainty for a few years, bouncing from town to town and job to job. I dated several times, even had moments of romance, but nothing meaningful took root. I had no deep interest in starting over with someone else, in building a new life. My heart was not made for breaking more than once.

Those first years alone were the unhappiest of my life, and I carried a heavy burden of guilt for our failure. I began to believe it was impossible for me, not only to fit into a relationship or a job but to fit in anywhere.

Then, I was hired at Midwest Stable Platforms. A week with the company and I realized I'd found a place that was different from everywhere else I'd been. My coworkers made me feel like I belonged somewhere. The nomadic lifestyle also turned out to be a perfect match for what I needed most: to live for today and only today. Now, traveling to a new place every couple of weeks keeps my mind preoccupied, and in the present, leaving little time to feel sorry for myself or miss being in love. Where I go is decided by others now. I don't need to plan for or even to contemplate my long-term future, and I'm okay with that.

**The warm** copper moon above Pigeon Falls has climbed several degrees into the sky and gotten smaller and whiter as the angles of reflection continue to change. I wonder if Paige might be watching this same harvest moon, wherever she is. I also wonder if she's finally found what makes her happy. Although I'm no longer in love with Paige, I sometimes feel her absence. I'll be driving between projects and will look at the empty seat beside me and wonder what it'd be like if we were still together, back like it was in the beginning of our marriage, in the days before a cloud of unhappiness shaded her feelings. For those few moments when I'm imagining Paige beside me in my truck, life seems perfect. But it's impossible to sustain that illusion. It's a fantasy that lasts only as long as it takes for another song to come on my radio.

**Room 5** is home for the next week, a comfortable space that's square in shape and has an immaculately clean hardwood floor. The room holds a queen bed, one small writing table with a matching wood chair, an antique armoire in place of a closet, and two bedside tables with new but old-fashioned-looking lamps. It's enough furniture to fill the space but not feel crowded.

On one wall is a tall window with a view to the street. Long curtains in a floral pattern of varying soft tones of green and brown border the window frame. Above me, a light with three small shades hangs from the ceiling.

While unpacking my suitcase, I hear a car honk twice, but I pay little attention. When the sound comes a fifth time, I go to my window. Idling below in the middle of the street is a shiny black pickup.

A moment later, Candace hurries out of the Shoe and gets inside the truck, but before she closes the door, I can hear the man inside shouting. I can't make out what he's saying, but his words are being flung at our young waitress both in anger and disgust. After she closes the door, the truck accelerates loudly on its way out of town, a cranky diesel sound diminishing as the truck heads west on US 53.

# Part Two

# The Things We Make

## Friday, November 1

Our first breakfast in Pigeon Falls began Friday morning when the Shoe opened at 6:00 a.m. After eating, we formed a convoy outside, six pickups in a single file procession, like a wagon train. Driving solo to a jobsite every day uses more gas than carpooling, yet we rarely double-up. We need the equipment each of us carries in his own truck: families of saws, drills, light stands, and toolboxes, plus any extra clothes we might need.

As we head out of town, Eddie is riding shotgun with Warren in the lead. I'm at the back and still half-asleep. Since I stopped drinking coffee, due to my stomach problems, I've needed more time in the morning to wake up. I roll down my window and grab a breath of cool air.

The Sandberg farm is only a short drive out of town, just off US 53 on Sizemore Coulee Road, an old thread of blacktop marked by a faded green sign that would be easy to miss, except that Warren drove out to the farm before dinner yesterday and scouted the way.

Today is the warmest first of November in memory, and the grip of rubber on pavement still holds strong. No hard freeze has shocked the area yet. No black ice. Not even a single snowflake has fallen. All we contend with are the normal predawn shadows within shadows crouching along a new roadway. The sun won't rise until 7:00 a.m., though already there are hints of the coming day, the lifting bands of purple and pink to the east that outline a faint horizon. This far north in late autumn, the first signs of a new day hold a certain unknown, a host of shifting colors and silent shapes that tend to creep up on you, as if the morning must be snuck into existence. That's quite different from late spring and early summer, when flocks of excited birds herald in a new day with choruses of hungry chirps and mating calls, a thrill that can go on for an hour or more.

When we leave US 53, we turn onto Sizemore Coulee Road by way of an ancient bridge that's only wide enough for one vehicle to pass at a time. It spans Pigeon Creek, the narrow waterway that's followed us along 53 from Pigeon Falls. From what I can see from the old bridge, Pigeon Creek is nothing more than a knee-deep headwater. A map on my phone shows that the creek will widen as it moves downstream ten miles to feed the Trempealeau River and from there empty into the Mississippi.

Sizemore Coulee Road has not been paved in ages. It offers no shoulders or pull-outs. Beyond the tarmac, the ground to the left rises sharply along a long hedge of dogwood. To the right, the land slopes down to Sizemore Creek, a meandering trickle of runoff even thinner than Pigeon Creek.

At the third bend in the road, we come to a rusty red mailbox without name or number. I follow the others onto a narrow spill of gravel that leads into the Sandberg property. Twisting and turning through cropland like a well-worn belt, the long driveway finishes in a loop in front of a sprawling two-story house. A flagpole inside the parking circle flies an American flag that ripples smartly in a strong breeze. The flag seems oversized for the height of its pole.

The Sandberg farmhouse is unlike anything I've seen before. Its unusual design is an architect's theme park, a mishmash of competing styles that take me back to my Architecture 101 course at community college, more than two decades ago. At the structure's center is the home's original section, a simple two-story cream city brick box, dating to the 1800s. The first floor has a narrow window on either side of a ¾-size front door. Three similarly-thin windows spread across the second floor.

At some point, a tall porch and six Doric columns were added to the house, giving the center section a Colonial Revival look. Later, to the left, a strangely-Victorian-looking wing was attached, with three second-floor gables and a wide brick chimney with three smokestacks. The Victorian wing is the largest section of the house. A more modern one-story addition with a steel roof, redwood trim, and a lot of glass was added on the right, probably in the 1950s or '60s.

I've never seen a home quite like this one. Sure, a better carpenter might have bridged the different styles more tastefully, but even as the house stands today, it's an impressive and curious sight.

But the devil is always in the details. I've noticed that spindles on the front porch railing are missing. Paint is peeling off trim around the windows. Above the front door, a transom no longer holds true to its frame. Half of the central section's soffit has been painted beige to match the brickwork, but the other half remains untouched, now nothing more than flakes of faded white. Neither scaffolding nor painting ladders are anywhere in sight.

**Warren motions** for us to park around the flagpole. Two men are standing side by side on the porch. The taller is in his forties and hatless. He's dressed in a flannel shirt, insulated vest, and blue jeans. The much shorter man looks nearly sixty, if not already there. He's bundled in a blaze orange parka and matching hunting hat. He's two heads shorter than his companion and weighs a hundred pounds less. This second man has a red beard and puffed out chest, which makes me think of a miniature Viking explorer commanding an ancient sailing ship, his face pointed into the wind, his watchful eyes scanning the sea ahead for danger. But then there's the long, filtered cigarette wedged between this smaller man's stubborn lips, and the old Norse adventurer image vanishes.

Even though I've never seen either of these men before now, I know that the smaller of the two is the property's owner, Burnell Sandberg. The key to hierarchy here is not in clothing choice or body size. It's in the eyes. The smaller man's eyes are bottomless pinpoints, focused on our approach like a feral cat protecting its territory. The taller man's eyes are different. They are the accommodating eyes of a helper.

The rest of our crew have already climbed out of their trucks and are walking towards the house. I step out into a considerable wind that's blowing hard against my door and directly into my face. My nose reacts immediately, as if it's inhaling fire. My eyes tear up and my throat begins to throb. It's the burning stench of pig manure that I'm breathing.

I scan the property again and spot a concrete hog confinement farther off to the left, its gray walls still draped in early morning shadow and mostly hidden behind an earthen privacy embankment separating the house from the pig operation. At the near edge of the berm, three very old boat trailers, minus their boats, are nestled in a thicket of tall grass, the three skeletons nearly invisible. I also notice a tall concrete manure tank that's downhill from the hog confinement, its curved shadowy outline just visible in the arriving dawn.

Small-time pig operations with only a few hundred head, like this one on the Sandberg farm, are not as common in the Midwest as they once were. Back in the day, these concrete structures were the Cadillac of family hog farming, with state-of-the-art concrete construction and a temperature-controlled growing environment in a building a quarter the size of a football field. But by the start of the new millennium, almost twenty years ago, Big Pork had bought out almost every small family pig farm in the Midwest. The Sandbergs' operation is a stubborn holdover from an earlier time, but how much longer it can stay afloat is hard to say. I shield my nose with my coat sleeve and hustle to catch up with my crew.

"You boys are late!" Mr. Sandberg shouts and begins to descend a half dozen porch steps. Warren and the others are assembled in front of the house. I join them. The hollow sound of new boots clumping down the staircase draws my attention. Mr. Sandberg is outfitted in a fine pair of black Timberlands, with bright orange laces to complement his expensive parka and matching hat.

Already, nothing about our client makes me think he's an actual farmer. Apart from the wardrobe, a real farmer at Mr. Sandberg's age would have already worked decades managing uncooperative animals and lifting heavy equipment. Yet, Mr. Sandberg shows none of the common signs of that tough farm life, not the chronically swollen ankles and weak knees of a real farmer, or the tell-tale curve of a deteriorated spine. Neither does Mr. Sandberg carry the extra pounds around his waist nor the weary tilt of the head of a real farmer.

I quickly conclude that Mr. Sandberg lives on his property but rents out the cropland. I can't even imagine him as a hobby farmer, those people with good jobs in the city who like to touch the soil and drive tractors on weekends. The way Mr. Sandberg gingerly grips the railing and calculates each step coming down the stairs, I think this man's life has been one of soft shoes and cuffed pants.

"You're on my clock, boys!" Mr. Sandberg shouts in an octave half higher than I expect. "I don't tolerate lateness!"

Of course, we're not late. Our workday starts at seven. We're five minutes early. Warren knows it too, but instead of acting offended and kicking off our new relationship by way of a sarcastic comeback, Warren replies cheerfully, because positivity is one of the many qualities we like about Warren, one of the reasons why our front office made him MSP's office manager. "I've got 6:55, sir!" Warren says with a smile and points to his wrist.

"Here's some advice," the farmer grumbles, pushing back on Warren's niceness. "I keep mine twenty minutes ahead. Never miss anything that way." Mr. Sandberg has stopped at the second to the last step.

Measure for measure on level ground, everyone in our crew stands at least seven or eight inches taller than Mr. Sandberg. Even the new kid, Eddie, is four or five inches above him. But with Mr. Sandberg paused on the staircase where he is, he appears to have a height advantage over all of us. Yet even giving him the benefit of those two extra steps, Mr. Sandberg looks uncomfortable standing there. He awkwardly shifts his weight from leg to leg. He fidgets with his hands. He's also unsure what to do with his half-spent cigarette that he finally flicks to the ground. I'm not sure if I'm witnessing a man who's reluctant to talk to strangers or one who's trying to conceal the uncomfortableness he feels about his own body. Maybe both.

Warren steps forward. The rest of us form a tight semi-circle behind him. Warren offers his hand. "You remember me, Mr. Sandberg?" he says. "I'm Warren King, office manager for Stable Platforms. I was there in Davenport last week. When you signed the revised contract." Burnell Sandberg's small, pale hand reluctantly gives Warren's large, dark grip a quick shake. "Normally, they tie me to a desk," Warren laughs, "but given the circumstances surrounding your project, they sent me up here to lead the crew. Our company wants everything to go perfect for you, sir. How's the weather looking?"

"Next week's good," our client says. "Maybe a little rain midweek… if you trust the news. They say it's the longest summer in more than a century, but we'll see. *After* next week… well, that's another story."

"We'll keep our fingers crossed," Warren says with a smile.

"I don't believe in superstition," Mr. Sandberg clucks. "The weather changes fast around here. Four inches of snow fell on Halloween last year. That's why I need you boys to get here on time."

"Just show us the fastest way to the jobsite," Warren says. "We'll take it from there."

Instead of pointing us in a direction, Mr. Sandberg angles away from Warren and faces the rest of us. He raises his right hand, as if to take an oath, and then points an index finger skyward. "Number one," he says, "I don't care how you normally do things. On my land, I'm in charge. You got a question… you come see me. You got a problem… you come see me. You need something… you come see me. Are we on the same page?"

We nod and mumble that we understand, though I'm not sure what's happening. Once a project starts, crew members never interact with a client, let alone take orders from them. If a problem arises, then either our foreman or the front office handles it.

"Number two," Mr. Sandberg continues, now pointing two fingers skyward, "I don't give a damn what you call me. You can call me *Mr. Sandberg*, like your foreman does. You can call me *Burnell*. Around here, most people call me *Red*. It don't matter." None of us makes a sound or even stirs. "What matters is giving me a full day of work, every day you're here. If you boys do that, we'll get along fine."

Burnell, which is what I decide to call him, lights another cigarette. "When I say *full day*, that's what I mean." Burnell takes a long drag. When he exhales the wind grabs the smoke right off his lips and it disappears. "This deal came together last minute. When I talked about you last week with your people in Iowa, they told me you postponed vacation time to come work for me. I appreciate that, and for it, you'll be well paid. But I need this work to get done now. Which means, I need workers I can count on. Your owner assured me that's what I'd be getting."

Burnell takes another long pull on his cigarette. "Have you boys been to the State Fair lately?" he asks. If he's expecting us to respond, no one does. "Fourteen dollars for a lemonade… and I don't give a damn that you get to keep the cup."

There's probably a message in what Burnell is saying about the State Fair, but none of us picks up on it. We're waiting to be shown where we start working.

"*Fourteen dollars*," Burnell repeats to make sure we heard the price. Still, none of us says anything, or moves an inch. He curiously tilts his head. "Whatever," he sighs and turns back to the tall man still standing on the porch. "I'm taking these boys up the hill," Burnell calls at him. "After we're gone, carry over more firewood and stack it in the shed."

The tall man answers back, "Yes, sir, Mr. Sandberg."

Burnell faces us again. "Get in your vehicles and follow me up there." His hand holding the cigarette points back above the house, in the general direction where the north end of his valley rises in a steep ridge covered in more dogwood, yellow pines, and dead ash. At the same time, I sneak a glimpse to the west. The first rays of sunlight are brightening the tops of hardwoods positioned along the western ridge, their gold and red leaves exploding in late autumn color.

Burnell says nothing more, just finishes coming down the stairs and then moves past us before disappearing around a corner of his house. None of us are sure if we're to wait where we are or follow him around the house. The tall man on the porch, who hasn't moved since we arrived, is watching us, his arms folded across his chest.

"He goes to get the truck," the man calls to us, and I detect a foreign accent holding his words together. It's an old-world sound, perhaps Eastern European. "He comes. You follow him there." The man points behind him, exactly where Burnell indicated, up towards the top of the ridge.

"Thank you!" Warren smiles and waves back. "Let's go," he says to us, and we head for our trucks.

Walking to my pick-up, I think about Burnell's fourteen dollars for a lemonade. He was making a point about money, I guess, and money is why we're in Pigeon Falls. After seven long months on the road, all of us were expecting to start our winter break this past Tuesday night, but here we are instead, mostly because the money we've been promised for this extra week in Pigeon Falls is too good to pass up. It's only a quick thought I have about all the extra money that I'll have in my bank account, a week from now, but it's one that gives me a little extra comfort.

As I wait in my truck, I survey the rest of Burnell's holdings laid out in an early morning light that's continuing to gather around the property. To the right of the farmhouse stands a pole barn. The paint on its aluminum walls was once sunflower yellow. You can see traces of its glossy shine around the edges. After countless Wisconsin winters, however, most of the color has faded to a dull beige, the color buttermilk takes when it's been left out overnight.

Looming behind the pole barn, a navy-blue silo rises like a giant turret 80 feet into the sky. In a story about chivalry, the silo would serve as a perch for lookouts protecting the castle and valley. A single blue silo like this one was once the premier benchmark for a prosperous farmstead in the Midwest, the one structure every young farm family hoped to own one day. Those silo dream-days are artifacts of the past, however, just like Burnell's old hog confinement. If you've traveled through the region recently, you've probably seen plenty of these blue giants spread across the horizon and sitting dormant. Today, a single blue silo on a small property is just another reminder that family farming in the Upper Midwest is in decline.

In a swirl of dust, Burnell emerges from around his house. He's sitting high in the driver's seat of the finest truck I've seen in a long time, an enormous F-350 super duty crew cab. He's got double rear tires, LED roof rack, and a bull bar out front. The cherry red vehicle is dripping in shiny chrome, looking like a mammoth polished bauble whose only function is to impress. This red beauty is not a work truck, something meant to get dirty. It's a show truck, an adult toy. It's the owner's personal statement that says, *I can buy whatever I want*. Gems like this one cost $80,000, twice the price of my truck. Stenciled on the front door in gold lettering is *Sandberg Renewable Energy, LLC*.

Burnell isn't the first eccentric CEO or wind farm manager we've worked for, though from what I've observed so far, he's the oddest client I can recall. He seems to be a man with one foot locked in the past, with his aging pig farm and run-down house, and one foot pointed towards the future, with his fancy clothes and plans for a state-of-the-art wind farm. He's bought a glitzy truck, yet his house and yard are falling apart. His new clothes are trendy and expensive, while the outbuildings on his property are holding on by a stitch.

What's unclear is how Burnell bridges this past and future, how he lives in the here and now. What I'm beginning to wonder is, *is this Burnell's business model?* Use something until its brilliance fades and then dump it off to the side and chase the next shiny object passing by? I can't help but wonder what Washington bureaucrat approved loaning Sandberg Renewable Energy, LLC, a mountain of money to build six commercial wind turbines.

The red F-350 skids to a stop on the gravel circle and blasts its horn. Buck is parked next to me. He nods at the impressive truck and gives me a thumbs up. Burnell signals for us to follow him back towards Sizemore Coulee Road, so Warren and Eddie take the lead for our group and stay on the tail of the thundering truck, with Skinny a couple of lengths behind them. Manny has pulled in behind Skinny, followed by Buck and then Carson, and then I bring up the rear.

At a spot where clusters of weeping willows kneel against the ditch that runs parallel to the long driveway, Burnell turns a hard right over the culvert. If he wasn't leading the way, we'd never have noticed that there's a dirt path bisecting Burnell's farmland on the floor of the valley.

I'm the last to make the turn as our caravan cuts across two large parcels of land, what earlier in the season was corn to the north and soybeans to the south. A gnarly oak stands out in the middle of the south field. A hundred yards beyond is another lone tree. A third and a fourth are farther away. All are surrounded by nothing but empty field, a string of garrison outposts holding watch in a desert of dirt.

At the far side of the valley the path begins to rise and follow the natural curve of the landscape, all the way to the top of the escarpment. Minutes later, we arrive on a plateau overlooking the entirety of Sizemore Coulee. Burnell has turned off his engine but remains in his cab, talking on a cell phone. We get out and cluster on the edge of the ridge, waiting for our client, while enjoying a bird's-eye view of the area. Off to the south is a stunning display of other coulees, a full set of ancient ridges and valleys that time immemorial and endless flowing water have carved out of the earth.

Below us, Burnell's valley is laid out as a rectangle that's longer north to south. The sharp angle of the drop from where we stand to the valley's floor makes the descent seem precarious, even though the distance is only four or five hundred feet. The sun is up now but still low on the horizon. Even so, it's shining right in our faces, which makes it difficult to see the farmhouse and hog confinement below. I also try to locate the path we took across the fields but can't see that either. Atop the plateau, a stiff breeze pushes against our backs as it rushes across the highland and then cascades over the ridge and down into the valley. It's not something that's strong enough to push us over the edge, but it's the strongest breeze I've ever felt on a jobsite.

*Working with the wind.* For years I've hated strong winds. I can't concentrate in them because the pressure they put on my body is both annoying and distracting. Even so, it's a love-hate relationship I have. Wind energy is what gives me a paycheck. And while the wind can wear me down, for others it lifts them up. I notice a pair of red-winged blackbirds chasing a hawk not far above us.

"Check it out," Carson says, gazing in the opposite direction of the valley, back across the plateau to the northeast. "We're good to go." In the distance, tracks from the movement of heavy machinery crisscross the flat earth. Excavators have come before us and dug a big pit in the ground. Assuming they followed MSP's specifications, the pit is 85 feet in diameter and 12 feet deep. The earth movers have left behind two tall mounds of dirt. The highest is a pile of brown subsoil and rocks that rises 20 feet to its peak. The smaller mound is darker topsoil, 10 feet tall. Inside this deep pit is where we'll build our platform for the wind turbine tower that will rise above it.

Standing between the pit and our parked trucks is an encampment of MSP equipment that goes with us everywhere we go. It was delivered a couple of days ago. It includes a tan single-wide trailer, which is the foreman's office and our refuge in case of rain. On its side in large white letters is *Midwest Stable Platforms, Davenport, Iowa*. Next to the trailer rests a green porta-potty, and alongside it stand pallets of framing lumber and steel reinforcement bars.

On the largest pallet is tethered a 12-foot-tall cylinder made of welded rebar. We call this structure *the cage* because, well, it looks like a giant bird cage. There's also a loaded flat-bed trailer not far away and a 40-foot shipping container just beyond. Skinny sometimes refers to our company as the home of Midwest Bedouins, since our lifestyle is transient, our equipment is portable, and we take with us only what we can't do without.


**Burnell has** finished his phone call and is walking towards us now. "They dug the first hole last Saturday," he says. "Did a good job, I guess."

Warren says, "I see the access road over there." He points beyond the earthen pit to a white strip of fresh gravel a hundred yards away, with the tail end disappearing over a soft rise on the plateau.

"I had them start that road a couple months ago. It connects to the county highway at the back of my property," Burnell says. "You can drive up here that way if you want. Depends on where you're staying. Are you boys shacked up at the Motel 6 in Waterford?"

"At the Horseshoe Inn in Pigeon Falls," Warren says.

"Fancy-fancy," Burnell quips. "In that case, you'll want to come through my coulee. It's ten minutes quicker."

We're anxious to get to work, but Burnell tells us to follow him. He stops on a piece of open ground between our trucks and the pit, out in the full force of the wind. "You feel that?" he says, extending his arms out to his side as if the robust current is going to lift him into the air.

"It's quite the breeze, Mr. Sandberg," Warren says with a too-nice smile. Warren wants to start working.

"Damn right," Burnell grunts. "Wind don't blow like this anywhere else in the county." Burnell takes out a cigarette. "I came close to selling this property more than once. *That* would've been the mistake of my life." As he lights up, he turns away from the wind and cups his hand to protect the flame. "You know, the geography up here is unique to my property. It's because of the shape of those hills over there." He points with the glowing tip of his cigarette. "The drift line is only a few miles north of here. Glaciers came close but never touched my coulee. For some reason, God decided to gift me and my family a natural wind tunnel. Some days the wind blows hard like this, and other times it's even harder, rushing through as strong as a raging river. Either way, it never fucking stops. You feel it, right?"

"I feel it, sir," Warren says. "It's strong, for sure."

"That wind nearly drove me loony when I came up here as a boy," Burnell continues. "Took me years to realize what the wind was trying to tell me..." He inhales again and speaks through the smoke he exhales. "*Enn-err-gee,*" he says. "I'll make enough energy up here to power most of the county. Six incredible turbines strung out along my ridge. Maybe even more than six someday. We'll see."

Warren says it sounds like a plan and tells Skinny to get started checking the inventory of everything that's been delivered from

Iowa. Warren's trying to get us started, to politely move us forward, while not wanting to be rude to our new client. As Skinny is walking to the foreman's trailer, Burnell's eyes take a sudden interest.

"You sure he works *construction?*" Burnell remarks with a mocking rise in pitch on his last word. Burnell's subtlety vanishes as he teases a couple of steps of his own, an exaggerated swish added to his gait, like a little dance. We're only 30 minutes into our first day here, and already we're running into a big problem with our client. But no one says anything because, one, all of us have pretty thick skin and, two, we've encountered worse insults than this on the road. Unfortunately, our silence proves to be a mistake. It's left Burnell thinking he has license to continue down the same path. "The tattoos and earrings," he chuckles, "is that still a thing?"

Though the comment is about Skinny and directed towards Warren, I'm feeling that the disrespect is meant for all of us. "Mr. Sandberg, Stable Platforms doesn't care about earrings and tattoos," Warren replies. "We need to get to work."

"Exactly!" Burnell says as if he and Warren see eye to eye, which they don't. "This is *hard* work, Mr. Foreman, so I got no problem with how someone looks, what words they call themselves, all of that nonsense. But are you sure *he's* got what it takes to do this job? Tall as he is and light-footed, hell, he can't weigh more than a buck fifty."

The farmer's comments are upsetting me, and by my co-workers' looks, I can tell they're feeling the same. This is why MSP crews don't interact with clients. We don't want to hear what some of them have to say about us, or about anything else for that matter.

Skinny, by his own testament, has never weighed more than 170 pounds, and at 6'4" he appears delicate, almost breakable. His Willie Nelson-style beard and ponytail, his ear studs, tats, and neckerchief add to that whimsical appearance, yet anyone who's worked with Skinny knows he's a smart and steady hand and, after Carson, the strongest man among us, even stronger than Buck, who has never in four years beaten Skinny in a match of arm wrestling.

"His name is *Skinny Martin*," Warren says, putting extra emphasis on those last two words. "Skinny's an outstanding worker. And if it weren't for him, none of us would be here right now. Skinny's the one who talked the crew into building this platform for you."

Burnell clears his sinuses and spits to the ground. "Fair enough. As long as I get 110%, I don't care what people do on their own time."

Warren is doing his best impression of a career diplomat, working to minimize conflict and keep peace on track. "You'll get 110%," Warren says. "You'll get it from all of us."

Burnell flicks away his cigarette. "I'll take your word for it," he says and sets off for his truck, but immediately turns back. "Just so you know, I talked to the ready-mix folks yesterday. They have no problem with doubling the order."

Warren looks at us and then at Burnell, and then back at us, but we stand there mute. We're as puzzled as Warren is. "You doubled what order?" Warren asks.

"Your order for cement."

"I don't follow you," Warren says. "The concrete we ordered with you Friday afternoon, when you were in Davenport, it was the right amount."

Now the confusion on Burnell's face matches ours. "Didn't you talk with your people in Iowa yesterday? Or the day before?" he asks.

"I was in Indianapolis for three days," Warren says. "No one called me."

Burnell wipes away a droplet of spit or tobacco that has caught on his lower lip. "Look over there," he says and points to the far northeast corner of the plateau, three hundred yards away. None of us noticed it earlier, when that part of the plateau was in early morning shade, but there in the distance, now lit in fresh sunlight, stand another pair of recently dug mounds of dirt, one brown pile and one black, identical to the two mounds of soil near us.

Burnell takes out another cigarette and lights up, his departure delayed again. "That's where my second tower goes," he says.

Warren searches for something to say, even though the response he seeks is unreachable. His words have been lost in the maze of confusion that comes with monumental miscommunication. Burnell exhales another cloud of white smoke. "Because the weather is looking so good, I called your boss in Iowa on Tuesday. With you boys coming here anyway, I asked about getting a second tower put up."

"You want *two* towers now, not one?" Warren says.

"I told them I'd pay extra for everyone's troubles."

The news of two towers has stunned us. It's impossible that Davenport didn't let us know of such a significant change in plans. "Your owner cleared it with the tower company," Burnell continues. "He said if everyone here agreed, we can push ahead with a second tower. If we do that, I'll put in writing that your company is guaranteed to build all my other platforms. I assumed you knew that. That's why you're here."

"We know nothing about it," Warren says. Burnell shrugs his shoulders and takes another long pull on his smoke. "This crew signed on for one extra week of work, not two. They have families."

"The excavators came out yesterday and dug your second hole," says Burnell, ignoring everything Warren just said.

"In two weeks, the weather could…" Warren is doing his part to push back, but Burnell interrupts.

"I know all about laying cement in cold weather," he says, impatiently. "But that's what got me thinking. There's no snow in the forecast. Not even a hard freeze. We're in the middle of a damn heat wave."

Burnell turns to favor the rest of us. "Boys," he says, "if there was ever a time to build something, it's now. Strike while the iron's hot.

Your owner told me you're his best crew. He thought you'd be up to the challenge. That is, if the money's right. And I can guarantee you, the money's right."

Burnell looks to Warren again, expecting him to make the final decision, but Warren's an office manager, a team builder, and a careful planner. He does things thoughtfully and by the book. He doesn't like surprises, and he doesn't make choices on his own for other people.

"Look, I'm willing to boost everyone's wage another $30 an hour on the second job and twice that for overtime," Burnell announces.

A quick calculation lifts my imagination to a new level. I'll make $90 an hour. $120 with overtime. That kind of money is unheard of in our line of work. Burnell draws on his cigarette again, savoring the smoke before exhaling. His tiny eyes probe us, waiting for someone to say something.

"I'm a generous person," he says finally, sounding a bit offended with us for remaining silent, maybe for not thanking him. "I've heard I could be the most generous person in this county, maybe the whole state."

Under his breath, Manny swears in Spanish. I can't tell if he's happy about the money or upset by the insincerity dripping from Burnell's lips. Warren notices Eddie fidgeting with his hands. "You having second thoughts, Eddie?" Warren says. "This isn't what I told you we'd be doing."

"No second thoughts," Eddie says. "I'm just wondering. That $30, it's extra from our normal pay?"

"It sure is," Burnell says, brightly.

"Just that extra is more than my mother makes at her job," Eddie says. "Sure, I'll do it."

"That's the spirit," Burnell crows. "Who *doesn't* want to stay?"

The amount of money to be made is beyond reason. Again, no one utters a word. And no one asks if there's enough time to build a second platform before the weather turns cold, even though it's the first thing we should be wondering.

"I'm all in on green energy," Burnell says, "have been for a couple years now. Only an idiot doesn't understand that green is the future. You know, Wisconsin has never seen anything like what I'm putting up here, and you boys will be making history. This is going to be the most beautiful wind farm in the state."

Burnell smiles proudly. It's a genuine smile, mostly tongue and teeth. Yet while we're anxious to get to work, Burnell's eyes are still measuring us. The victory smile stays on his face until his gaze stops again on Eddie. "How old are you, son?" he asks.

Eddie takes a step forward. "I'll be nineteen in January," he says.

Warren has already anticipated Burnell's next thought. "Don't worry about Eddie," Warren says. "He's young, but he's a terrific worker."

"He doesn't seem old enough to be out here."

"He's old enough and you're going to need him with this change in plans."

"Where are you from?" Burnell asks Eddie.

"Chicago."

"Chicago?" Burnell shakes his head. "Is this what you plan to do with your life?"

"Sir?"

"Is cement work your career path?"

"No, sir." Eddie says. "I want to help people."

Eddie's answer gives Burnell pause again. "Help them do what?" he says.

"You know, I want to make a difference in their lives."

Burnell laughs so hard he almost drops his cigarette. "Young man, I've heard that nonsense before. I've got a son who...." He drags on his cigarette again and then waves the thought away. Burnell's scrutiny of Eddie passes. His eyes move over to Manny. "Is the money I'm paying enough to make a difference in your life, *amigo*?"

Manny doesn't answer. It's impossible to know if Burnell is making fun of Manny or showing him he knows a few Spanish words. I've worked with Manny for six years. I can tell already that he's hating Burnell. Fortunately, the farmer's attention doesn't linger long enough to give Manny an opportunity to tell him what he's thinking. Burnell continues down the line, gives me a quick pass, as if I'm not worth a complete stop, and settles his scrutiny on Buck.

Buck Taylor is a big man. Before deciding that a full four years of college classes were not in his life plan, Buck was a linebacker for two seasons at Central Montana State University, starting every game. He's still in game shape and displays the thick neck and muscular shoulders of an athlete. Carson is standing beside Buck. Burnell has noticed Carson too. Carson never played college football, though he could have and probably at a big school. He has the same powerful look as Buck's, but he's heavier and taller, and he carries himself with more streetwise confidence. Both men stand a couple inches over six feet.

Burnell shifts a step to position himself up close and right in front of both Buck and Carson. They tower over the farmer, yet Burnell shows no worry. "You two boys look like you got a decent chance of getting this job done," he says. "Maybe I should pay you more and pay the others less." Burnell doesn't wait for Warren to respond, as I'm sure he expects Warren to do. Instead, Burnell turns and looks back across his valley that spreads out below us.

The sun is fully above the horizon now. A cloudless sky is turning robin egg blue, and everything's pointing to a beautiful day ahead. From our vantage point, I can just make out Sizemore Coulee Road and its junction with US 53. A distant vehicle reflects sunbeams off its windshield as it moves east along the highway.

Skinny comes out of the trailer and sticks a flagpole with the Stars and Stripes attached into a holder next to the door. The sound of the trailer door closing draws Burnell's attention back to us. He waves Skinny over. Burnell's chalk white cheeks are glowing pink in the stiff breeze. He reaches a hand under his parka and pulls out a thick fold of green bills held in place by a silver money clip. He undoes the clip and peels off one crisp $100 note after another, handing a bill to each of us. When Skinny arrives, Burnell hands him one too. Skinny looks at me with a confused frown.

Other than Eddie, the rest of us haven't agreed to anything yet, but Burnell already knows we're going to build his two platforms. The money is too good to pass up. He returns the silver clip to his pocket and snuffs out the last of his cigarette in the dirt. "Okay then," Burnell says. "Get to work. It's already quarter to eight."

We watch the farmer drive away, retreating back along the dirt trail where we came up the escarpment. Warren explains the second tower to Skinny and the extra money we'll be earning. I follow the descending red truck as it gets smaller and smaller, until I lose it in a thicket of gray branches far in the distance. "Allrighty-dighty," Skinny says and neatly folds the new bill and sticks it in his front pants pocket.

I know what Skinny's thinking: *when people hand you money for no reason at all, who's to complain?* Skinny has no problem with building a second platform. He'll just have to change the date he picks up his new boat in the Ozarks.

"Call your families and let them know we'll be here longer," Warren says, trying his best to sound upbeat. "I need to talk to the front office and see if we can get another body or two to help."

"Wait," Carson says before we start off. "Is it me, or is something off big time with this Sandberg guy? You said it last night, Skinny."

"Ignore Mr. Sandberg," Warren says. "We've handled worse." He hands Eddie a yellow hardhat to match the rest of us, required dress on a jobsite.

"He's majorly different," says Carson.

"Carson's got a point," says Skinny.

"Come on, guys. Let's get to it," Warren coaxes Carson and

Skinny, resting an arm around each of their shoulders. "We'll be out of here in no time."

On the way to my truck, I'm thinking about what Carson just said. Our new client does seem different, even a little strange. The weird house, the posturing, the way he throws money around. I try not to judge other people, since I have enough faults of my own, but Carson makes a good point. Burnell's behavior bears watching. At the same time, truth be told, I can't stop estimating all the money I'll be making here.

*Shooting grade.* As our crew's surveyor, I make sure the platforms we build are perfectly level, which is a simple way of saying that I determine boundaries and elevations. In addition to shims, measuring tapes, and chalk lines, my main tools include bubble levels and a tripod-mounted laser. Bubble levels are rectangular beams 2, 4, and 6 feet in length. You can buy them at any ACE Hardware. Like what a mason does, I use a bubble level for close-in work, when something needs an extra-fine calculation. The laser, on the other hand, is a digital piece of equipment that's powered by a computer chip. It gives me a fast way of shooting grade over a wide area. The laser level has two parts: the tripod mounted laser and a hand-held measuring rod.

MSP builds a hundred wind turbine platforms each season. Once completed, a platform looks like a 10-foot-high dome made of super-strong concrete that's been poured around a mesh of steel reinforcement bars. After the concrete has dried, we refill the pit with the soil that was removed, and then another company follows us in a few weeks to raise the tower and add the blades and energy-producing turbine at the top.

Building a platform is a meticulous process. Every calculation must be exact, each piece of support steel perfectly placed, and each load of concrete the correct consistency of cement, sand, gravel, and water. Being off an inch or a percent isn't acceptable. The wind towers that attach to our platforms stand 290 feet tall and weigh 180 tons. Our platforms must be strong enough to keep the towers from falling over, even during a tornado or a blizzard.

**With Burnell** finally off the plateau, we get to work. I unload equipment from my truck, while the rest of the crew organizes their own responsibilities, such as setting up a chop saw, charging batteries, segregating framing materials, connecting generators. It takes Skinny another hour to inventory the construction materials stacked next to the foreman's trailer and those on the flatbed and inside the shipping container.

On every project, our crew's first big step in building a platform is laying down a "mud mat," a flat three-and-a-half-inch-thick subfloor of poured concrete at the bottom of the pit. A mud mat gives us a level surface for everything else we'll build above it. It also keeps us from slopping through muddy ground if it rains. Because we're on a very tight schedule for this project, the mud mat for the first tower was poured earlier in the week by a company out of La Crosse. It has already dried and is rock solid. I recheck its measurements. The local company did their job well. The mud mat is ready to be worked on.

Warren and I drive to the second pit and discover that the mud mat for it hasn't been poured yet. There's only the big hole in the ground and two piles of fill dirt nearby. Warren gets on his cell phone to the local concrete company and explains what we need. He's assured that trucks of mix will start arriving by 11 a.m., which means we need to act quickly.

Buck, Carson, and Eddie load lumber onto the bed of Buck's pickup. They meet us at the second pit. Manny has brought his miter saw. I set up my tripod and laser on the dirt floor of the second pit, at the center. Manny miter cuts 2x4s into edge pieces. The rest of the crew stake out a 75-foot diameter circle on the ground and begin to assemble the 2x4s into a perimeter that's three-and-a-half inches high. This circular frame will contain the fresh concrete that we'll pour for the second mud mat.

With my measuring rod in hand, I walk around the 2x4 circle and call out height adjustments, at 1-foot intervals. Buck and Carson move up or down the 2x4s held in place by steel spikes. This is how we work at MSP: precise, steady, operating as a team. I double-check each measurement. Measure twice, cut once. It takes an hour to get the frame exactly how we want it.

Next, we level the ground inside the wood frame. With my measuring rod again in hand, I walk a spiral out from my tripod at the center of the circle. The laser and rod communicate together and tell me where the high spots are on the dirt floor. Where the ground is too high, Buck, Eddie, and Carson shovel away dirt, filling a wheelbarrow several times. This takes another hour before the second mud mat is ready to be poured.

The morning is passing fast and we're working at a good pace. We return to the first pit. I use my measuring tape and colored chalk to mark on the mud mat, that hard concrete floor, where the first strands of rebar will be laid out. Although the air temperature on the plateau is only 58°, the sky is clear, and the morning sun feels warm on my face. We're making progress, or as Skinny likes to say, *Life is good.*

By 10:30 a.m. the air has warmed, and I'm dripping in sweat. Warren shouts that it's time to take our 15-minute morning break. We assemble at the foreman's trailer and sit together on lawn chairs on the southside of the trailer, our faces fully in the sun's glow, our bodies out of the wind. Manny is wearing a Cowboys jersey, Carson a Harley-Davidson tee-shirt, Skinny a white tank top. Some in the crew drink coffee or Coke or Mountain Dew. Skinny pops a can of Red Bull. I pour a cup of chocolate milk from my thermos. We're as united and committed as the best-ever tailgate party at a ballgame.

Buck has taken his boom box from the pit to where we're sitting.

It's tuned to a country music station. Mornings we play country, afternoons classic rock. Sad ballads and love songs. It's a negotiated arrangement that appeals to all our tastes. Skinny's the only one of the crew who smokes. He removes a thin cigarillo from a colorful case and lights up. Although we have only fifteen minutes to relax, it's enough time to lean back and catch our breath.

We're barely settled in when distantly the sound of an approaching vehicle commands our attention. It's a throaty chorus of deep notes foretelling something powerful climbing the path up from the valley. I vaguely recognize the oncoming roar, but before I can place it, Burnell's red pickup crests the escarpment. He parks next to where we're sitting and shuts off his engine. Except for Chris Stapleton's pleading voice escaping Buck's radio, the plateau is silent. Sitting on the passenger side in the red truck is the same tall man we saw with Burnell on the porch earlier this morning.

Burnell pops out of his truck and greets us with a whiny bark. "What in Sam hell is going on up here?" The tall man gets out too and comes to the front of the truck, where Burnell waits. "Turn that fucking music off!" Burnell's irritated voice strains to reach the lower level of its narrow register.

Buck turns off the boom box, and for a moment the air becomes eerily quiet. Burnell's face is flushed, his body quivering. Then, he squeals, "You boys are here only a couple hours and already taking a fucking break?"

Warren is inside the trailer and has heard Burnell's tirade. He bursts through the trailer door. "What's the problem?" Warren asks and hurries down the wooden steps, a pencil in one hand, a calculator in the other. The rest of us are already on our feet and putting hoodies back on, then safety vests and hard hats.

"Look, Mr. Foreman," Burnell says. "I'm not paying your boys to get a goddamn suntan. I thought I made myself clear. We don't have time to spare. These towers need to go up now!"

"Mr. Sandberg, everyone who works for us gets one fifteen-minute break in the morning and one in the afternoon."

"Is that a government regulation?"

"No, sir. There's no government regulation for coffee breaks. It's company policy."

"How do I know they haven't been on break since I left?"

"Sir, we've already done a lot this morning. Go look for yourself. We're setting up rebar for the first platform. We already laid the forms for the second mud mat. Concrete will be here in a few minutes." Encased in the warmth of his parka and matching cap, Burnell stands frozen for a moment. Warren's logical explanation seems to have taken him by surprise. A small hand then escapes its orange protective pocket and points at the tall man planted next to Burnell.

"I brought Albert up here to introduce him," Burnell says. "Albert's my hired man. He runs my hog operation and oversees the Guatemalans working for me. Albert comes from Hungary, but he knows English."

We cautiously eye the foreign man, who stands at attention beside his *patron* like a mercenary soldier. Albert is about my age, mid-forties, and even larger up close than he looked standing on the porch. His hair is dark brown and cut short, framing a weather-beaten face with long 1980s sideburns extending to his chin. He's as tall as Skinny, but twice as wide. It's obvious in his shoulders that Albert's a man who is used to handling physical labor. We could use him on our crew, in fact. His rough and drawn face suggests a back story of struggle, possibly a family history long planted in subsistence agriculture. He reminds me of old photos from the Great Depression, portraits of American farmers struggling to squeeze whatever they could out of stressed crops and tired animals. Albert doesn't move a muscle or return our gaze. He's a statue with eyes fixed on the wall of the trailer behind us.

"Understand this," Burnell announces. "Whatever Albert tells you, it comes from me. If Albert says to do something, do it."

Burnell's prickly eyes give us a slow once over and then he shakes his head in disgust. Nothing more needs to be said. He returns to his truck. Albert follows. Before getting inside and while perched on the running board, Burnell decides he has one more thing to say. "Do I have your attention now?" he squawks.

The farmer doesn't wait for an answer. He powers up, and as he drives away, I'm left with a sick feeling in my stomach. I see it in Eddie's face too and across Warren's brow. To Burnell's way of thinking, we've crossed a forbidden line. To him, we're all shiftless losers. We've been caught red-handed, lounging on the job and wasting Burnell's money. It isn't true, of course, and Warren's explanation about company policy helped defend us some. Still, none of us like being thought of that way. We're too proud of the work we do to be shamed, even by a guy like Burnell Sandberg, yet I feel the weight of disgrace anyway.

"What a joke," Carson says, as he climbs into his truck to drive back to the second pit.

"A fucking asshole is what I'd call him," Skinny adds and then stops at the front of his truck. "See how he stood with his hand in his pocket? Looks like Napoleon." He mimics Burnell posing fiercely like the diminutive French emperor.

"You're right," I say. "You know, in real life, Napoleon was a terrible person."

"That fits," echoes Carson and the others nod in agreement, but before the dialogue goes too far afield, Warren brings our focus back on what's most important.

"The first load of mix will be here in a few minutes, fellas. Let's get ready."

We wait at the bottom of the second pit, our hands fitted in rubber gloves, our feet buried in knee-high boots also made of rubber. Manny had an extra set of rubber gloves and boots in his truck that he's given to Eddie. "Always wear rubber," Manny warns him.

"This shit will eat your skin."

The first truck backs up and the driver gets out. He unfolds a long metal chute that's attached beneath a rotating barrel that holds ten cubic yards of ready-mix concrete. It's my job to check every truckload to make sure the concrete we're delivered is the consistency we require. It's called a *slump test*, and I do it on the first few pounds of mix coming out of the drum. The load passes my inspection, and then the driver points the end of the long chute over the 2x4 frame on the floor of the pit and lets the mix run.

One pull of a lever and wet concrete slides down the chute, hitting the ground with the sound *plop-plop-plop-plop*. It's the sound that begins every great wind farm, and for me, it brings a thrill that never gets old. It means that concrete is flowing on a new project, the start of another platform going up, the building of something from scratch.

A thick gray mound begins to rise at the point of delivery. Buck, Carson, Eddie, and I shovel and rake the heavy mix into the wooden form we've built. The large 2x4 frame slowly begins to fill. Our bodies move to the beat of another country tune playing on Buck's boom box. Manny and Skinny have positioned themselves on either side of the chute. With a long pole called a *screed*, they smooth the surface of the wet mix, using the top of the 2x4 frame as a guide, keeping the surface level. Screeding is an art form that requires a steady hand and an eagle eye. Jimmy Gilligan was a specialist at it, but with Jimmy in jail, Manny has the lead, with Skinny as his assistant.

A second truckload of concrete follows the first. As Manny and Skinny smooth the surface of the evolving mud mat, the rest of us keep shoveling and raking fresh mix away from the delivery point. Lifting shovels of concrete is painful enough on our backs and legs but having to wade through an ankle-deep sea of the mix makes the job even harder. By the third truckload, Eddie is having trouble keeping ahead of the flow.

Skinny calls out, "Eddie, you're on a hill! Move that shit!"

Eddie responds by shoveling faster. It's clear to all of us now that Eddie isn't used to physical labor like this. A few minutes go by and Skinny calls again. "Eddie, you're still too high!" Eddie does all he can to move the heavy gray sludge down the line, but his arms are limp, his knees wobbly.

Skinny calls again, "You're still up on a hill, man!"

Eddie never stops shoveling, never looks up, but he calls back over his shoulder, "I'm standing on a hill, Skinny, because I'm shorter than the rest of you!"

For a moment no one says anything. Then Skinny stops screeding and begins to laugh. Manny puts down his end of the screed and starts laughing too. Soon, we're all laughing, Eddie included. This is the moment Eddie joins our crew. From here on out, we treat him like he's been part of our team from the beginning.

**After the** last driver has washed his chute and the truck is driving away, Manny and Skinny start *magging* the mud mat's wet surface. Magging brings the *cream* or liquid of the concrete to the top and gives a slab its smooth surface. Magging is done with a *float*, a flat bar of magnesium attached to a long aluminum pole. Like screeding, magging requires a special talent to do it right. Skinny and Manny are very skilled at it.

It's past noon when we finish the mat and leave it to dry. I'm returning tools to the shipping container when I notice Eddie and his shovel reclining on the pile of topsoil next to the first pit. His eyes are closed, and his arms are spread wide. Warren has also spotted Eddie. We go over and recline in the sun too, on either side of the teenager.

"You tired?" I ask. Eddie remains silent, doesn't even open his eyes.

"You did good work this morning," Warren says.

"My feet are frozen," Eddie mumbles.

"Two hours in wet concrete can do that," Warren says, "even on a warm day."

"I can't feel my arms."

"That's your muscles growing," Warren tells him. "Every day out here, you'll get a little stronger. By next week, you'll look all pumped up, like Superman." Eddie opens his eyes and looks skeptically at Warren. He's not buying it.

"Sun feels good, doesn't it?" I say.

"I guess so."

"Come on," Warren says to Eddie and pulls the kid to his feet. "Let's get some lunch."

**Driving back** to Pigeon Falls takes us ten minutes from the plateau, which is twenty minutes roundtrip. With parking and hand washing, that leaves about half an hour to order lunch and eat it. It's not a lot of time but enough. Crews often break into small groups for meals, depending on what kind of food they want. In Pigeon Falls, as in the other towns where our crew has worked, we always eat together, not because there are only a few places to find food, but because we prefer not to split up.

Candace isn't working when we get to the Shoe. Instead, we're helped by a woman in her 70s whose nametag reads *Dot*. Dot's hair is gray and neatly permed. She greets us as at the back of the dining room and hands out menus, then takes our orders and a few minutes later returns with our food. "Is Dot short for Dorothy?" Skinny asks.

"It is, hon," she replies and sets a plate in front of him.

"My mother's name is Dorothy," says Skinny. "They call her *Dot* too." As many meals as we've eaten together, I can't ever recall Skinny mentioning his mother's name. He keeps family details pretty much to himself. He adds, "It's not a name you hear much anymore."

"No, not so much," Dot says and then asks, "Aren't you the boys working on those windmills out at the Sandberg farm?"

"That's us," says Warren. I know Warren doesn't have the heart to correct Dot, to tell her that *windmills* are for grinding things like grain or corn and wind *towers* are for generating electricity.

"Does Candace have the day off?" Carson asks.

"She only works evenings. She's on the schedule tonight." Dot sets down the final plate of our order. "Enjoy!" she says and leaves.

**It's 2:00** p.m. when we get back to the jobsite. A large blue crane has arrived while we were at lunch, and it's standing now along the rim of the second pit. Sunlight glints off its long neck that's stretched over our deep hole in the earth. For me, seeing cranes in the wild like this, surrounded by pine trees and tall grass, is a stunning sight, not only because their elongated bodies move in elegantly odd angles through the air, but also because they are so foreign to the natural landscape. We couldn't get by in our work without the help of cranes. At their tallest point, with their necks fully extended, the cranes we use stretch 72 feet from front to back. They're beautiful to watch as their hydraulic booms and cable pulleys twist and turn gracefully, while lifting thousands of pounds of rebar in one smooth sweep of the neck.

The crane operator who brought this machine is a local, thirty-something man named Bud. He wears a white ball cap over long hair that's tied in a ponytail. Bud's puffing on a vape cartridge at the back of his heavy-equipment trailer when we return from lunch. He gives a friendly wave as we approach. For the rest of the afternoon, Bud steers the crane's long blue neck over the first pit as it sets bundles of rebar at the bottom.

While the second pit is drying and everyone else is working with Bud, I'm alone at the center of the first pit marking more chalk lines on the mud mat, indicating where the first rods of the rebar will go. We call these bottom rods *bearing bars* because they'll bear much of the weight of the platform. Bearing bars weigh 85 pounds each and take two men to carry. They're placed four feet apart on the mud mat and elevated on steel supports three inches high. We raise them off the floor so concrete can fill in below the rods and prevent weak spots.

A dusky sun has sunk behind the western tree line by the time the crane finishes lifting its last bundle of rebar. Bud's done for the day and takes off, though the rest of us still have more to do. We continue to assemble the mesh of steel rods that's begun forming atop the floor. Wherever two rods intersect, we twist-tie them together with steel cables. Then, we add 55-pound rods at 1-foot intervals between the heavier rebar in order to build more strength.

No one has taken a break since lunch. Skinny swore while we were eating that he'd work non-stop all afternoon, and he's fulfilled that pledge. Whether it was to avoid another confrontation with our client or to prove he could work without a rest, Skinny never explained. Either way, we followed his lead. Burnell drove out twice to check on us. Both times he was alone and never got out of his truck. He simply perched above the pit and watched us working below, all the time talking on his phone.

Closing in on 5:30 p.m., Warren claps his hands and calls, "Let's light 'em up." We wheel a portable gas generator to the edge of each pit and set up LED stands along the rims. These are powerful security lights that will run all night. Almost all the daylight has abandoned us by the time we switch on the LEDs. Only narrow ribbons of orange and red remain in the west, where sky meets land. Even so, the colors are hugely vivid, as if someone has lit the horizon on fire.

Intense sunsets, like the one I'm seeing now, are short-lived this far north in late autumn. They're measured in minutes, and before you know it, they've slipped away, and the world has become impenetrably dark. I prefer the sunsets of early summer instead. That's when sundown lasts an hour or more and is painted in wide brush strokes of magenta, my favorite color, that gauzy compromise between purple and pink. Magenta offers the softest shade of twilight during the year, something that's especially comforting on the eyes at the end of a tiring day. It's a hue that makes me wish that summer went on forever.

Those magenta sunsets always leave me feeling satisfied in what I've accomplished during the day, that the hard labor I've put in was worth the effort. I might be tired at nightfall in summer, but I'm always eager for the next day to begin, because a magenta sunset makes me believe that tomorrow will be just as fulfilling as today was.

That's never the case in autumn, with its shorter hours of daylight and brief sunsets. By fall, my body and mind carry months of strain and fatigue. I'm no longer excited about the days ahead or eager to accomplish anything more. These short-lived sunsets in autumn do little for me. I only want to crawl into bed and sleep, a feeling that is even more undeniable this year, what with all the troubles that have been going on in my stomach.

**After showering,** we gather for dinner in the Shoe. Eating together is the one thing I do look forward to throughout the season, even when I'm tired. Sharing a meal is a family ritual, and this MSP crew is my family when I'm on the road. Entering the dining room, I pass the same bartender from last night. He waves in recognition, and I wave back. I find a seat at our usual table, between Warren and Skinny. Tonight, Buck is posted next to Eddie, who's hunched over his placemat and looking so still that I wonder if he's breathing.

A paper insert to my menu announces the evening's special: *Friday Fish Fry*. I'd forgotten what day of the week it was. In Wisconsin, the Friday fish fry is an honored tradition and a treat for our crew whenever we're working in the state. Over the years, I've learned that for more than a century restaurants throughout Wisconsin have been serving fish on Fridays. The tradition began in the 1800s, with immigrants from Germany and Poland. Their

Catholic faith prohibited them from eating meat on Friday. Over time, the practice of eating fish on Friday found popularity throughout the state, regardless of one's religious or ethnic background. Today, a Friday fish fry in Wisconsin is like a town hall meeting, bringing together people from near and far. It's a time to reflect on work and school and family life, the perfect end punctuation to the past week.

In fact, I've yet to come across a tavern or supper club in Wisconsin that doesn't have a Friday fish fry on its menu. A typical plate includes beer-battered perch or walleye with a side of tartar sauce, a heap of french fries, a slice of buttered rye bread to dislodge throaty fish bones, and cole slaw served in a small dish or a plastic cup. Though, as much as I look forward to these Friday meals when we're in Wisconsin, the way my stomach's been acting lately I'm having second thoughts about eating anything fried tonight.

Before we order, Manny takes a call from Rita and steps outside to talk. I make a second pass through the menu. Upon returning to our table, Manny says, "Rita's worried. She thinks the baby might come anytime. She's making me nervous."

"What're you waiting for?" Warren says. "Go down there and be with her. It's not a problem."

"Yeah, brother," Skinny says, "we've got everything covered up here."

"Not with two platforms, you don't," Manny says. "You need all of us, and more."

"What's the hold up with Davenport?" Carson asks. "They gotta step up and get us some extra bodies. Manny's gonna to be a father. He needs to be there."

"It's okay," Manny says. "I came to Pigeon Falls *because* of the baby. The extra money will help. I've got to stay."

We talk for a while about hospitals and the cost of raising children, though Warren's the only one among us who's ever been a parent. Eddie adjusts the position of his head on the table, and I know he's alive. "You holding up okay?" Skinny asks him. He whispers something back that none of us can make out, other than it sounds like exhaustion. Buck balls up a paper napkin and tosses it at Eddie, hitting him on the head.

"Come on, Eddie," says Buck. "Today wasn't that bad. You were shoveling shit like a pro! Once you get back from Hollywood, you gotta come work with us." Eddie raises his head off his arms just high enough to grin.

Carson is texting furiously. We can hear his fingers clicking against his phone screen. "You got a nibble?" Skinny asks.

"This time, something's gonna happen," Carson assures us. "I can feel it."

"We've heard that before," I remind him.

"Yeah, but she's the first *nurse*," says Carson.

Candace arrives with a tray of beverages. She circles the table, placing a bottle or glass in front of each of us. I get a glass of milk. Skinny a Dutch import. And on and on around the table. The thing is, we haven't given Candace our drink order. So, here she is working from memory and giving us the same beverages that we ordered last night. For Eddie, she puts down a can of orange Fanta and a tumbler of ice. "Sweet," he says, lifting his shoulders off the table.

"If you guys don't want what you had last night, I can change it," Candace says with that smile of hers again. "Since we're busy, I thought I'd get you started with something I knew you liked. Sorry that I don't know your names yet."

I can't ever recall a time when a waitress remembered our drink preferences the day after our first night in town. No one asks her to change the order, though we share curious glances around the table. "Darling," Skinny says to her, "Do you memorize the drinks for every customer?"

Candace's smile hasn't let up, and it's radiating ample kindheartedness across the table.

"Memorizing stuff keeps my mind working," she says. "Waitressing is kind of boring, you know."

"But how do you know you'll see the people again?" Buck asks.

Candace shrugs. "If I didn't exercise my brain, I couldn't do this job very long."

We tell her our names, and she tells us that she's been waitressing at the Shoe for almost five months. Before starting here, she says, she completed two semesters at the state university in Eau Claire. "College didn't fit you?" Warren asks. He finished his own business degree by taking night classes for several years.

"I loved college," Candace says. "Someday, I'll go back. Just don't know when."

We give her our meal orders. I can't resist the fresh perch but take only half an order with no fries or cole slaw. I add a vanilla shake. "Remember, tomorrow night's our big, big special," she says. "Spaghetti and ribs, all you can eat. We'll have a full house for sure. I'll reserve this table for you."

**Moments later,** and before we get our food, the sudden awareness of a shared danger ripples through the dining room. A commotion is brewing up front near the bar. I turn to see our waitress's halo of bleached blonde hair in the middle of the disturbance. Candace is trying to break free from a man who has a hold on her wrist. The man appears to be late twenties, early thirties. He's good-looking, with strong features. He stands as tall as Candace but is wide in the shoulders and beefy in the neck and arms. Most notable is his trim dark beard and the red ball cap he wears backwards.

The bearded man draws Candace closer and pushes a thumb into her arm pit. It's an odd grip, some kind of martial arts or police technique that makes my stomach churn. He has her subdued now, unable to free herself, but she says nothing until he presses deeper and then she cries out. The room quiets. A couple of older men in the middle of the room rise from their tables. Candace removes her cell phone from her apron pocket and hands it to the man in the red cap. He stashes the phone inside his jacket.

The bartender has moved towards the trouble like saving grace, coming from the far end of the bar in a flash. "That's enough, Jared!" he commands, loud enough for everyone in the room to hear. He reaches under the bar and pulls out a long piece of wood, a milled table leg. He strikes it hard against the bar top. "Let her go! Now!"

The bearded man lets go of Candace's wrist but gives her a little shove for good measure.

"Can I have my phone, please?" she asks, seemingly more annoyed than anything else.

He ignores her question but warns, "Make sure you're ready when I come to get you, not like last night." Candace retreats and exits the room through a door to the kitchen. Eddie is looking nervous, unsure what's happened.

"It's all right, Eddie," Warren says.

I hadn't noticed until now, but Skinny left our table during the commotion and has joined the bartender up front in a face-off against the bearded man. He's standing only an arm's reach from him. "You've got no right treating her like that," Skinny says.

The bearded man points to the wide gold band on his ring finger. "This is all the right I need."

*Outsiders.* Whenever our crew comes to a new town, we try to remain low key and off the local radar. We don't want to cause waves. We're outsiders, and we understand what that means. Getting involved with townies is not good for our business, and it can be dangerous.

But here's Skinny in the middle of a storm, face-to-face with a man who's just roughed up his sweet young wife, who is also our waitress. Skinny is six inches taller than the bearded man in the red cap, but his adversary is twenty-five years younger and outweighs

Skinny by fifty pounds. The man clenches his fists against his chest, daring Skinny to spar with him.

"Get out," the bartender says in a calm but controlling voice. "Right now, Jared, or I call the sheriff." The bearded man makes a threatening flinch towards Skinny and the bartender, but it's only a tease. He then starts to nod, as if his head is keeping time to a tune that only his ears can hear. The stare-down draws out with no one budging.

Then, the man unclenches his fists and lets his hands drop to his sides. He zips his coat slowly, as if he has all the time in the world, and then pivots on his heels, military style, and leaves through the front door. The silence gripping the room holds another moment, and then conversation starts to fill in again as the bartender returns his club under the bar.

Moments later, Skinny returns to our table and sits. "The bartender's name is Mike," Skinny begins. "Seems like a good guy. He says the piece of shit up there was Candace's husband."

"How's she doing?" Warren asks.

"She's embarrassed more than anything. Mike says they've been married only a few months." Skinny motions us to follow him, and we move camp to a corner of the bar while we wait for our food. Skinny buys everyone but Eddie and me a shot of Jägermeister to take the edge off. It's a fresh 2% and a Fanta for the two of us. The bartender puts down his bar towel and accepts a shot as well. He's interested in talking.


**It's a condition** in small Midwest towns served by only one high school that you can learn all you shouldn't about the town, in a single night at a bar.

Mike tells us the husband's name is Jared Vreelander. The Vreelanders are a high-profile family in Trempealeau County, with Jared's father owning a big car dealership in Bridgewater. After high school, Jared enlisted in the Army. When he was discharged, he went back to living at home and started working for his father. That's when he spotted Candace. She was a cute eleventh grader, and he was a twenty-seven-year-old Army veteran, a full ten years separating them. In no time, Jared was picking Candace up after school, taking her where she needed to go, buying her things she otherwise wouldn't have had.

Mike accepts a second shot and fills in more of Candace's backstory.

Raising her six older siblings had been a strain on Candace's parents. It nearly broke them. By the time Candace came along, her parents had stopped meaningful parenting. Even today, Candace's parents don't like Jared, but there's the rub. His family is prominent, and he has the money to take care of her in ways they can't.

"A couple months ago," Mike says, "Jared started coming in every night. He's always been a dick, especially after he got discharged. But he'd sit here at the bar and if she acted too friendly with a customer, Jared would tell her about it. Two weeks ago, Candace said something back and he grabbed her by the wrist, almost twisted her arm off."

"We saw that bullshit move," says Carson.

"I threw him out," Mike says. "We can't have that in here."

"*Es un veradero pendejo,*" says Manny.

"I also let the sheriff's office know. They were going to tell him to shape up, but like I said, Jared's always been a dick."


**Tonight, before** falling asleep, I lie in bed thinking. Not about my visit to the clinic and the mystery behind my stomach pain, but about our young waitress and her husband. What happened tonight happened in public, in front of thirty or forty people. It's tough to imagine what happens between Jared and Candace when no one is watching.

If Jared had never spotted Candace in high school, I'm thinking, maybe her life would be different now. Maybe she'd be just another college coed on her way to somewhere else, and not the victim of a violent partner. There's still hope for Candace, of course. Maybe she'll find a way to leave her husband. Maybe the court will catch up to Jared and punish him. Maybe he'll be struck by lightning. It's a lot of maybes, though only one thing is certain. Before any of that happens, Candace will continue to hurt.

As my brain processes the threat that Jared poses and my eyes adjust to the darkness filling my new hotel room, I take note of the room's peculiar shadows that seem to be encircling me. Caught in a slit of light escaping the drawn curtains, the shadow cast by my armoire looms high in one corner, looking down on me. The half open door to the bathroom spills its own shady outline across the floor, an irregular figure that's only inches from my bed. And outlines of assorted shadows on the ceiling above me and made by the hanging lamp and its trio of pleated lampshades, appear like three fat spiders dangling from a dark thread. I pull the thick comforter up to my neck and close my eyes, immersing myself in the safety of sleep and the absolute quiet of the village of Pigeon Falls.

Before drifting off, I recall a line from something I heard on the on the radio yesterday, during my drive from the clinic. It went something like, *What doesn't kill you makes you stronger... yeah, yeah, yeah.* It's a catchy maxim, but not true for our young waitress, Candace. When it comes to abuse and a bully like Jared Vreelander, what doesn't kill you just makes you suffer longer.


## Saturday, November 2

Over the years, I've witnessed thousands of early morning skies, all sorts of fascinating color combinations and cloud formations. What amazes me still is how every now and then I'll come upon a color palette I don't recognize or a new cloud shape that bends my imagination. Today is one of those rare mornings.

I pause for a moment on the plateau above the Sandberg farm to marvel at the evolving sky. Layer upon layer of various shades of gray hang above the horizon to the south, everything from silver to pewter, from charcoal to ash. In the narrow space that's left between the gray clouds and the darker land, today's harbinger of dawn is sprouting, a burst of blinding yellow light so special, I'd put it close to the color of joy. The brightness is more than overpowering, wedged between the clouds and the land, I can only look at it for a second before turning away. Even so, it's more than enough grandeur to put anyone in a good mood for the day ahead.

**After laying** down bearing bars, our next step in constructing a wind turbine platform is to add the heart of what will be our concrete and steel anchor. It's the large cylinder of welded rebar that resembles a giant bird cage. MSP's cages are pre-assembled in Davenport and trucked to our job sites. The cage for the first Sandberg platform is resting on a wood pallet beside the foreman's trailer. The cage for the second platform is only being loaded onto a trailer in Davenport this morning and won't arrive on site until later this afternoon.

One function of the cage is to protect the tubes of PVC conduit that will hold the main electrical cables for the tower. The cage is also the central support structure we'll use when building the rest of the platform. Dimensions for cages vary across the industry. At MSP, ours run 12 feet tall and 10 feet in diameter.

My immediate task this morning is to locate where the first cage will sit on its bearing bars. When I finish marking the outline, Bud works with his crane to lower the large cylinder of steel onto the profile I've chalked. While the rest of the crew steadies the heavy parcel, I use my 6-foot mason's level to make sure the vertical sides of the cage are perpendicular. Manny inserts steel shims as needed around the base, hammering and readjusting until we have the cage standing exactly how we want it. Then, we anchor it to the bearing bars with dozens of steel twist ties.

Burnell pulls up at ten, as we're all walking to the foreman's trailer. Warren has insisted we not go without coffee breaks anymore. It's not good for us, he told us, and it sends the wrong message to MSP's customers. Nevertheless, the timing of Burnell's arrival couldn't be worse. Surprisingly though, he ignores our approach and hurries up the stairs and into the trailer. Albert and a boy in his early teens get out of Burnell's truck and stand beside it. The boy is a smaller version of Albert, with the same shoulders, head, and big hands, so I assume the youngster is Albert's son.

The morning air is warm now, and the sky has cleared of clouds. I open a bottle of water and drink, while enjoying the sun's rays. No one dares take out a folding chair or remove his hoodie. As close as we are to the trailer, it's easy to overhear what's being said inside. Warren is telling Burnell that some of the rebar for the second platform won't arrive for two days. The supplier shipped the wrong bearing bars to Davenport.

"This is unacceptable!" Burnell shouts at Warren, who assures our client that we can find a work-around, that we won't lose any time. But that's not an answer that satisfies Burnell. "Call your boss. I want to talk to him," he says. Warren tells Burnell the office is closed on Saturdays. "Then call him at home, goddamnit! I don't have two days to wait!"

Warren calls MSP's owner at home. I only hear Burnell's side of the conversation, but it's enough for me to roll my eyes and shake my head. Burnell complains about Warren's leadership. He refers to us as *bums* and claims that we spend half our time sitting around doing nothing. Burnell says he won't accept any more delays. "I have a contract!" he shouts.

I share a nervous look with my co-workers, who've also been listening in. Never have we had a client as out of control as this one. Part of me wants to laugh at what Burnell is saying, maybe make a joke about it, because all of it is ludicrous. But Albert is looking directly at me, as if he can read my mind. I silently look away.

When Burnell exits the trailer, he's still angry. His hand quivers while grasping the staircase's side rail. As flushed as his face is, his head seems ready to explode.

Manny calls over to Burnell when he's halfway down the stairs. "Why do you say those lies?" Manny asks. It's a question, I believe, we've all been wondering, but only Manny is bold enough to ask right now. Burnell stops one step from the bottom of the stairs.

"What are you crying about now, *hombre?*" Burnell asks.

"Why do you have to insult us?"

Burnell chuckles. "Mind your own fucking business," he says and continues towards his truck.

But Manny doesn't let it go. "My mother says, *Se cazan más moscas con miel que con vinagre.*"

Burnell opens his door. "I don't *Español,*" he snickers, though I'm not sure him not understanding Spanish is true.

"It means, *You catch more flies with honey than with vinegar.*"

Burnell puts a leg up on the chrome foot rail of his truck. "Thanks for the Spanish lesson." He speaks in a high-pitched whine that suggests sarcasm and arrogance. "Let me ask you this," Burnell adds, as he's about to get into his truck, the side door already open. "You born in this country?"

Manny replies rapidly in Spanish. It's a lengthy response. I understand none of it.

"Didn't think so," Burnell scowls. Manny says nothing more, only zips his hoodie. "Now, that's more like it." Burnell appears self-satisfied, as if he should congratulate himself for putting Manny in his place. He turns his focus on the rest of us. "You boys need to follow your buddy here. Zip up and get back to work. That's an order."

Burnell slides into the driver's seat, just as I'm realizing that

Manny isn't heading back to the pits. He's on a path towards Burnell's truck, quickly closing the forty feet that separates them. Manny starts cursing in Spanish, phrases we all recognize, even if some of the nuances aren't clear.

Burnell notices Manny through his windshield. As he's climbing back out of his truck, Burnell shouts, "If that's how you want to play it, bring it on!" Burnell jumps back down to the ground and starts moving towards Manny, who is almost at the red truck.

*Fighting with locals.* Other MSP crews I worked with over the years, though never this group, would get into a dustup now and then. It was always against townies in some sketchy place and about nothing important, just an unfortunate yet inevitable consequence of a traveling culture crossing paths with a local one. Some amount of alcohol usually figured into those confrontations. Fighting's not the smartest way to address a problem, of course, but it gives the most immediate relief. At MSP, as is true at other construction companies, there's an unwritten pact: *Always protect your brother.* If an outsider confronts a crew member, then the rest of the crew comes to his aid. This developing battle with Burnell is different, however. Never, until now, has a crew member squared off against a client.

**Like the** rest of us, Albert's been watching the situation unfold and rushes to take a defensive position between his boss and Manny. Only six feet separate Manny and Albert, close enough to see that the difference in their sizes is unambiguous. Albert stands half a foot taller and outweighs Manny by fifty pounds. Albert's son has joined his father on the front line. We hurry over to support Manny, just as the door to the foreman's trailer bangs open.

"Guys, guys, guys!" Warren calls to us, while hurrying down the stairs. Panic is fueling his rapid decent. Fortunately, Warren's mind is not guided by panic, but by reason.

"Come here, please," Warren says to us. "I have something important to share with you."

We hear Warren but hold our position. Eddie is beside us too, standing between Buck and Carson. Like Albert's son, Eddie is lending a helpful hand to whatever's going on, but I'm certain neither he nor Albert's son has a completely clear idea why he's standing there in a face-off and what's about to happen.

"Come, come, come," Warren chants amid a fierce accompaniment of hand clapping.

Skinny sighs and is the first to turn away from Albert. Then, Manny turns, and the rest of us back off and follow them to where Warren waits at the bottom step of the trailer. "See you later, Mr. Sandberg." Warren waves with a nervous hand that moves erratically, like it belongs on someone else's body.

Keeping a watchful eye on us, Burnell, Albert, and the boy climb back into the red truck, its powerful engine starting with a huff. Warren continues waving until the truck is on the path pointed down the side of the escarpment. Warren then takes in a deep breath with his eyes closed. His body continues to tremble.

"That was close," Warren says finally, but he's still shaky. "I don't know what that guy's problem is, but I do know he's an *idiot*."

Warren pauses again to catch his breath and settle his balance. "Just so you know," he says, "everyone in the front office is aware of what we're dealing with here. Stable Platforms is not in the business of giving away business, but the president just told me he'll stop the project... if that's what we want. We can tell Mr. Sandberg we've had enough. We can pack our equipment and head home."

Warren lets the idea of leaving sink in for a moment.

Then, he tells us, "I know I'll feel great getting away from here. At least for a while. But if we quit, you need to know that sorting out the Sandberg LLC contract will be a nightmare for our company and cost some serious lawyer money."

The rest of us are still fuming. We're not thinking about contracts and lawyers. Adrenaline pulses through my body. Its narcotic warmth has reached my fingertips and flushed my face.

"I don't like Mr. Sandberg any more than you do," Warren goes on. "So, we've got to figure this out. What do you want to do?" None of us is sure what the next step should be. We've never been in a situation like this before.

"That shit bird disrespected Manny," Carson says. "Before Manny it was Skinny. We heard on the phone what he said about us being *bums*. Client or not, I'll fight his sorry ass."

"I'm ready to call it quits," I say.

"Same here," says Skinny.

"No disrespect, boss," Carson says, "but if Jimmy Gilligan was here, that little prick would be in the hospital and so would his hired man."

"That's exactly what I'm worried about," says Warren. "They'd be in the hospital, and you'd be in jail."

"I get what everyone's saying," Buck says, "but if I'm being honest, I want to finish the job we started. I can put up with the farmer's bullshit. I need this money. I'll never make hourly like this again."

Manny steps forward and touches his hand to his heart. "*Muchas gracias*, my brothers." He takes his phone out of his coat pocket and holds it up. "Rita keeps texting. She's scared about the baby. That's what upset me. She wants me with her. I have to go." Manny shakes his head. "I'm also thinking, if I go, maybe that *pendejo* will calm down."

Manny turns towards Warren. "Boss, if I leave, will I lose my job in spring?"

"No, you won't," Warren says. "I can talk to Davenport. It'll be all right."

Either way, Manny has no choice, and he gets it. Family first, whatever the risk. "I gotta do this," he says and fist-bumps each of us. He hugs Carson last. A minute later, Manny's in his truck and driving away. Warren wants to know who else is leaving and who will stay. We talk it over and decide to keep working. We solemnly walk back to the first pit, and Warren returns to the trailer to refigure our work assignments, down one good man.

**After lunch,** the episode with Burnell is behind us, and we start building what we call the *nest*. The process begins by attaching long strands of rebar in a complex web around the inner cage. A nest is huge, 56 feet in diameter and 8 feet tall at its crest. It's the skeleton for our platform. When finished, and before we fill it with concrete, the nest of rebar will look like the home for a giant mother bird, albeit upside-down. On most jobs, it takes us eighteen hours to finish one nest, and that's with a full crew. On this job, we don't have that much time.

When Warren emerges again from the foreman's trailer, he comes to where we are in the pit. He shows us a new work chart he's drawn and says he's hopeful we can finish the first nest in a day and a half, even with Manny gone. It's an ambitious goal, but we trust his calculations and buy into the plan.

I keep an eye on Eddie all afternoon. He's been with us only two days, yet if I were giving grades for effort, Eddie would earn an A+. The kid pitches in and never stands around waiting to be told what to do, which for an eighteen-year-old is remarkable. He always carries his fair share of any load, and he never complains. Best of all, he catches on right away.

When I started with MSP, I knew a lot about surveying but nothing about building platforms for wind turbines. It took me a week to learn what Eddie has picked up in two days. Adults complain how video games and social media have made teenagers unable to think for themselves, how they're incapable of doing anything hands-on if an electrical outlet isn't within a short cord's reach. If that's true, Eddie is an exception.

And now, just as twilight is arriving and we're walking around the jobsite, moving among the shifting patterns of early evening shadows, Eddie's the first to notice the headlights from a flatbed trailer pulling onto the far side of the plateau from the county road. It's the driver from Davenport bringing the cage for the second platform. His arrival lays out our last two tasks for today. First, we have to set our night lights around each pit. Second, we have to get that second cage off its trailer, so the driver can return to Iowa.

As I stand with Eddie watching Bud and his blue crane lift the heavy load of steel and set it on the ground beside the second pit, Eddie asks me, "Have you been a surveyor a long time, Tom?"

"Since before you were born, I guess."

"Is it what you always wanted to do?"

"I was never sure what I wanted, Eddie. Not until I started shooting grade. The job's been good to me. So has Stable Platforms. I think I've been lucky finding what I like to do and doing it with a company I like working for."

Since I have the opportunity, I ask Eddie, "How's everything going for you? Are you adjusting to being away from Chicago?"

Eddie thinks for a moment. "It's hard getting used to how quiet it is here," he says, finally. "And how dark it gets. But I'm starting to like it."


**Leaving the** plateau, I look across the distant ridges and into the clear night to the southeast. Barely recognizable in all that darkness is a small feather of light a couple of miles away. It's floating like a faint amber mist between earth and sky. It's coming from the mercury vapor lamps that brighten the streets of Pigeon Falls. Somewhere under that glow, I know that warmth and good food await me.

As I drive down the escarpment, I look to see what ambient light might be coming from the towns spread along US 53 in the other direction of Pigeon Falls, places like Waterford, Templeton, and Bridgewater. But with so many hills and valleys out there, and a road that meanders from one coulee to the next, I'm unable to detect any brightness escaping in the west, only undefined darkness.

US 53 parallels Pigeon Creek for several miles east and west. When I get to US 53, I turn left towards Pigeon Falls. Pigeon Creek runs so close to the highway that even at night I can see the water's surface glimmering in the wash of my headlights. As I draw closer to town, I look for a waterfall or dam that might give the place its name. The nearer I get to town, the more I expect to spot something. But I arrive in Pigeon Falls having never encountered any falling water along the way, and I wonder how I could have missed it.


**The Saturday** night special of all-you-can-eat spaghetti and ribs is what the rest of our crew is looking forward to, what they've been talking about since breakfast. I'm eager for the special too, not because I'm starving, which I am, but because Candace was so excited for us to try the meal. I'm also anxious to hear what Skinny has to say about pairing pasta with barbecued ribs, because Skinny is a kitchen encyclopedia when it comes to food facts, and he owns a discriminating palate that he's developed over many years of travel. His father was military, and the family moved a lot.

So, add to that his work in construction, and Skinny's been on the road most of his life. He's tasted food at the best and worst restaurants in all fifty states. He can tell you a dozen ways to make chili, red base and white, with noodles and without. He can tell where in the country you are if you order a hoagie, grinder, po'boy, or sub. He knows what sets a frappé apart from a milk shake or smoothie, and he can tell you how they fill pierogies in Pittsburgh and what meat to pair with collard greens in Alabama. And if you let him, he'll talk your ear off about herbs.

Skinny has said several times that the labor of a skilled chef is no different from that of a skilled concrete worker. You get out of it only what you put into it. In other words, a tasty meal isn't made by throwing together a list of ingredients, any more than building the foundation for a wind turbine is just slopping around some rebar and concrete. Good food, like a well-built platform, involves the use of skillful techniques and a thoughtful process. Gathering and measuring and assembling are as important as finishing.

At every restaurant we visit, Skinny analyzes the menu and critiques the food he orders. Many times, I've watched him select only a green salad and a bowl of soup, rather than swallow another mediocre cheeseburger or basket of greasy chicken strips. So far at the Shoe, Skinny has had only one comment about his meals here: "The food's more than decent."

According to Candace, the Shoe's cook starts smoking his ribs early Friday afternoon. And his pasta sauce is an old family recipe that simmers all day Saturday. Skinny remarked to us that such a lengthy preparation is a hopeful sign the meal will be above average. Also worth noting is the size of the crowd when we arrive at the Shoe. Every chair in the room appears taken, even those along the bar. Candace forewarned us that the *Special* would fill the place, and she was right. Fortunately, we have our table reserved.

Entering the Shoe, I spot a vase sitting atop the bar in the place where the jack-o-lantern had sat two nights before. The vase is stuffed with a fistful of red long-stemmed roses. I also detect a sweet and unusual aroma circulating in the air, an intoxicating marriage of oregano, thyme, and barbecue sauce. We put off showering and take turns washing hands and faces in the men's room. No one in the restaurant pays attention to how we look. They're too busy attacking mounds of pasta and racks of ribs.

Candace brings our drinks. Nothing is said about what happened with her husband and her cell phone the night before. A lonely bottle of Corona remains on her tray. "You're missing someone," Candace says, looking around the table. "It's Manny."

"Manny had to leave," Warren tells her. "His wife's having their first baby."

Candace takes Manny's bottle of Corona off the tray and raises a salute. "Here's to Manny and his family," she smiles and clinks glassware around the table.

None of us bothers with the menu. Everyone orders the Special, though given my ongoing stomach issues, I ask for a kid's portion that's easy on the sauce. Warren excuses himself from the table. When he returns, he tells us we have an okay from the Shoe to keep our rooms an extra week if we need to.

"Anyone notice the roses?" Skinny asks.

"Mike says, Candace's husband left them," Warren reports.

"Figured as much."

Carson asks, "You think Jared roughed her up when she got home?" We pass that possibility around the table a couple of times. I notice Eddie listening intently, though he says nothing.

Buck brings up the memory of a waitress we had in Missouri last year. "Remember her?" he says. "She had bruises like that too."

Carson sets down his drink with a purposeful clunk on the table. "Fuck her husband," he says. "She's gonna get hurt bad. I know it."

In a soft diplomatic voice that ignores Carson's agitation, Warren says, "Okay, guys, I'm not going to kid anyone. I'm not sure if we can finish two platforms in time. I'm getting worried about the weather."

Disregarding Warren's statement and more determined than ever to follow his previous line of thought, Carson says, "All I want is a couple of minutes with him. No more than five."

"I've been looking at long-range forecasts," says Warren, pushing back. "I just don't see these warm days lasting much longer."

"Five minutes. That's all I ask."

"Listen," Warren says, finally. "What happens with our waitress is none of our business." Warren has added new weight to his words, using a commanding voice unlike anything I've heard from Warren before. It's steady and impactful, an emerging leader's voice.

He adds, "Our job here is to build platforms, so... *Stay. Focused.*"

Silence rules for the moment. Warren's message is clear: Keep away from Candace's marital problems.

When our food arrives, we wait for Skinny to try a bite and give his assessment. Candace and another waitress stand nearby, curiously watching the ritual. Skinny takes a fork of spaghetti, twirls it around the sweet spot of a spoon, and then daubs it with a little extra red sauce. "Bronze cut noodles," Skinny says in appreciation. He then chews in slow motion, just as any connoisseur worth his salt would. "Savory sauce," he adds and chews some more. "I can tell it's been mellowing all day, and with what? Bay leaves, dry red wine, a pinch of sugar... maybe some lemon zest?"

Skinny can be a character when he has center stage. His fingers pinch off a hunk of the meaty ribs and he feasts on it.

"Come on, Skinny," Carson pleads, "my plate's getting cold."

Skinny raises an index finger. Wait for it, he chews, wait for it. Eddie is smiling broadly, enjoying the show. Skinny swallows again. Smudges of barbecue sauce paint the edges of his moustache. He strokes his mouth with his napkin.

"Trust me, fellas," Skinny declares. "I've had worse."

We dive in. The pasta and ribs taste as good as Skinny predicted. Carson and Buck request second plates. The food is so delicious and light on my digestion that I'm convinced I could eat as much as I wanted without discomfort, though I'm not going to risk it. Candace brings Eddie a second orange Fanta.

"Compliments to the chef," Skinny says to her.

"When I came here as a girl," Candace tells us, "Max had to go to the Twin Cities to find real parmesan and tomatoes that didn't taste like wax. Now, he can get everything fresh in Eau Claire." She watches us eat for another minute and then leaves again. I'm wondering if anyone else has spotted the eye contact growing between Candace and Eddie. The moments are brief, lasting only an extra second or two, yet I'm certain something is developing between them.

Buck says, "I think you're right, boss. With Manny gone, it'll be impossible to get both platforms finished in time."

"I didn't say it was impossible, I'm just not sure of it."

"You still bugging Davenport for help?" Carson asks.

"Non-stop," Warren answers, "but it might be just us here."

"That's because Red Sandberg is a horse's ass," Carson adds.

"And that's why we have to stay clear of him."

"Leave the husband alone. Leave Burnell alone. Jesus, Warren."

"Carson, we don't want a war."

"Well, it's starting to seem like one."

"Carson, we *don't* want that," Warren responds firmly. "I'll interact with Burnell from now on. And yeah, Buck, I *am* betting we can finish on time. Weatherwise, the coming days still look good."

Warren pushes his plate aside and unfolds a paper napkin into a large white canvas that he spreads out on the table. Warren smooths the creases, and with a blue Sharpie from his pocket protector he begins to draw. After sketching a long horizontal line with a box-like indentation at the center, he says to Eddie, "Look here. This is what we accomplished yesterday and today."

The horizontal line Warren has drawn represents the plateau, and the indentation is one of our pits. Warren adds more lines along the indentation for the mud mat and bearing bars. As Warren's lesson continues and the portrait develops, Eddie takes a keen interest in it all.

"This is what's left," Warren says. Atop the bearing bars he draws a large cylinder that's cross hatched. "This is the *cage*," he says. "We set one up this morning." Warren subdivides the cage with a dark horizontal line, creating a shorter cylinder at the top. "This is the *crown*. It's the only part that sticks above ground. It's where the wind tower will attach to the platform."

The picture continues to take shape. Diagonal lines of rebar bow outwards and connect the sides of the cage to the mud mat. Other lines are added horizontally. "This is all rebar, and it forms a dome. We call it the *nest* because upside down, well, you see that's what it looks like." He turns the napkin for Eddie to get a better look.

"The nest gets filled with concrete," Buck says. "When the concrete is hard, the weight of a platform will hold a wind tower to the ground. The rebar is what makes it super strong."

"Almost everything we do is underground," Warren says and points to his original horizontal line across the napkin. "When we're done, the platform gets covered in dirt, everything except the very top of the crown."

Warren's portrait isn't finished. After he shades in dirt around the platform, he adds a tall tower above the crown. He then draws a nacelle at the top of the tower, a sleek elliptical shape like an egg, and finishes by adding three long skinny blades.

"Inside here is a turbine." Warren points with his pen at the nacelle. "Wind turns the blades. The blades turn the turbine. That's how electricity is generated. Three weeks after we leave here, the turbine company will come and erect the tower. By then, the concrete will be completely cured." Warren pushes the napkin towards Eddie. "Not too complicated, right?"

Eddie looks at the drawing and studies its parts. "How much electricity does one tower make?" he asks.

"Each turbine generates enough electricity to power a thousand houses," Warren says.

"Burnell will sell power to the local utility for a pretty good chunk of change," Skinny adds.

"And the power company sells it to their customers."

"These wind towers cost a lot, right?" Eddie asks.

"Yeah, a lot," Warren agrees. "Bigger ones even more." Warren then explains what he learned in Davenport last week, how Burnell received start-up money from the federal government, enough financing to build six towers for his wind farm.

"People in Washington want more renewable energy in rural areas of the Midwest," Warren says. "Mr. Sandberg got a loan to do that."

"You saw that new truck he's driving?" Skinny asks Eddie. Eddie nods. Skinny then says, with a sarcastically greedy grin, "Your government money at work."

"Government money is also paying our wages," Warren points out.

"Just saying, boss. It's a mighty fine truck for a man whose house is falling apart."

"Why is everyone so interested in getting this done before winter?" Eddie asks. "These towers still work in winter, don't they?"

"They work all year long," Warren says. "It's the concrete that's the problem. Concrete needs warmth to set right. If the temperature falls below 40°, we have to stop work. You can add a chemical to concrete to make it harden in cold weather, but if you use rebar, like we do, that chemical eats away the steel."

"It's why you don't see concrete highways being built during winter in northern states," says Buck.

"Or wind farms," adds Carson, who then lets his raised forearm fall to the table like a wind tower toppling over.

*Finding one's legacy.* Tonight, before falling asleep, I lie in bed thinking about Warren's napkin drawing of a wind tower and the one important thing Warren didn't mention to Eddie, that the platforms we build are intended to last for many decades, long enough to outlast even our own lives. It's a thought I come back to now and again, and it's something we've talked about as a crew.

For some of us, especially those of us without children, the wind towers we help to put up will be the only evidence that remains of our time on Earth once we're gone, the only proof that we were here. It's not only why we like building platforms, it's why the quality of work we do on them is so important to us.

With my eyes closed, I try to imagine every tower we've built. Hundreds of them out there turning 24/7, unstoppable, spinning forever, as if there really is such a thing as perpetual motion. I imagine them all together, one massive wind farm spread out across the country's heartland, row upon row of white towers and their long thin blades, wind energy as far as the eye can see. Each slow tumble of a blade becomes a miraculous confirmation of what we've built, confirming some new law of physics and the future passing of time. It's comforting to think like that, about what I'll leave behind someday.

Then, as I'm about to pleasantly drift into sleep, my fantasy future vanishes. Life is never that easy, of course. Instead of feeling satisfied, I'm confronted with new thoughts about Candace and her abusive husband. At dinner, we agreed to give Jared a pass for now, even though none of us believed this would be the last of the ugly stains on Candace's slender young arms.

We can't kill Jared, so I ask myself, what should a stranger do if they suspect someone is suffering ongoing domestic cruelty? Should they counsel the victim and try to get her to leave her abuser, maybe get her to seek help at some agency or hospital? Should a stranger inform law enforcement in the hope that the perp can be scared straight? Maybe a group of strangers, like our crew, should conduct a group intervention? Confront the abuser and persuade him to stop.

Or, as Warren suggests, is it better for strangers to just stay in a secure lane and mind their own business? When I consider all the options, each of them – except murder – ends up being a lukewarm remedy and leaves me feeling anxious, unable to fall asleep.

*Right or wrong.* Doing things right and not doing the wrong thing are straightforward commandments I've lived by for a long time. Unfortunately, the right and wrong ways to solve some problems, like the problem of Jared Vreelander, aren't always clear cut. Lying in my bed now, more awake than I was a few minutes ago, my thoughts circle in a convoluted spiral that gets me nowhere. Any of our options about Candace and Jared could be right, or wrong.

The only thing that's clear to me is that we're not Candace's family, not her neighbors, and not her co-workers. Our crew is concerned about her, that's a given. But we're nothing more than short-term acquaintances, travelers passing through Pigeon Falls on our way to somewhere else. We're here one week and gone the next. Soon, our project on the Sandberg farm will finish, and our recollections of this place will grow fainter and fainter by the day, eventually dissolving into the memories of every other place we've already passed through. And even if we do contact the police or confront Jared Vreelander before we go, will it even matter? I don't see Jared becoming anything different from who he is, not tomorrow, not ever.

And as I again begin to drift closer to sleep, I'm less and less sure about what we can do or should do or must do about him.

## Sunday, November 3

*Spring forward, Fall back.* With our adjustment for Daylight Savings Time, we gained an hour of sleep overnight, so I begin today a little more rested than yesterday. When we leave the Shoe after breakfast and head out to the jobsite, the streets of Pigeon Falls are not clothed in darkness as they were at this time yesterday. Today, the streets have already bid farewell to the night and stand alight in the soft blue-gray hues of the coming dawn. Normally during the construction season, Sunday is a day off for us, a free day to catch up on personal business, like paying bills and doing laundry. On the Sandberg project, however, we are working every day of the week. There's no time off for anything. There's barely enough time for us to catch our breath.

When I drive onto the plateau, I see the American flag that

Skinny had posted outside the foreman's trailer being pummeled by an incredibly strong wind. It's even more powerful today than it was yesterday. Swap-swap-swap-swap. The flag struggles valiantly against the blows. My years with MSP have taught me to pay attention to the wind. It's a valuable skill, knowing how to read its changing speed and direction. While the weather app on my cell phone is useful in many ways, nothing tells me more accurately the kind of weather that's approaching than what the wind is doing. A shift in direction can indicate that warmer or cooler weather is not far off. A sudden change in velocity can signal a storm is near, or better yet, that one has finally passed.

The wind on the Sandberg property, however, has me stumped. It blows as hard as ever, and it never stops. Normally, a breeze this powerful would foretell a changing forecast, a front coming through, a new weather pattern emerging. But up on the plateau now, I scan the sky over Trempealeau County and everything as far as my eyes can see is clear and blue. Despite the immense power this wind is showing, no new front is lurking on the horizon. No significant change in weather appears imminent. So, it gets me wondering, will my skills at reading the wind be of any use this week?

Our first task this morning is adding additional rods of rebar to the first nest, aligning one long piece of steel beside another, working from the inside out. An hour into the morning, Warren emerges from the trailer, clapping his hands. "I've got some good news!" he calls to us, as he makes his way down the earthen ramp to the floor of the pit. We gather around him.

"Is the front office finally sending help?" Carson asks, hopefully.

"No, not yet," Warren replies, and then after a slightly dramatic pause, he announces, "...We're ...getting ...another ...raise!"

It's not the news any of us expected, and our collective look of disappointment tells Warren as much. But he won't be deterred in delivering his dispatch. He explains that with Manny gone and us having to pick up his portion of the work, Davenport wants everyone on the crew to share in what Manny would have earned. "It's another $13 an hour, until they find us some help," Warren says, cheerfully.

"All this money talk is making my head hurt," Carson remarks, unimpressed. "Why is it so hard to get someone up here?"

"They're working on it," Warren assures us. "It's just that we only have one other crew still on the road, and they're in southern Illinois."

Buck tells us that he already contacted friends of his. "Everyone's started on vacation," he says. "They don't want to come back until spring."

"We're here less than two weeks," I point out. "Do they know how much money we're making?"

"I told Lammers and Billy Robinson about the money," Buck says. "I know they need cash. But they said coming up here isn't worth the aggravation. They've already heard about Burnell."

"And there you are," says Carson.

"Was the raise your idea?" Skinny asks Warren.

Warren admits it wasn't a hard sell with the front office. Burnell has been calling and leaving messages a few times a day, naming lawyers and threatening legal action. "They're feeling a lot of pressure," Warren says. "They want us to finish up as soon as we can."

While Warren is talking about overtime, I'm doing the math. A $13 an hour raise could mean an extra $1,000 on top of everything else we're earning. That's a nice bonus. But I agree with Carson. The extra money is becoming a distraction.

"Mother Nature doesn't care how much we're paid," I say to everyone. "If we get no help, does Davenport really think we can finish two platforms before it's too cold?"

"I don't know," Warren admits. He points over head at a serene sky that's cloudless and sharply blue. "But the sun is shining, and the wind is out of the west. The forecast for the coming week is still looking good. I think Davenport is betting we can finish on time."

I never thought I'd tire of Warren's optimism, or anyone's for that matter, but the likelihood of completing *both* platforms is seeming less and less realistic now. Then, what?

**One more** thing needs mentioning about the wind, something that is rarely said those conversations. Just as important as speed and direction is how the wind can affect a person's emotions. Wind flow against the body makes many people anxious and irritable. When I shot grade for a road construction company in central Illinois, before joining MSP, I was out in the open all day. When the wind was strong and gusty, I made more errors than when the air was calm. When my equipment was pummeled by the wind, I was often forced to retake measurements. The added hassle wasted time, of course, but it also upset me. It made me feel defeated. There's no way to win against a wind that wants to fight you.

Even worse was when I was out in the open and there was a constant breeze. The endless pressure on my head made my mind wander. At times, it even made me dizzy, and I had to sit down. There were days when all I thought about was the wind. I've heard claims that long ago on sailing ships, relentless breezes, the kind that last for days or weeks on end, made sailors lose their mind. Some even jumped overboard to free themselves from the wind. Fortunately, at MSP we spend most of our hours below ground level, where the wind blows over our heads and not directly on our bodies. The difference can be life changing, or as Jimmy Gilligan once put it, "If not for the pit, we'd all go crazy."

Wind aside, it's a beautiful Sunday, the finest day since we arrived in Pigeon Falls. When we break for lunch, the sky is clear blue, and the air temperature has climbed to 67°. Feeling a bit more optimistic about reaching our goal of two platforms, I drive to town with my windows down and radio blaring. The Shoe has laid out a Sunday buffet brunch with everything from eggs and waffles to beef tips and mashed potatoes. The dining room is nearly full.

We're halfway through our meal when Burnell walks in. Carson is the first to spot him. "Holy shit," Carson gulps. "Get a load of this."

Burnell is on his way towards our table in the back. It's too warm for his parka and hunter's cap. Instead, he's parading between tables in a shiny black leather car coat and matching cowboy hat. His silver hat band is oversized and studded with pieces of polished turquoise the size of quail eggs. Silver-tipped cowboy boots complete the ensemble and make a tick-tack sound on the hardwood floor as he approaches.

"Must be coming from church," Skinny says.

"Or the clown rodeo is in town," remarks Carson.

Burnell greets us with that edgy smirk I've come to recognize as forewarning, an unconscious signal he gives that says another unpleasantry is about to escape his mouth. After the confrontation yesterday, the last thing we want is another argument with our client. Anyway, him showing up here gets me wondering. Is Burnell so arrogant that he assumes he can bully us in the Shoe, a public place where we won't dare make a scene? I glance across the dining room, expecting to see Albert bringing up the rear, the faithful wingman protecting his master's back again. But Albert is nowhere to be seen. Burnell is flying solo.

"Coming from Sunday service, I passed by the ridge," Burnell says. "You boys should be pouring cement by now. What's the problem?" Around our table everyone puts down their fork.

The question about pouring concrete is ludicrous. Like any know-it-all, Burnell knows very little. He has no idea how we construct the foundation for a wind turbine, what we do when, or why we do it. He talks as if building a tower platform is as simple as laying the slab for a backyard patio. And it irks me that he still doesn't know the difference between concrete and cement.

I know it's a harsh assessment, but I'm starting to see Burnell less as the person that I thought he was, a super-stressed farmer who's desperate to right a failing farm. More and more, I'm seeing him as a wannabee genius entrepreneur who's really nothing but a phony and a fool.

"Mr. Sandberg," Warren says, "we're more than halfway done with framing the first platform. After that's ready, we'll fill it with concrete. Remember, we're down a man."

"That's on you, Mr. Foreman. I can't help it your man walked out on his *compadres*."

Warren refuses to be drawn into another battle. He replies with his typical positivity, after all, he's the son of a minister. "We're on schedule, sir," he says.

Burnell takes a step closer to our table and insists, "I still see a slowdown."

"What slowdown is that?"

Burnell doesn't answer. He folds his arms over his chest and glares with his pinpoint eyes at Warren. "Maybe I should find a company that actually does what I pay it to do," he says.

Unfolding now is the kind of pathetic moment MSP crews will retell for years. Burnell fingers the brim of his fine hat and waits for a reaction. He's bluffing, and we all know it. This late in the season, there are no other concrete builders in the Upper Midwest who could take our place. Without us doing the work, no towers will be rising in Pigeon Falls, and no turbine blades will be generating electricity, until next April at the earliest. If Burnell breaks his contract with MSP, I'll be thrilled. We all will. That'll let us off the hook, and we can head home tonight. But Burnell's threat is as hollow as he is.

What surprises me, though, is hearing Warren call Burnell's bluff. "You're right, Mr. Sandberg," he says. "You should find another company."

I expect Warren's reply to stun Burnell, as it has me, perhaps force our client to take a step back. But retreat is not in Burnell's repertory. Instead, Burnell doubles down. "I could find a better company. I could even find the perfect company. Except your owner signed a goddamn contract with me," Burnell says. "Do you boys want to see *Midwest-Stable-Platforms* in court?"

We've arrived at another fork in the road. What's that Middle East saying about someone never missing an opportunity to miss an opportunity to make peace? That's Burnell Sandberg to a T, a sad man with an appetite for creating conflict when none is necessary.

I suspect Warren has finally reached his limit and is ready to turn on Burnell, to throw up his arms and tear him a new one. But that's not Warren, of course.

Instead, Warren turns to Buck and calmly says, "Can you pass the ketchup, please?"

Buck looks at Warren, pauses in disbelief, and then hands him the red plastic bottle. Warren squeezes a glob onto his plate, up tight against his side of golden fries. He sets the bottle back on the table and then picks up the longest fry on his plate and whisks it across the top of the mound of red. Warren acts as if he's eating at the table alone, where there's no antagonist standing over him and no friendly eyes waiting to assist him. He puts the fry in his mouth. Two bites it takes. He chews. Nothing more to say.

Once again, Warren has made the best possible decision, another testament to his diplomat's instinct and him being the son of a pastor. He whisks a second fry over the ketchup. The rest of us follow his cue and resume eating. Sometimes, the best diplomacy isn't rooted in the prolonged push and pull between contenders, those drawn-out negotiations that end in compromise and exhaustion. Sometimes, victory can be had by doing nothing more than savoring french fries with a side of Heinz.

Moments later, Burnell slithers out of the Shoe, and not long after that, we're done with lunch and back on the plateau.

**By late** afternoon we've finished the rebar frame for the first nest. Then, Skinny and Warren insert PVC conduit and cabling for the tower's wiring. The rest of us double-check every cross piece of rebar to make sure each one has been twist-tied securely. The first nest is now ready to be filled with concrete, which we'll do later in the week. Neither Burnell nor Albert has come to the jobsite all afternoon, and by the time night arrives and we're leaving the plateau, we're grateful for that unexpected gift.

**On the** road from April to October, a crew's daily routine is simple: *work, eat, sleep, repeat.* When Skinny and I walk into the Shoe, it's after 6:00 p.m. Candace is near the bar and notices how tired we look. "Been a rough one?" she asks. I give her a weak one-thumb-up, and as I follow Candace to our table, I realize how much I've been looking forward to seeing her again. I'm still unsure what it is about this young woman that interests me so much, but seeing her tonight, I feel like I've gotten my second wind for the day.

Skinny is not far behind me. When we get to the table, he asks Candace, "You ever get a night off, dear?"

"Usually, Sundays, but I picked up an extra shift tonight." She hands us menus. "Skinny, are you saying that you're glad to see me?" Candace asks with a big smile.

"You betcha, young lady," Skinny replies and Candace's smile grows even wider.

**Our meal** proceeds uneventfully, from start to finish. There's no drama in the air tonight, and after dinner everyone but me heads upstairs to his room. I'm low on gas, so I drive a few miles down US 53 to Waterford to fill up. When I return to Pigeon Falls, my tank full again, I park across from the Shoe. As I'm walking towards the stairs leading up to the second floor, I pass in front of the large picture window that looks onto the Shoe's dining room. I notice Eddie and Candace sitting side by side at a booth near the back of the room. The restaurant is otherwise empty, except for a few stragglers still at the bar.

Even though the booth where Eddie and Candace huddle together is bathed in shadow, the couple's faces are aglow in the cool white light of a cell phone screen, leading me to conclude that Eddie and something on that screen are why Candace picked up an extra shift tonight.

**Crews relax** in different ways before bed. Some play video games or watch TV. Others like playing a few hands of cards, poker mostly. For all of us, there are the usual texts and calls to family and friends. I like to read from my phone or listen to a podcast in bed, mainly articles and shows about history and travel. On some crews, you'll find a few workers who drink more than they should, but not many, and no one in our crew had ever gone overboard with alcohol, until Jimmy Gilligan's sudden fall. Heavy drinkers never last long on one of our crews. No one wants the headaches they bring. As for illegal drugs, it's one-and-done at MSP, the only rule the company won't bend.

Before getting into bed, I sit at the writing table and phone my father. Because I'm on the road from April to October, I only see him once or twice a month, so to keep in touch, I try to call him every few days when I'm gone. Over the last few years, my father has been in a gradual decline. For a man who claims to never missing a day of work, my father's body and mind at 80 are letting go. His memory has clear days now and cloudy ones, but it's mostly cloudy for his body. My father has started wearing hearing aids, and he walks with a cane now. His daily routine includes help from my sister, who lives nearby.

My call is answered on the second ring. I remind my father where I am and ask how his weekend went. He's never been as far north as Pigeon Falls, so I describe the Driftless Area and the Horseshoe Inn. Near the end of our conversation, I ask if he has a joke for me tonight.

**Telling jokes** before bed is a ritual my father started when my sister
and I were children, soon after our mother passed. I was twelve at
the time, my sister fifteen. Our mother's absence had hit us hard.
She'd been the rudder that kept our family on course, so the first
few months without her, my sister and I started to drift. I don't
know how my father came up with the idea, but he discovered that
telling us a joke or two at night, before bed, smoothed out our day
and brought us closer together. The jokes he told us were silly and
uncomplicated, usually only one- or two-liners, little kid jokes. It
was our father's comical routine that we looked forward to, more
than the jokes themselves. The ritual lasted a few years and only
ended when my sister moved out and got married.

After my father retired, I convinced him to revive the tradition
for me. I was on the road a lot, and he was growing more and
more depressed about not working anymore. Now, the punchline
sometimes doesn't match the joke he's chosen, and many of the
jokes he tells I can recall hearing as a kid. But that isn't the point.
Telling a joke now is more a way for him to settle his mind before
falling asleep, than it is for me to settle mine.

**Over the** phone, my father tells me a couple of one-liners to warm
up, and then he says, "I got a good one for you, Tommy."

"Okay, Dad, I'm ready."

There's a moment of silence and then he says, "I saw these geese
flying over the house today. They were headed south for the winter."

"We see them up here too. It's that time of year."

"You know those V formations they make, Tommy?"

"Yeah, Dad, I see them all the time. What's the joke?"

"Well, do you know why one side of the V is sometimes longer
than the other?"

I'm wondering now, is this his joke or is he off on a tangent again? Lately, that's been happening more and more often, him getting lost in his thoughts. I go with the flow and let my father take me along with him on the question about geese. I'm expecting to hear something about wing aerodynamics and lift, or maybe a little-known fact he heard about celestial navigation related to migrating birds. Or it could be some other unconnected piece of trivia. It's anyone's guess.

"I don't know why one side of the V is longer than the other," I say.

"It's longer on one side, Tommy," he says, followed by a perfect pause on the other end of the line, one beat, then two. "Because the longer side has more geese."

I hear my father start laughing. I can picture him sitting in his La-Z-Boy or at the kitchen table. He's got half a bowl of something salty near him and the last of a cool drink, which he's put down so as not to spill, because he's laughing so hard.

"You got me, Dad," I tell him.

"That's a good one, isn't it, Tommy?"

"Stellar, Dad."

I end the call without reminding him of my visit to the clinic, even though I want to talk about it with him. My father has heard from me previously about my stomach pain, but at this point, without something definite, there's no reason to have him worrying over empty speculation.


## Monday, November 4

Mid-morning, we're preparing the palettes of rebar for the second pit when Warren calls us together at the foreman's trailer. Burnell and Albert are waiting there, and my first guess is that our client has come to discipline us for some new slip-up. Our pace is too slow? We're talking too much, or not enough? The planets are out of alignment?

When we're all assembled outside the trailer, Warren says, "Mr. Sandberg has something he wants...."

Burnell interrupts. "Somebody, turn that goddamn music off!" A lively country song is playing from Buck's boom box that's propped on the flatbed where we were working. Eddie hustles overs and turns off the device.

"Listen, boys," Burnell continues, "Like I said before, I want my two towers up by Christmas. I want people around here to see what a great wind farm looks like. And I want them to know I've started selling electricity to the power company. That means, if you don't speed things up, none of that's gonna happen."

Wrestling his way back into the conversation, Warren says, "That doesn't mean Mr. Sandberg wants you to cut corners. He talked to the front office in Davenport this morning and offered to pay extra if we shortened our lunch breaks to 30 minutes and added an extra hour of work at the end of each day." My brain quickly untangles the odd proposal and immediately starts calculating the financial impact to my wallet.

Burnell butts in again. "That's right, shorten lunch and stay an hour more at night. But your owner, *in his great wisdom*, refused my offer. He said, you were working too many hours the way it was. He thinks adding more would be too tough on you." Burnell lights a cigarette.

"Well, I'm pretty sure you boys are tougher than that. I know you can handle an hour and a half more each day, and I sure-as-hell know you understand the value of a dollar."

"So," Warren says, "Mr. Sandberg came directly to me with his idea and asked me to present it to you."

Not waiting for Warren to present anything, Burnell says, "If you're up to it, we can do our own deal, on the side. If you agree to my proposal, I'll pay you cash for the time added to your day."

"Mr. Sandberg will pay everyone $180 extra, at the end of every day."

"That's *cash*," Burnell says. "No taxes. No government."

"I'm not arguing one way or another," Warren continues. "Stable Platforms has no part in this offer. In fact, I'd rather they don't know about it. But this deal is up to you. You can take it or leave it."

Skinny raises his hand like we're back in grade school. Burnell calls on him. "Thirty minutes isn't long enough to get to town and back for lunch," Skinny points out.

"I don't want you driving anywhere for lunch," Burnell says. "I want you staying up here on the ridge." Before anyone can ask if Burnell expects us to starve, he adds, "My wife will make lunch and bring it up here for you."

We look at one another, our curiosity piqued. Catered food at a jobsite? "Does your offer begin today?" Skinny asks.

"Joyce can be here at noon with your first meal," Burnell says.

Buck then asks, "So, you'll pay us cash every day and all we have to do is have a shorter lunch up here and stay an extra hour at night?"

"Isn't that what I just told you?"

We're all considering the offer. No wasted time driving to town and an extra hour of work at the end of the day. Neither change seems a problem. Skinny nods his head and then I do the same.

Warren claps his hands. "All right, back to work," Warren says. "Lunch at noon, at the trailer."

"Hold on," Burnell twitters. It appears that the best idea he's had all week has inspired another. "I'll also pay you $300, that's three hundred to each of you, one lump sum, if you work without that damn radio playing."

Carson, trying to get his head around the idea, asks, "You want us to stop playing music on the job?"

"That's right. No more music when you're up here."

Who's ever heard of an offer like this? Paying people to work without music? Who would even think of it?

"You don't like music, Mr. Sandberg?" Buck asks.

"It has nothing to do with what I like," Burnell growls. "Music's a distraction. It keeps us from focusing on what's most important. When you're on my clock, all I want you thinking about is building my wind farm."

"Mr. Sandberg, if your offer is *$500* to stop the music, we'll think about it," Skinny says. "We'll think about it *seriously*."

Skinny's counteroffer has confounded Burnell, though only long enough for him to light another smoke. "Okay, partner, five hundred it is," Burnell says as he exhales. "I'll leave you boys to talk it over. Let me know what you decide by close of business today. I told you, I'm a generous man. If you turn off that damn music, you'll each get an extra $500 tonight, in cash. But everyone needs to be onboard."

**For the** rest of the morning, we keep the boom box shut down, thinking about music instead of listening to it. When we break for lunch, Burnell's red truck is parked in front of the foreman's trailer. The thought of seeing him yet again today turns my stomach sour.

Between the red truck and the foreman's trailer, a long rectangular folding table has been set up, the kind you see at a church picnic or family get-together. Burnell is nowhere in sight. A middle-aged woman with long raven hair is standing at the folding table, along with Albert, and they're laying out real plates, real glasses and real silverware, nothing paper or plastic. Three white serving dishes covered in aluminum foil have been set at one end of the table. Warren is off to the side, opening our folding chairs.

When all of us are together, Warren says, "This is Mrs. Sandberg." He moves his arm in front of himself, as if he's welcoming the woman on stage.

"Call me Joyce," she says in a softly sweet voice that conveys a kindness we've not heard from her husband. "I'm sorry I didn't have time to make a dessert today," Joyce says. "I'll have one tomorrow."

I'm not sure who I was expecting when I imagined Burnell's

wife, but Joyce Sandberg is not her. She's of similar age and height to Burnell's, yet that's where apparent likenesses end. First, she has Native American ancestry. Her facial features speak to that heritage, especially her high cheekbones and dark hair, which is partially hidden by a stocking cap. A long braid carries halfway to her waist. Second, Joyce's skin isn't chalky white like Burnell's but a chestnut brown that matches her eyes. The deep skin color is partially related to aging from the sun, I believe, though there's also a richness to the tone that suggests her family line. Then, there's the coat she wears. It's an elaborate hand embroidered native design with tiny beads and fancy stitching that reaches almost to her knees. By the wear on the sleeves, the coat looks like it's been a reliable and often-worn garment for many years. On her feet are a pair of old black duck boots.

"Eat when is warm," Albert says, his English skills a work-in-progress.

The meal Joyce has cooked is also not what I was expecting. She pulls back the aluminum foil, revealing Swedish meatballs in an elegant mushroom and cream sauce, buttered egg noodles that look homemade, and steaming slices of freshly-baked multigrain bread. We're staring at a meal created in a real farm kitchen by a real farm cook. Everything looks fabulous, and there's plenty of it.

"Go," Albert says in his accented yet commanding voice. "You work in 30 minutes." Buck and Carson waste no time heaping food onto their plates, which seems to please Joyce because she's smiling now, though not looking directly at us. Her eyes are fixed only on the table.

There's more than enough food to go around, and it's almost medicinal in the way it soothes my tired body from the inside out. I expect Skinny to give a review, but he's too busy buttering a second slice of bread. Soon, she and Albert climb back into the red truck, with nothing more said to us, and drive away, Albert behind the wheel.

While we eat, the debate over Burnell's offer of $500 to stop playing music continues. "I like hearing music when I'm working," Buck says, "but I can leave it for 500 bucks. I need every cent I can get for my truck."

"I like the idea of no taxes," Skinny says.

"Am I the only one who thinks this is insane?" Carson asks. "The dude was already paying us too much. Now we're getting free lunch and money off the books. What's next, gold bars to sleep in the pits? I say, fuck him. We keep the music on."

"Even for $500?" Skinny asks.

"It's the principle," Carson replies.

By the end of the meal, we're ready to vote. Warren and I abstain. Carson votes for the boom box. Buck, Eddie, and Skinny vote to take the money. In the end, silence has won. I listen to Skinny talking to Eddie as we're walking back to the pit. "Son," he says, "that's the easiest $500 you'll ever make."


**The second** mud mat has cured. Its surface is as smooth as glass and hard enough to build on. I shoot grade on the mat after lunch and start marking our grid for laying down the second mesh of bearing bars. The rest of the crew is over at the first pit with Bud and his crane. The long blue neck is lifting steel fit-forms off the flatbed trailer and setting them around the perimeter of the first mud mat. Fit-forms are metal walls 36 inches high that can be joined together and secured with heavy-duty clamps to form a steel hedge around the base of a nest. Later, when we fill the nest with mix, the forms will hold the foundation of our concrete in place.

After chalking gridlines, I put away my measuring tapes and other tools and drive from the second pit back to the foreman's trailer. When I come out of the porta-potty, I pause at the edge of the escarpment to drink some water. Blotches of puffy cumulus clouds have been pushing across the sky since lunch, steadily replacing the wide-open blue with swaths of gray. On the few hardwoods still sunlit across the valley, clusters of autumn leaves are alive with color, though the late seasonal hues have diminished in their range and are relegated now to the paler varieties of orange and yellow.

Farther south, I spy a fence of evergreen pines, and for a moment, a single beam of sunlight escapes through a crease in the cloud layer and focuses its shaft of light on a blemish of white limestone high up on the face of the coulee, just below the pines. The rough stone sparkles like fool's gold in the sudden brightness, and for another minute I stand there and marvel at this magnificent light show. Then, just as suddenly as the light appeared, the cloud layer regains control of the opening, and the sunbeam is snuffed out. I return to my truck to head back to the second pit.

I've just put my truck in gear when I spot a car parked behind the foreman's trailer, a small sedan almost hidden by our shipping container and the pallets of rebar piled next to it. I pause to look closer. The car is an older foreign model whose silver body seems in good shape, showing no obvious signs of rust or damage. Eddie is leaning against the car's front fender, along with Candace, who is dressed in her waitress uniform. She hands Eddie a small package that's wrapped in brown paper and tied with string, like a present. In return, he hands her something unwrapped, maybe a magazine or thin catalogue. Then, she gets in the car and drives away, not down through Burnell's valley, but north off the plateau, by way of the gravel service road.

Later, when I'm back in the pit, Eddie comes and asks if I need help. I show him what I'm doing, and he pitches in. Making sure no one else can hear us, I say to him, "I think I saw our waitress up here a while ago."

"Yeah," Eddie answers with an awkwardness in his voice, maybe a tinge of embarrassment that someone saw them together. "Candace was on her way to work." He reaches into his pocket and pulls out a thin paperback. "She gave me this." Eddie shows me the cover. It's the book *The Prophet* by Kahlil Gibran. "You ever hear of it?" he asks.

I vaguely recall the title from during my two years at community college, before I transferred to tech school. "I think it was popular when I was in school," I say. "Maybe it still is. I don't remember much about the book."

"Candace wants me to read it. She said it's good for when you're trying to figure out things in life, like I am."

"It sounds like the perfect gift," I tell him. Eddie slides the book back into his pocket. He mentions nothing about whatever it was that I saw him give to her.

While we're all busy in the pits, twilight tiptoes onto the plateau. We set up our portable light stands and continue working into the dark. It's our first evening with the new schedule, adding an extra hour to the workday.

At 7:10 p.m., Albert drives up in an old Dodge minivan and parks where we're gathered outside the foreman's trailer. Warren has already exited the trailer and locked the door. Albert comes to Warren and hands him a short deck of white business envelopes. Warren opens one and pulls out a sheaf of tens and twenties. He counts the money, $180, one person's compensation for the extra time put in today. No taxes. No hassles. Just cold cash. Warren deals an envelope to each of us and keeps the open one for himself.

"The music radio," Albert says. "You bring it, yes or no?"

"We've decided that we will work without music," Warren says.

"Yes, radio?" Albert responds. His English comprehension and Warren's statement are not in sync.

"No radio," Warren says slowly, to help Albert out. "No radio. No music."

Albert nods his understanding and reaches into his coat pocket and takes out a thick roll of $100 bills. We form a queue. "It's a bread line," Buck says. "You guys get it, right?"

Albert deals out money, money, and more money. In one hand I hold five crisp one-hundred-dollar bills and in the other a white envelope thick with tens and twenties. I cram it all in my front pants pockets, as Albert is returning to his van. He gets in and drives away. No one on our side says another word. It's as if talking about it now might wake us up, and we'd discover the extra cash was all a dream.

Minutes later, I'm leaving the plateau and except for the narrow wash of my headlights, it's pitch black all the way down the escarpment. The odd thing about being under a cloudy, starless sky out in back country on a night like this is the way my eyes adjust to the murky darkness. You'd think it'd be just the opposite from what actually happens. You'd think that far away from the afterglow of city lights, the night sky would be impenetrably dark, like a blindness. But that's not what happens at all. Instead of a total blackout, the starless sky out here actually lightens as my eyes adjust to it, turning into a medium shade of gray that's something close to the color of slate.

The land at my feet, on the other hand, does just the opposite. It descends into a shapeless sea of nothingness, a void that's so dark a person can't even see where he's stepping. All to say, what I've learned over the years is this: *at night, out in the countryside, watch where you're going.* The truest form of darkness, when you're out in the middle of nowhere, is found not in the heavens, but on earth.

**Due to** our longer workday, we've had to push back our dinner time at the Shoe. Regrettably, no one remembered to let the cook know we'd be arriving late. Warren and I enter the Shoe and remove our coats. Mike is behind the bar. He says to us, "Good thing, Candace heard about your extra hours." Warren realizes his mistake and apologizes to Mike for not calling. Warren then goes off into the kitchen to apologize to the cook as well.

Once we're seated in the back, Warren says to me, "My bad. I should have remembered to call them about the new schedule."

"It's easy to forget," I tell him. "You've got a lot on your plate."

"Still, it bothers me," Warren says.

"You know, when people get out of a normal rhythm, like we are now, mistakes happen."

Warren nods. "How do you think Mike knew about our change in schedule?" Before I can answer, Candace sets a tap beer in front of Warren and a milk in front of me. She asks if the rest of the crew is coming to dinner, though I figure she's mostly wondering where Eddie is.

"They'll be down in a minute," Warren says.

Candace's cell phone buzzes, and she removes it from her apron pocket. She turns away to answer the call, but we can still hear her side of the conversation. "Yeah, I took my car tonight…," she says. "I just felt like driving… of course I'll be home… soon as I'm done here." Candace drifts away from our table and then we're out of reach for whatever else is said.

Dinner goes by without a hitch. Everyone is tired and hungry. It's been a full day. While I'm eating and watching Carson text, I try to recall everything that has happened since breakfast. There's so much that it's hard remembering everything. There was the extra labor we had being down a man. We added fit-forms and more rebar. There was the ongoing drama that is Burnell Sandberg. We agreed to longer hours and more money. And then we met Joyce and heard her unexpectedly kind voice. We ate a delicious lunch. Later, in the afternoon, I saw Eddie and Candace exchanging packages like spies behind the foreman's trailer. And finally, before leaving the plateau, we traded our music for cash. A full day, and then some.

After dinner, I stay at the table when the others get up to leave. My sister has texted to tell me that my father fell in the yard just before dark. It isn't serious, she claims. I phone her.

"He's sleeping now," my sister reports. "Just a bump and a bruise.

He'll be fine."

We talk for five minutes. I learn that my father was on a ladder when he fell. "Thank god it wasn't a hip," my sister says and promises that she'll keep an eye on him.

After the call, I'm getting up from the table when Candace comes over and sits down across from me. "Hi," I say to her. "What's up?"

"Do you want another milk or anything?" she asks. I tell her I'm heading up to bed, that our new schedule has me even more tired than usual. "Let me get you a glass of milk," she says. "I want to ask you something."

I watch Candace head off to the kitchen. I still haven't figured out what it is that keeps me wondering about her, what it is that has me so intent on watching her move, but whatever it is, it's feeling more and more familiar.

Candace returns and sets the glass on a square bar napkin in front of me. She retakes her seat across the table. "You saw Eddie and me talking up on the hill?" I nod, while sipping my milk. I have no idea how she knows I saw them. Did Eddie tell her in a text? I never noticed them talking together tonight at dinner. "He said you know the book I gave him."

"It was mentioned in a course I had in school," I say. "But that was years ago."

"Well, I'm hoping he'll read it," she says. "The book's a little different, but it's good."

"Eddie told me he's planning to read it, so I think he will. What did he have for you?"

My question doesn't surprise her, not like it would if him giving her something should be kept a secret. "He wants me to look at a magazine about building model airplanes," she says. "He's been telling me how he flies them in Chicago. It's something he's very interested in."

"I didn't know he did that," I say and realize how little I know about Eddie. Candace bites on her lower lip, and for a second I notice that off-color tooth of hers again. Obviously, Candace has more to say, so I wait until she's ready.

While I'm waiting, I make note of a sweet vulnerability I detect in her youthfulness. It's an innocence one enjoys seeing in a woman her age, the ambiguous time between the end of one's teenage years and the start of actual womanhood. Yet, the more that I watch her, especially what I see in her eyes, I sense another side of Candace as well, an independent and strong spirit that counterbalances any vulnerabilities. She radiates a mature resilience and carefulness that come from years of fending for herself, a protective shield that was probably formed in her teens, or even earlier, when she figured out that no one was looking out for her, other than herself.

Candace is ready to say something again and starts with a deep breath. "Eddie told me he's going to California. Is he really going that far?"

"You know, Candace, I only met Eddie last week, that first night we had dinner here. Even so, I think if Eddie says his plan is to go there, then I believe he will."

Candace is quiet again. I let her thoughts continue to percolate.

"That's a good plan," she says, finally. "Going out there, that's a good plan." She folds her hands atop the table.

"I've noticed that the two of you are kind of friendly now. What is it that you like about Eddie?"

"Oh, that's easy," she says, taking less than a second to consider an answer. "Eddie's funny. He makes me laugh." It's not the response I was expecting. Aside from Eddie's one comedic moment on the jobsite, when Skinny called him out for standing on a too-high slop of concrete, I haven't seen any sense of humor in Eddie at all.

"Can I ask you something else?" she says.

"Ask away."

"I notice you drink only milk. And the food you eat is bland. And you don't eat much of it. Do you have a problem with digestion?"

Under different circumstances, the question would seem intrusive. I don't take it that way tonight. Candace is an intelligent young woman. She's been to college. We've witnessed her powers of memory with our drink orders. Now she's revealed her observational skills, as well. So, I say, "You're good at noticing things."

"You don't have to tell me. It's not a problem. I was just wondering."

In the last few days, I've become so immersed in the drama that is Burnell Sandberg and his wind farm that I've paid little attention to the on-going discomfort in my abdomen. I've been swapping one pain for another. During this time, I've also given little thought to the many serious disease possibilities that Dr. Welton mentioned. I've even forgotten to call and change the time of my return appointment at the clinic. Now, Candace's question about my diet has pushed layers of dread to the front of my thoughts again, like grainy photos from the past that are quickly brought into focus, only to reveal that they're actually images from today.

Not sure how to answer Candace, I take another sip of milk, a diversion that gives me a little extra time to consider her question. I've not spoken to anyone yet, not family or crew, about the roller coaster of emotions I was feeling during my drive last week from Fairview to Pigeon Falls. I could tap dance around my visit to the clinic and make up a story for her that would explain my food choices. But I realize that inside of me a subconscious need to share these worries with someone has been gathering the last few days. So, over the next 30 minutes, I tell Candace everything about my situation. Everything from the history of my discomfort to my visit to the clinic, even the worries that I'm guarding about my return appointment. Candace listens attentively throughout it all. For me, it's liberating to put everything on the table and have another person share in my uncertain journey, even if that companionship lasts only as long as it takes me to nurse another glass of milk.

When I finish my story, Candace reaches across the table and puts her hand on mine. Then she smiles warmly, though it's not her signature wide-mouth greeting smile, the one all teeth and innocent energy. Now, she's offering something I haven't seen from her before, a softer look of understanding and a smile that's driven by her eyes and meant as comfort. "I hope you get good news, Tom," she says.

"Thanks," I tell her and smile back, as best I can. "I hope so too."

## Tuesday, November 5

*Cool mornings, warm afternoons.* Such are second summers in the Upper Midwest. This unseasonably warm weather has been a godsend our first four days in Pigeon Falls. Daytime highs have been reaching up into the high sixties and staying well-above freezing overnight. We've seen no rain and little cloud cover. I tell myself, as I'm getting dressed, if the weather stays like this another week, we'll be in the clear. We will have completed Burnell's two platforms, as promised, and we can head home.

But that's wishful thinking, because at breakfast, Dot brings news of a change in the forecast. Overnight, an Alberta Clipper from Canada has slipped southward more than was expected, and the front is passing through the northernmost edge of Wisconsin today, carrying cooler temperatures and a thick blanket of clouds.

The really cold weather that's north of Lake Superior isn't expected to work its way as far south as Pigeon Falls, and no one is predicting snow or even an overnight freeze here. But the warning signs are clear. Autumn is nearly spent, which means the last few days for pouring concrete are upon us. And because of this new front, rain is also on the way. No one can tell us yet how much rain we'll get, but it's expected to arrive late Wednesday or early Thursday. Up on the plateau, I double check my phone app. Just as

Dot said, rain is showing an 80% chance tomorrow night.

The bearing bars that had to be reordered for the second nest arrive by semi-trailer at 9 a.m. Bud and his crane offload the bundles and pile them on the floor of the second pit. At noon, Joyce brings another outstanding meal. We've asked Bud to join us at the trailer, but he wants to call his wife from the crane and eat the sack lunch she's made for him.

Joyce has come alone with her food today, no Burnell or Albert. She's waiting at the folding table when we arrive. The aroma from the meat she's cooked is intoxicating, a sweet gamey smell like nothing I've experienced before. "It's bison," she tells us.

For Eddie, Warren, Carson, and me, eating bison is something new. Skinny and Buck have had it before and are anxious to dig in, so we let them fill their plates first.

"Hop to it, boys," Skinny says, after only one bite. "This is a treat."

Joyce doesn't leave immediately, as she had yesterday. Maybe it's because she's alone now. No one is looming over her. She's removed her hat and is watching us from the far end of the table.

"Are you originally from around here, ma'am?" Skinny asks in a formal voice, the respectful way you might talk to a teacher or an elderly neighbor, even though Joyce is probably only a few years older than him.

Skinny possesses a special talent when it comes to starting a conversation with a stranger. Just as cooing reassures a restless infant, Skinny's soft Georgia accent has even the most apprehensive adult feeling at ease. While part of this conversational talent is revealed in the soft sound of his voice, an even larger share comes from his body language. Skinny doesn't have a gift of gab as much as a gift of trust and respect. When Skinny is listening to someone, he always maintains eye contact, leans in towards the person, and keeps his hands open and out in front of him. Even though they're simple and subtle cues about his intentions, they're effective. And he's using them now to let Joyce know that he cares what she has to say.

"My family comes from north of here, farther up near Rice Lake," Joyce replies. "There's a lot of Ojibwe in that part of the state. I still have cousins up there, and my brother lives in Birchwood."

"Your family's been in Rice Lake a while?" Skinny asks.

"I'm not sure how long," Joyce says. "No one kept records that far back. But before this was Wisconsin."

Burnell's wife is a handsome woman, though her eyes are cautious eyes, alert to the strangers she's not yet sure about. Even so, her face cannot hide the optimism she's carried with her for a lifetime, the hopeful look of the long-time family farmer who hasn't given up. When she smiles, the age lines around her eyes and mouth tell me she's someone who's spent a lifetime pulling more goodness from life than it holds and still believes the best is yet to come.

Although the backs of Joyce's hands are a bumpy roadmap of purple veins and darker sunspots, her fingers are beautifully long and thin. Right now, those fingers are intertwined at her waist. As for Joyce's eyes, even as guarded as they remain around us, they are crystal-clear and shine with the same rich glow as her hair. Today, her long strands of hair are braided in two plaits, which are tied with thin strips of red-dyed cowhide. The braids carry down the front of her beaded knit sweater, with the ends falling a foot below her shoulders.

Joyce uncovers a plate of chocolate chip cookies and says, "Red and I met at a high school football game. My brother was playing. I moved down here when we got married, and I've been here ever since. That was 37 years ago."

Joyce sets the plate of cookies in front of us and then returns her hands to her waist, comfortably clasping them there. She seems pleased at how much we're eating. No one speaks for a few minutes, then she asks, "What do you men think of these electric windmills?"

One of the most important things I've learned while working for MSP is that a crew member never discusses the merits of our product with a client. We leave that to MSP's people in Davenport, because across America today, communities are divided over the use of fossil fuel, wind power, and solar. Talking about them can turn into a heated debate, even an opportunity for confrontation. Being part of MSP's leadership team in Davenport, Warren knows the company's talking points, so we leave it to Warren to answer Joyce. He jumps in.

"Tell me what you'd like to know about them," Warren says.

"Do you think a wind farm's a good idea?"

Warren ponders her question before answering. "I think renewable energy's the future, Mrs. Sandberg. The wind farm you're building up here will provide clean energy for a lot of homes and businesses in this part of the state. People around Pigeon Falls will benefit from your towers for many years to come."

Joyce is listening attentively to what Warren is saying, though she's also started to wring her hands. "Air pollution from power plants is helping to kill the planet," Warren continues. "What you and your husband are doing is good for the environment, and the people who live here."

"These towers are really tall, aren't they? Won't they change how everything looks?"

"I've talked to people who live near them," Warren says. "They tell me no one notices the towers after a while. Some even say they're attractive, you know, how elegant they look and how gracefully they spin."

"I suppose so," she says.

Sounding like he wants to be helpful, Eddie jumps into the conversation and announces matter-of-factly, "I read some complaints online, such as each year the blades on wind turbines kill half a million wild birds."

Eddie's words have taken Joyce and the rest of us by surprise.

Our crew stares at Eddie, as Joyce covers her mouth with her hand. "Oh," she says, "that's awful."

What Eddie's just revealed is totally accurate information, but definitely not on the list of MSP's talking points. We've rarely heard Eddie say anything around us, and when he has, it's never been controversial. Now, he's informed our client that the product we're building, for her and her husband, kills innocent birds, many tons of them. But Eddie remains upbeat, having no idea how provocative his remark was. He looks to Warren, maybe expecting him to elaborate on what Eddie must assume is common knowledge, but Warren doesn't respond.

"After you drew that picture on the napkin for me, Warren," Eddie says, "I wanted to learn more about wind energy, so I did some research on my phone."

More times than I can count, I've heard the details about dead birds and other arguments against wind energy that Eddie has discovered, things like the machines are noisy and a stain on the natural landscape, that wind power is the latest gimmick power companies offer the public to justify rate increases and boost profits.

"But you know, Mrs. Sandberg, it's okay," Eddie continues. "I also read online that cats kill a thousand times more birds every year than wind farms do. *A thousand times more.*"

In the wake of a half billion dead birds, I want to say something uplifting, anything positive to reassure Joyce that a wind farm is a good idea, but my mind goes blank. No one else seems able to rescue wind energy either. Or soften what Eddie has said.

Joyce speaks again: "Red wanted these windmills to go up so fast. I wish we'd have talked about it more."

I glance at my watch. It's 12:40 p.m. Our lunch has gone ten minutes longer than planned. Even though we're on the tightest of schedules, no one appears interested in ending our conversation with Joyce.

Trying to guide the conversation down a different path, I say, "Why *did* your husband want them to go up now? We had you on our schedule for spring."

"The government money only arrived a week ago," she says. "It came earlier than we thought it would. Burnell was afraid the government would find a way to cancel everything and take back the money if we waited until spring. He said we had to start building now."

"Makes sense," Buck says, seemingly trying to be sympathetic. "That's government for you."

"Red also said these towers will change our lives. But I don't know if that's a good thing, or not."

"They'll change your life in a good way, Mrs. Sandberg," Warren tells her. "They will."

In the distance, we hear Bud's diesel engine start up. Vibrations from the crane rumble across the plateau with enough force to rattle the window in the foreman's trailer.

"We better get back to work," Warren declares, clapping his hands. "Bud's ready for us."

We thank Joyce for lunch, and as the rest of the crew drives over to the second pit, I sit in my truck. I need to call the clinic to push back my return appointment.

**All afternoon,** we make good progress. Joyce's delicious meal and our not having to drive to town for lunch have opened unexpected reserves of energy in all of us. And just as Burnell wanted, not listening to music has also helped us focus solely on the job in front of us, though by mid-afternoon I've also noticed that we've stopped talking to one another.

You might think we'd talk more without music, that we'd fill in the silence with conversation, but we don't. The rest of the afternoon continues to roll out in this muted way, and after a while, I feel like I'm laboring alone. A solitary and soundless emptiness has taken hold of me. With friends working right beside me, it's illogical to feel as isolated as I'm feeling now, so I say nothing about it to anyone.

Then, out of the quiet, I notice the high-pitched pinging sound of a hammer pounding a nail. Then, the whoosh of a shovel cutting dirt. Determined footsteps are shuffling their comings and goings. A toolbox opens and closes. Up on the nest, someone sighs, and I know whose breath it is. Behind me, there's the creak of a wooden pallet followed by a clang from steel batting steel. When Eddie groans, I finally understand what I'm listening to. *The music of work.*

All around me are the daily melodies a construction crew makes when building something important. I've heard these tunes a thousand times before, but until this afternoon, I never stopped to listen to them. This afternoon's absence of conversation and the jailing of Buck's boombox had me feeling uneasy. It had my mind wandering in places I'd rather not go. Now, each whirl of a drill is brightening my mood. Each turn of Bud's crane is lifting my spirits. Up on Burnell's plateau, we're making our own playlist, a construction crew's playlist, and if I had the right words, I could sing along.

**Carson calls** to Eddie across the pit, "Hey, Eddie, tell us about yourself."

"Good idea," says Skinny. "Tell us about your family."

"And what it's like in Chicago," adds Buck.

Since this project began, we've already discovered a few things about Eddie, but only a few. For one, we know he's a quick learner. In no time, he's caught on to how we do things on a jobsite. He's also shown he's a self-starter, retrieving a tool without being asked or holding something in place. We know he was the night manager at a dollar store and he's just out of high school and on his way to California. But that's about it.

Given this opportunity to speak, Eddie perks up, and I wonder if maybe he too has missed hearing conversation all afternoon. During what's left of the day, he answers everything we ask him.

Eddie tells us that his lighter shade of skin comes from his father, who is white. Eddie and his brother haven't seen their father since he left Chicago, when Eddie was three and his brother was five. Eddie and Anthony were raised by their mother, with help from her parents. They all live together in a two-floor walk-up on Chicago's southside, in a neighborhood called Avalon Park. Eddie's mother works as a dental hygienist. His grandfather is a machinist in Gary, Indiana, twenty miles away.

We also learn that the genesis of Eddie's dream to see California came in middle school, when he learned about the Pacific Ocean in geography class.

"What's so special about the Pacific?" asks Skinny.

"I want to swim in it," Eddie says.

"You're near Lake Michigan," says Buck. "That's not much different than an ocean."

"The ocean has salt water," Eddie says. "Your body floats in salt water. The best place in the world to float in is the Dead Sea. That's in the Middle East. But the oceans are good too."

We contemplate the floating idea for a moment and then Buck asks, "You're gonna go to Hollywood, right? See some stars?"

Eddie laughs in an embarrassed way and shakes his head, which tells me that him visiting Hollywood is probably also on his list of things to do when he's out there.

"You planning to work in California?" says Carson.

"Maybe, if I stay long enough."

Eddie goes on to tell us about the dollar store, how he started with sweeping floors and stocking shelves. He then moved on to cashiering, before being promoted to night manager. "How come everything's not a dollar in those stores?" Buck asks, which I think is funny, but Buck didn't intend the question as a joke.

Before Eddie can answer, Carson interrupts. "You got a

girlfriend?" I wonder if Carson has noticed what I've been seeing between Eddie and our young waitress.

"Nothing steady," Eddie replies.

He goes on to tell us that his grades in high school were good enough for college. Math was his favorite subject. And he was president of the Highflyers, a club where students build remote-controlled model airplanes powered by gas engines.

"I joined my sophomore year," Eddie says. "We fly drones too, but they're too easy. They fly right out of the box. I like to build a plane myself. I like cutting the wood pieces by hand and gluing them together. That way, I don't know if it'll fly, until I try it."

Talk turns to Eddie's older brother, which takes us into nightfall. Anthony works the counter at a Popeye's Chicken and cooks at a diner part-time. "Anthony wants to open his own restaurant," Eddie says. "He already has his menu picked out. My mom thinks, it's like… *fifty pages too long.*" Eddie's over emphasis on those last words gets us laughing.

When we stop for the day, darkness covers every square foot of ground between the two pits and the foreman's trailer. I'm reaching into the back of my truck, while stowing away a toolbox and my hardhat, when a new pain shoots across my hips and carries down my right leg. It feels hot and sharp, like the jab of a long needle.

Since I carried a lot of rebar today, I'm thinking the pain must be coming from over-exertion, though it's nothing like any pain I've felt before. And it's not at all like my stomach problems. I try to stretch it away, but that doesn't work. All I'm looking forward to tonight is a quick meal and the comfort of my bed, but the sleep part will have to wait. Warren has created a new work schedule for us, and he wants to explain it at dinner.


**I order** a bowl of chicken soup with extra saltine crackers and a vanilla milkshake. Warren passes around copies of his latest spreadsheet. The changing weather pattern has him worried again.

His previous work plan gave us nine days from today to finish the two platforms. The latest weather forecast is now warning of a hard freeze and 30% chance for snow at this time next week. If that prediction holds true, there won't be enough time to finish both platforms before it's too cold. In other words, we'll be forced to halt construction until spring.

We're discussing ways to increase concrete deliveries when a man bursts in through the front door of the Shoe. "Mercy House is on fire!" he shouts and hurries back outside.

Mike, at the bar, springs into action. He grabs his coat and takes off after the man. A couple sitting in a booth up front rush after Mike. Even though none of us know what Mercy House is, Carson and Buck grab their hoodies and follow the others.

Candace has stopped bussing dishes and gone to the front window. Eddie is immediately at her side, stretching his neck to see what's happening up the street. Skinny, Warren, and I are standing at our table now.

Eddie looks back at us and calls, "Something big is burning!"

The rest of us have our coats on now and go outside. Only a block away, flames are escaping second-floor windows on an old two-story brick building. A dense white cloud of smoke is rolling in slow-motion down the street towards the Shoe. We head uphill towards the blaze.

Across the street from the burning building, displaced adults and children are already shivering in the chilled air. Some are coughing. Youngsters are crying. Some of the dislocated are barefoot and clothed only in pajamas. Warren, Skinny, and I watch as devilish yellow flames crackle and dance along windows on the second floor.

First responders arrive, one pickup and then a second, both skidding to a stop in front of the building. A sheriff's car is right behind them, followed by a lime green fire truck. Firefighters unroll their hoses, attach nozzles, and connect the equipment to spigots on the truck. Neighbors from nearby houses congregate on porches and lawns. The sheriff deputy gives Skinny a flashlight and reflecting vest and tells him to go to the end of the street and keep curious drivers from turning towards the fire. The deputy brings blankets from his trunk and tells Warren and me to distribute them to the people shivering on the lawn.

As I'm handing out the blankets, I notice Albert across the street. He's leading three men, two women, and a child from the back of the burning building. They disappear down a side street, as an old woman is wheeled out the front door on a stretcher, two EMTs performing CPR.

Candace, Eddie, and Mike are standing on a driveway and talking to some of the women and children from the building, when the deputy announces there are LP gas tanks on the southside of the building. Mike quickly leads the group down the sidewalk and then up the steps and into the Shoe.

I continue to watch the fire hoses attack the flames. Rafters pop like campfire kindling. I shuffle over to an older man who's gazing at the fire from his front lawn. He tells me that a hundred years ago Mercy House was the finest hotel in the area, a favorite stopping off point between LaCrosse and Eau Claire. In the late 1940s, the building was converted to apartments.

Today, he says, the building houses laborers from Mexico and Central America who work on dairy farms and small businesses in the surrounding communities. Off the top of my head, I ask the older man if the residents displaced by the fire are in the U.S. legally. It's a dumb question, I guess, and the man glares at me. He wants to know if I'm from the government.

"Of course not," I reply. "I work construction. I was just wondering."

"Well, we don't ask questions like that around here," he says. "Reliable workers are hard to find. We try to keep ours." I nod and walk back to the Shoe.

**The dining** room has been turned into a safe haven. Lights have been dimmed and chairs and tables moved against the back wall. A collection of blankets and quilts and knit throws have been laid down to soften the hardwood floor. The youngest children lie curled beside their parents.

Warren enters and joins me at the bar. Candace and Eddie are sitting against one wall with four young kids in front of them, second or third graders by my estimate. Warren and I watch Eddie read a story from the large book he's holding on his lap, while Candace turns the pages. "They work well together," Warren says of our young couple. Skinny enters and tells us the fire fighters are finally winning.

I'm about to head up to bed when Jared Vreelander stomps in from the street. He pays no attention to us, just scans the dimly lit room until he spots his wife. He calls to her, "Candy!"

When a reply doesn't come right away, he calls louder. "Candy, let's go!" Candace stands and walks over to her husband. "Get your stuff," he tells her.

"I need to stay," Candace replies. "We're reading to the children, 'til they fall asleep. They're pretty upset."

"I'm sure whatever you're doing is *really important*, babe, but let's go," says Jared. The sarcasm in his voice cuts like a razor blade, and I'm reminded that a jerk never sees himself as other people do. Jared dangles his truck keys in front of his wife. "I went through hell getting here," he tells her. "Had to park on 53."

"Jared, please… these kids."

"*No*," Jared says. "They've got it under control. Trust me."

"Come on, Jared," she pleads. "They've been through a lot. I can get a ride home later."

Warren, Skinny, and I are seated only a few feet from the couple. Jared exhales in one dramatic stream of coarse air. "I'm not going to tell you again, babe. We're out of here."

Skinny slides off his barstool and needs only two steps to get to

Jared. "Come on, man," Skinny says to him. "Your wife wants to help the little ones. Let her stay awhile."

"This is none of your business… *man*."

"I know it's not. I'm just saying. These families lost everything tonight. They've got a rough road ahead."

Jared ignores Skinny. "I'm waiting, Candy," he says.

Candace folds her arms over her chest. "I'm staying," she replies in a firm tone. "I have to."

Jared grabs Candace by the wrist. It's the same maneuver we've seen him do before. He twists her arm into a submissive angle. She is instantly under his control. "Hey!" Warren shouts. "Enough of that!"

At the same time, Skinny has reached out and put a hand on Jared's shoulder. Jared tries to shake it off, but Skinny's hand is going nowhere. Another thing to mention about Skinny is that he can be stubborn. He doesn't give up once he's committed to something important, especially when he feels someone is being treated poorly.

Jared spins around and pulls back his fist, about to hit the face of a man who is twice his age. But Jared hesitates. There's no punch thrown. He's noticed movement at the front door. Carson and Buck have entered the Shoe, and already the space between Jared and them has closed. The two would-be footballers stand on either side of Jared, up close and personal, like a sandwich. Two hunks of white bread around a slice of gouda. Jared relaxes his punching arm. His hand lets go of Candace's wrist. "We'll talk when you get home," he sneers and quickly exits the Shoe.

Candace rubs blood back into her hand. "I don't know why he's like that sometimes," she says, and then touches Skinny on the shoulder. "You're my hero."

I watch Candace leave us and return to where the children are listening to Eddie read from the storybook. My eyes follow her, as she gracefully navigates the exhausted bodies scattered around the floor. Then, as she's about to sit down, *everything-I've-been-wondering-about-our-young-waitress* makes sense. The puzzle pieces that I've been unable to put together since our first night in Pigeon Falls fall into place. The answer to the enigmatic *why?* of, why have I been so captivated by this young woman?

Now, I see it all clearly. The familiar sway of her hips and how she crosses her legs when she sits on the floor. The special twist in her delicate neck as it slopes to meet her shoulders. There's the narrowness of her long forearms. Her hourglass waist and how it curves at a unique angle around to her thighs when she bends over.

All the while I was watching Candace move across the dining room in real time, broken memories of mine from long ago had begun to resurface. It was like I was looking back at my life through a kaleidoscope, one fragmented hint after another. The clues went all the way back to the time when my ex-wife and I were not much older than Candace is now.

What I've realized is that from the neck down, Paige and Candace share the same body. Not some spooky approximation of height and weight, *but the same body.* They share the same measurements, the same angles and curves, the same graceful movements, and the same beauty. I know everything about the young body I've been watching in the Shoe, because it's Paige's body.

This long-coming realization is giving me an eerie chill and the upside-down feeling that comes with melancholy. I now ask myself, how many times did I see Paige walk across a room, bend to pick something up, or raise an arm? How often did I enjoy watching the smooth angles in her shoulders, her legs, her hips? Because the two women's faces, voices, hairstyles, *and especially their smiles*, are nothing alike – not even similar – I couldn't make the obvious connection between Candace and Paige. Not until an apartment fire. Not until now.

And suddenly, it all seems obvious.

"That guy's a punk," Carson is telling Skinny. "Completely

worthless. He has no clue how to treat his wife." Candace is reading from the book now. Eddie turns the pages.

"Brother, you got that right," Skinny says, "At a minimum, a woman requires two things: *respect* and *affection*. Those aren't negotiable. If you can't give her that, then you've lost her. And once a woman's lost, getting her back is as hard as, well, you know, finding a swan in a snowstorm."

"I know what you're both saying, and I appreciate it, but we still need to stay out of this," interjects Warren. "Believe me, I worry about her too, I really do."

"Boss, the person to worry about is whoever crosses him next," Skinny says. "Jared's dangerous."

The conversation over Jared's abuse of his wife and Skinny's honor code on how to treat a woman continues a while longer, while I turn to watch a nearly perfect reproduction of my ex-wife as she reads a picture book to displaced kids. It's a vision of Paige that's as close to real as anything I've experienced in years.

**When I** get to my room, I discover a text from an hour ago. It's telling me to phone my sister. Even though it's late, I make the call. Shannon answers on the second ring. "Are you still up?" I ask.

"Dad's in bed," my sister says. "His cut needed a couple of stitches, and I think he's still a little confused from when he hit his head."

I don't recall my sister mentioning that my father hit his head in the fall or cut himself. Shannon's tendency to minimize medical conditions unnerves me at times. She's been that way as far back as I can remember. To my sister, a cut is always a scratch, no matter how deep it goes. A sprain is a tweak. The flu is only a pesky cold. And aches and pains will take care of themselves.

We've argued over word choices many times. I think she's like this now because of how close she was to our mother years ago, throughout our mother's illness. Shannon was never willing to believe our mother was sick enough to die.

"Dad might have a concussion," I tell her.

"They ran tests but didn't find anything," she says.

"Well, keep an eye on him, okay? It doesn't sound right."

"I check on him every two hours, Tom," she says with a defiant tone to her voice. "It's what the doctor recommended." Shannon then changes the subject, as she often does when she loses control of where a conversation is going. "Dad told a joke today," she says.

I could turn the conversation back to my father's condition and ask for more information. I could try to pin my sister down on the number of stitches he got or press the point about using language correctly, but I'm worn out and don't want to start an argument that I'll probably lose. Instead, I go in her direction. "What was his joke?" I say.

"Dad asked, *Why is the cookie sad?*"

"That's a joke for kindergarteners," I tell Shannon. "I think Dad's regressing."

"He's not regressing. It's just one of his favorite jokes."

"I've heard it before."

"We've heard them all before, Tommy. Do your part."

"Okay. Why was the cookie sad?"

"Because it was feeling crumby."

"Shannon, that's exactly how I remember it."

*Losing a parent.* I was twelve when our mother died. A few years before then, the home insulation company in New Jersey, where both our parents had worked, shut down. This meant our family no longer had a steady income. During the next year, our parents chased one dead-end job after another. They talked about selling the house and moving into an apartment, getting a cheaper car, cutting back on food and clothes, and going without extras. Then, my parents started to argue. Our once perfect life was falling apart.

Soon after the arguing started, my mother's coughing got

worse, and the lung cancer diagnosis came not long after that. She couldn't work anymore, and my father's job wasn't paying enough to keep us afloat.

A decade earlier, my mother's brother had moved to Rockford, Illinois, and started his own business installing furnaces and air conditioners. He arranged for my father to come work for him. The job paid well enough to make ends meet and provided health insurance. When we moved to Rockford, my mother was in her third round of chemotherapy. My sister was starting high school, and I was eleven. Rockford was a good town, and my father liked his job, but my mother never got better and died the following year.

After she was gone, we stayed in Rockford, and my father raised Shannon and me alone. He never remarried, and as far as I know, he never went on a date. He too, I suspect, was destined to have one companion in this lifetime.

**Shannon is** aware of my trip to the famous clinic and asks, "What did the doctors tell you?" I explain as little as possible and tell her I have to wait another week for the test results. "Don't worry," she assures me. "You'll see, everything will turn out fine." I hang up, worried that my sister has escaped into an existence where denying any bad news is her only way to survive.

I jump in the shower a second time tonight, this time to rid my body and hair of fire smell, and then go to my bed and pull back the puffy down comforter. Sometime earlier today, my old sheets were exchanged for a new set. The scent of new linen smells fresh and clean, like spring water. I slide inside.

## Wednesday, November 6

A home fire tears at the soul of a neighborhood. It's a shared violation of protected space, a misery that affects everyone living nearby. The feelings of danger and defeat that a fire brings are felt in the community long after every flame has been put out and smoke no longer rises from the ashes. Leftover visual reminders of a fire are bad enough, with charred beams, broken glass, and twisted metal. But it's the lingering odor, the scent of irrevocable change, that hurts even worse.

This morning in Pigeon Falls, fire smell clings to every tree and lamppost. The pungency lurks like an invisible menace around every corner. On my way to breakfast, I gaze uphill towards Mercy House and the streamers of caution tape that surround the wounded apartment building like wrappings of yellow gauze. Inside the perimeter tape, disfigured sofas and mattresses, scorched tables and chairs lie lifeless on the dark lawn, a sight no different from a harbor of crushed boats pushed ashore during a killer storm and left abandoned.

I'm the first to arrive for breakfast. Dot is almost finished prepping our table. She goes to get me a glass of milk. When she returns, she says simply, "Quite the night," and sets the glass in front of me.

"You hear anything new?" I ask her.

"Red Cross came around midnight and took everyone to Harrison," she says. "They turned the high school gym over there into a shelter."

"Does anyone know how it started?"

"My nephew rides a ladder truck," Dot says. "He thinks some wiring in the attic was bad. Lord works in mysterious ways, don't you know."

Warren arrives and says that Eddie was up late and is still in bed, which I figure means that Candace also got home late. Dot sets down her last set of knife and fork. "How're those windmills coming along?" she asks.

"Our part should be done early next week," Warren says. Dot asks nothing more. Buck and Skinny sit down at our table. According to Warren's revised spreadsheet, we're still on track to finish on time, though just barely. The first nest is ready to be poured, and the bearing bars for the second platform are in place. We'll finish installing half of the second nest today and complete the rest of it tomorrow. We can start pouring concrete for both nests on Friday.

**Mid-morning, we're** laboring in full sun. I check my phone app. It's 61°, warmer than expected. I remove my hoodie.

The rebar we use to build a nest is pre-shaped in Davenport, and depending on a rod's function, it can be bent at a sharp angle or curved elegantly like an archer's bow. Some rebar ends are threaded so they can be inserted into the cage like a traditional bolt and secured with a washer and nut. To save us time, the ends have been painted an array of colors, corresponding to the bar's length, thickness, and type of bend. From a distance, the tips of rebar that are stacked in bundles on a pallet next to the foreman's trailer look like the colorful brushstrokes in a kindergartener's primitive painting of a rainbow.

Our afternoon's workload continues like the morning's, a mix of lifting and hauling and connecting. A shift in the wind cuts across the plateau at 4:00 p.m., and the temperature falls ten degrees in half an hour. Everyone notices. "It's the rain coming," Skinny remarks instinctively, verbalizing what we're all thinking.

Burnell stops by the plateau at sunset, just as a wall of dark clouds is rolling in from the west. In the descending twilight, I watch him park outside the foreman's trailer. He honks his horn. Warren comes out, and Burnell hands him our white envelopes. Burnell then drives over to our pit and gets out. He stands up on the edge, looking down at the rest of us working in the shine of the spotlights. I suspect he's not only noting our progress, but also making sure that we're all still here and no one has turned on the boom box. After a few minutes, he leaves, though not by way of the escarpment. He exits with four rear wheels spinning a cloud of dust on the gravel access road that leads out to the county highway, at the northside of his property.

**Back in** Pigeon Falls, I'm first to finish showering and come down for dinner. I take a chair on the far side of our table and rest my back against the wall. It feels good to relax. Candace brings me a chocolate milkshake. For a moment, I consider telling her my recent discovery, that I've realized how her body and my ex-wife's body are a perfect match. I quickly recognize how inappropriate that would sound.

Instead, I ask, "Did everything go okay when you got home after the fire? Your husband left here pretty upset."

"I didn't go home," she says. "I stayed at my sister's. This morning, when I got back, Jared acted like nothing had happened. He's kind of unpredictable like that."

"I'm glad you're okay," I say. "It was nice how you and Eddie read to the children."

"They liked Eddie," Candace says. "He could speak Spanish."

"Spanish?"

"Yeah, he's really good. We didn't have any foreign languages at my high school."

Warren comes and takes a seat, and Candace goes to get him a beer. Warren and I are talking about progress on the nest, when an older man from across the room walks over to our table. He's moving with the help of a cane. Under the blue blazer he's wearing is a yellow golf shirt, buttoned to the neck. "Are you the fellas out at Red Sandberg's farm?" he asks.

"We are," Warren says. "We're with Midwest Stable Platforms, in Davenport. We build foundations for wind turbines."

"Concrete and rebar, that's hard work," says the man.

"Yes, sir."

I study the old guy. There's a lot of character in his features. Larger than average ears, a crooked nose, dark bushy eyebrows that might never have been trimmed. His shoulders curve inward, but they still show good muscle tone, to me a sign he could have spent his life working construction himself or doing heavy lifting in a factory. Something tells me he wasn't a farmer, maybe it's the golf shirt.

The man is doing his best to keep his free hand from shaking but it refuses to cooperate, so he makes the hand a prisoner of his coat pocket. How the man's neurological condition figures into his work history, or his retirement plans, is impossible to know, but that doesn't keep me from wondering.

When the man speaks, his words are clear and carefully chosen, not a single syllable missed or out of place. It's obvious the guy's mind is still in the game, even if his body is on the bench. He asks, "How much does one of those towers cost? You know, the whole package."

"They cost a bunch," Warren says.

"I know, it's a lot." He's acting light-and-easy with us, yet I can tell his question is serious. "But about how much are we talking?"

"Ballpark figure?"

"Yeah, ballpark."

"To build a wind turbine the size Mr. Sandberg is putting up, it's about one and a half million… each."

The old guy is silent for a moment, probably running the numbers in his head. Then, he says, "I heard Red's putting up six."

"That's correct," Warren replies. "Six of them. When all's said and done." Warren isn't breaking any confidentiality agreement between Burnell and MSP. The number of towers going up outside Pigeon Falls isn't a secret, considering the public permits and notices Burnell had to work through before the project was approved.

The man has both hands in his jacket pockets now, and his cane is leaning against our table. He seems a little wobbly on his feet without the help of the cane. "You want to have a seat?" Warren asks.

"That's ten million, give or take," the man says, more to himself than to us. "What a shame."

"I'm not sure I'm following you," Warren says.

The man hesitates in replying. I'm thinking he's about to pick up his cane and head back to his table. A woman his age is sitting up front and has turned around to look for him.

"It's such a waste of money," the man says finally, and instead of leaving, he pulls out a chair at our table and sits down. "I've lived my whole life in this town," he says, settling into the chair. "For as long as I can remember, the Sandberg family has been chasing one get-rich scheme after another."

"Didn't know that," Warren says. Warren maintains a distance in his voice, refraining from discussing the private life of a client, something he doesn't want to do.

"Well, it goes back even before my time," says the old man. "And every big idea of theirs ended in failure." His gaze goes from Warren to me and back to Warren, and then he shrugs. "Food for thought."

The man turns to look towards the front of the dining room again, checking on the woman I assume is his wife. She's facing the front, and Candace is pouring her a coffee refill.

"You might not know this, but Red's grandfather, Swede Sandberg, he bought that property from the Sizemore family during the Depression. Got it on a steal. The Sizemores had a big mink farm out there, but Swede didn't like mink, so he took down the pens and started cash cropping. My grandfather knew Swede pretty good.

"Then after a few years of cash cropping, when his profits weren't big enough, Swede got the idea of selling fishing boats from his home, what with all the rivers and lakes, you know. For several years, he had big boats out there, small boats too. A whole lot of boats. It was quite the operation, and Swede did well for a while.

No one else was selling boats around here."

I recall the rusted boat trailers I saw on our first day out at the farm, three cast-offs in a sea of tall grass.

"But fishing boats didn't make the family rich enough, I guess," says the man, "so Swede ended up selling some of their land."

"Farmland?" I ask.

"A hundred acres on the southside of 53," the man says. "And another hundred, closer to Waterford. That was after land prices shot up after the war."

The man is quiet for a moment. He taps his fingers on the table and then touches his cane, gathering his thoughts, I think.

He says, "Swede's son, Edge, was just like his old man. Told everyone he was going to build an empire. Edge started a slew of door-to-door businesses. Fuller Brush. Amway. Encyclopedias. Had salesmen covering the whole county and then some. Edge was good at talking with people, very cheerful, you know."

"That was Burnell's father?" I say.

"Yeah, Edgerton. But Edge's businesses all sputtered out, just like Swede's did. That's when someone convinced Edge to invest what money he had in pork. He put up that hog confinement and told everyone that one day pork would be as expensive as steak. Long story short, when Red took over the hog business, it was down to a hundred head."

Skinny arrives at our table. The old man shakes Skinny's hand and keeps talking.

"Now, Red's a very clever guy, always has been. He figured out how to bring in workers from Europe to take care of the animals. Cost him pennies to do it. For years now, his hired men have been running the show out there. That's what keeps the family afloat."

"So, what does Mr. Sandberg do?" I ask.

"Like his dad, Red's never been one to get his hands dirty. He's always worked outside jobs, mostly retail. I guess he's into technology now."

"You know a lot about the Sandbergs," Skinny says.

"And they know a lot about me. When you live in a town as small as Pigeon Falls, you know most of everything about everyone."

What the old man has told us has drawn me deeper into Burnell's history and raised my curiosity. I consider keeping a certain question to myself, but the opportunity to ask it is too good to pass up. I say, "How did Mr. Sandberg convince the government to lend him so much money?"

"I've been wondering that too," Warren says. "Normally, we work with electric companies or co-ops, not with private parties."

The old man raises a shaking hand. For the brief time it takes him to rub together his thumb and index finger, the man's hand stops trembling. "It's all money and politics," he says. "Red Sandberg knows important people, his so-called *board of directors*."

Warren and I look at one another. We're skeptical, Skinny even more so. There must be more to the wind farm's financial backstory than a case of *who you know*.

"Six wind turbines?" Skinny says, "that's a lot of government money for one person to get, even with politicians on your side."

"His wife is Chippewa, you know," the man says. "Full blood." There's silence at the table while we connect the dots.

Warren asks, "You're saying, Mr. Sandberg got millions of dollars in government loans because his wife's Native American?"

The man taps a shaky finger to his forehead. "Red did nothing illegal, as far as I can tell. Rumor is, he even mortgaged his house and property."

"Expensive clothes... Fancy new truck..." Skinny sounds like a district attorney addressing a jury.

"Maybe some of those things that he's buying isn't right, but what do I know?" the man says. "Red's new business needed a truck, so he bought the best he could find. Is it a waste of taxpayer money? Sure, it is. But fraud?" The old man shakes his head. "Red's not going to jail for leather seats in a work truck."

Buck arrives and sits at the table. The old man says hello.

"It's more the whole shebang that don't feel right, you know? Red's just gambling with money that's not his." The old man takes out a wrinkled handkerchief. "You know what he knows about wind energy, don't you?" He blows his nose. "Nothing."

As Carson arrives, the old man gets up from the table. "At least, you fellas know what you're doing out there," he says and takes hold of his cane again. "Nice talking to you."

I watch the old man leave. On the way back to his wife, he passes Eddie who's coming towards us. When we're all seated, Warren, Skinny, and I share the story the old guy told us about Burnell and how he got his wind farm money. Carson then gripes about Burnell taking advantage of a program meant for minorities, and Skinny is worried that the Sandbergs could lose everything they own on the family's latest get rich plan. But Warren goes in another direction.

"Of course, there's all that," he says. "Or we can look on the bright side. People around here will be getting clean energy."

A light rain begins to fall while we're eating dinner. It's nothing much, just a sprinkle at best, barely enough to streak windows and dampen the roads. When we finish our meal, the others go off to their rooms, but I remain at the table to check phone messages. I'm also hoping Candace will come over. I have something I want to say.

When she stops by the table a few minutes later, she asks, "You want anything more to eat or drink?"

"No," I tell her, "but I want to thank you for the other night. You know, listening about my medical condition."

"No problem." She smiles and then mentions how Eddie needs to open a bank account. She says he's been using his mother's account, but now he wants one of his own. "Do you think I could pick up Eddie at lunch sometime and take him to the bank?"

"That's a great idea," I tell her. "I'll let our foreman know."

Since I can't watch Candace anymore without also thinking of Paige, I'm not sure how to start what I'm about to say. I decide to just go for it. "What's up with your husband, Candace? I mean, he doesn't treat you very well."

Apparently, I'm not the first to ask about Jared's poor behavior, because Candace nods knowingly. A few customers are still finishing meals. Candace says that if I wait until they're done, she'll come back and talk with me.

So, for the next fifteen minutes, my eyes follow Candace as she winds around the dining room, clearing tables and settling bills. The smooth bends her hips and shoulders make are so obvious to me now, the gestures of her hands and neck so unmistakably Paige's, that I wonder how I didn't make the connection sooner. Movements like hers have been in my head for half my life.

Candace finally returns to where I'm waiting and without another prompt starts talking about Jared. She begins by telling me that Jared had a tough time growing up, that he never fit in with other kids. She says he was always getting into trouble because he was misunderstood. Her rationalizations sound naïve. I know Candace is smarter than that.

"He's abusing you," I remind her.

"He doesn't realize what he does," she says. "It just happens, you know. He always says he's sorry."

"It's not right, Candace. That's not how a good marriage works."

"Well, the big problem is Jared's dad. His dad makes him angry, but Jared's afraid of him too. It's gotten worse since we've been married." I can tell Candace has recited these excuses before. How much she actually believes that her husband's behavior is even somewhat justified is harder to tell.

"Abuse can happen to anyone, Candace, even normal people with normal lives."

"Jared's dad told him college was a waste. That's why Jared

enlisted. But the Army was a big mistake. Too many dumb rules."

The inventory of Jared's grievances with life continues, spoken through the mouth of his young wife. He doesn't like selling cars. He doesn't like people telling him what to do. He wants to move far away. His dad expects him to take over the family business. Jared hates the family business."

Candace pauses, shakes her head. "Jared's not good at selling anything," she says.

"Do you ever wonder how things would be if you'd never met him?"

Candace shakes her head again, more vigorously now. "Jared coming into my life was a miracle," she says. "By the time I got to high school, my parents had no energy for me. They'd been through it all with my brothers and sisters. From junior year on, Jared came to everything I was in. Softball. Choir. All my dance competitions. He took me places and bought me stuff I couldn't afford. Jared cares about me."

I ask, "When did he start twisting your arm?"

Candace's sweet voice goes silent. I know she's not searching for a month and day. She's trying to reconcile the elephant-sized inconsistency in her story. "Was it before you got married?"

It takes a while, but she tells me a lot about how things started going downhill with Jared during her first year in college, how his anger started coming out. "Maybe I didn't see everything like I do now," she admits.

"Has he ever hit you?"

"Oh, no," she says, too quickly, and I'm hesitant to believe her. "But he has strong hands. He knows how to get me to do what he wants." She gently pulls on her sleeve to cover the multi-colored bruises on her wrist, but there's not enough fabric to hide them all. She rests her hands in her lap.

"Have you ever talked to a counselor... or the police?"

"I'd never let it go so far that I had to call the police."

I lean in, as if to share a secret. "You know, everyone on my crew is worried about you." Candace looks surprised. "They are, really. Do you ever wish you never married him?"

"No," she says, and again I'm reluctant to believe her. "But even if I did wish that, I can't change what's already happened."

Candace thinks for a moment and then asks if I ever heard of something called *Amor Fati*. I haven't. She learned about it in a philosophy class this past spring semester. "It's Latin for 'love your fate,'" she says. I tell her I have no clue what that means. "It's an *amazing* idea. It's even helped me make sense about Jared."

"How so?" I'm genuinely curious.

"I used to blame myself when Jared got angry. Like it was my fault because I didn't prevent it. Even when he twisted my arm, I thought it was my fault. But I realize now that bad things happen to everyone, including me. It's part of our fate. It's part of our life story."

"You mean, you accept his abuse... because it's going to happen anyway? That's not right."

"No," she's quick to correct me. "That's more like *fatalism*, when you believe your future is already decided. *Amor Fati* is different. What it's saying is, don't stress over bad things that happen to us. In fact, we should even *love* them because they can make our life better."

"*Love* them?"

Candace explains that with *Amor Fati* you're supposed to learn from the bad things that happen to you, especially the experiences that hurt you. That way, you can keep those same bad things from happening in the future. You can make your life turn out better, turn out happier.

It's obvious that Candace was a top student in college. She remembers a lot from her philosophy course, even as much of what she's describing flies over my head. As I'm admiring her excitement, I notice again her top front tooth that's a little too white. Because of her stunning smile, it's easy to dismiss one substitute voice in an otherwise perfect choir. Now, with her sitting directly across from me, only three feet away, that outlier is impossible to ignore.

Soon, I'm barely listening to what Candace is saying about philosophy. I'm more curious about the tooth that's been replaced. Did she lose it as a little girl tumbling out of bed? Did she ride her bike into a tree? Has she been unwilling to brush and floss properly? Knowing Jared's anger, I also contemplate darker possibilities.

As she's saying something about *personal responsibility*, I interrupt her. "Can I ask you another thing?"

"Sure, what?"

"What happened to your tooth?"

Candace reflexively runs her tongue along her top teeth. She raises her upper lip with a grin that offers me an unobstructed look at the replacement part. "In eighth grade," she says, "an angry girl in gym class elbowed me in the mouth." She looks away. "They didn't get the color right, did they?"

"It looks good," I tell her and offer an accepting smile, though she sees right through my embarrassed lie, which causes her own embarrassment to return.

"Anyway," she says, rubbing her tongue along her upper row a second time, "that tooth I lost is part of my life story too, just like everything else. Doesn't help to get down about it."


**When I** leave the dining room, the evening rain is no longer the light and misty patter it was during dinner. Coming down is a substantial shower, though nothing close to a full-blown storm. If it continues into the morning, we'll have to break out our rain gear.

I open my room window a foot and lie in bed listening to raindrops falling beyond the screen. In no time, I can distinguish what's landing on nearby roofs from what's pinging against cartops or sliding through branches and leaves. I'm reminded of the work music from yesterday afternoon. How every tool, every movement, every outdoor surface produced its own unique sound.

Fortunately, no other noises are in competition with the rain concert outside my window tonight. There's no thunder or wind rustle, no rumble of car engines or idle chatter on the street. For now, my mind is clear of any distraction. All I hear is the serenade of a late autumn rain, millions of drops falling steady and true on a small village in rural Wisconsin, a night concert as comforting as a bedtime story. As I listen to the calming notes, I let myself drift into sleep.

# Part Three

# The Spill

## Thursday, November 7

Sometime during the night, the tranquil melody that had lulled me into such a peaceful sleep turned into a tempest. The pounding force of a full-blown storm wakes me an hour earlier than usual. Rainwater has spilled over the floor under my desk and created a puddle that stretches a yard away from the wall. I hurry out of bed and close my window. Outside the Shoe, water is pooling on the sidewalk below my room. A gutter filled with leaves has caused runoff to overflow the curb and stream across the sidewalk. I get dressed and gather my rain gear.

The dining room opens for breakfast at 6:00 a.m. Although I arrive a few minutes earlier, I'm pleased to find the front door unlocked. Dot is busy preparing tables, methodically distributing placemats and flatware like a seasoned floorman dealing hands at a blackjack table. "Good morning," I say, and she returns the greeting. "Never expected so much rain."

"One thing about Wisconsin, hon," Dot replies. "If you don't like the weather now, wait a few hours."

On my way to our table, I notice something I'd paid little attention to before this morning. It's the gallery of 8x10 black and white photographs on the wall to my left. I detour over to take a look at the ten frames that are arranged horizontally along the wall, each one shoulder high. In the first frame, I recognize the front façade of the Horseshoe Inn, though in the photo the place is named *Maddsen's Rest Stop and Delivery*.

The building's front windows are smaller in the picture than they are now, and the front door was all wood back then, not today's double-wide entry made mostly of glass, but the outline of the place is the same. Two men stand solemnly out front of Maddsen's, both with long uneven beards, high-waisted pants, black suspenders, and white long-sleeve shirts. The scene I'm looking at is more than a hundred years old.

The next black and white is a high angle shot directed on two dirt roads meeting in a T intersection. In the distance, a horse and buggy wait, unattended. The setting looks like the spot where US 53 and County 121 come together now. In the third photo, a narrow two-story building has a sign over the front door reading *Pigeon Falls Meat Market*. Another sign, this one much smaller and in the window, says *Open To All Paying Customers*. I continue through the display of local history. Next photo, two horses are hitched to a hay wagon parked in front of a shed. Beside the hay wagon is an old black jalopy. It's early 1900s. A sign posted on the shed's flat roof reads *U.S. Post Office*. In another picture, ten children stand outside a small church. They're holding paper certificates waist high. To the side, a bald bespectacled pastor stares humorlessly at the camera. Everyone is dressed for Sunday service.

"That was ages ago," Dot says. She is right behind me now, taking a break from setting tables. I swivel towards her, just as her finger settles on a man in the next 8x10. "This handsome guy is my great grandad. I never met him," she adds, sadly.

In the photo, eight men pose shoulder to shoulder, each in an identical heavy coat and pointed hat. Two men in the middle, one being Dot's ancestor, hold the ends of a small American flag. Penned in white ink near the bottom of the frame is *Pigeon Falls Volunteer Fire Brigade 1902*.

"I'm fourth generation Pigeon Falls," Dot says, proudly. She and I are still alone in the dining room. "My great grandbabies are seventh gen."

As we move along the wall, Dot goes on to tell me that her ancestors came from Norway, in 1885, and how she worked in Waterford as an elementary school teacher for forty-four years. At the end of the photo lineup is a view towards Pigeon Creek, where the stream widens into a long pond with a two-story wood structure next to the pond, what looks like an old mill. "Back then, was there a waterfall around here?" I ask, pointing at the photo. "You know, the *falls* in Pigeon Falls."

Dot laughs. "If I got a dollar for every time someone asked where the falls are, I'd be rich." My confused look prompts her to explain how the village got its name.

In the mid-1800s, Dot says, the land for miles around was all brush and forest. No white settlers had come here yet, only hunters and trappers passing through. One autumn day, two hunters camped along a stream they'd been following for some time. The next morning, a flock of pigeons settled in an old tree next to the men's campsite. More pigeons arrived throughout the day, and by dusk the old tree held more birds than leaves on its branches. Overnight, the weight of the birds must have been so great that a huge branch broke off and thousands of birds either fell to the ground or flew away. The odd event inspired the hunters, Dot says, and they named the place "Pigeon Falls."

Her story finished, I stare at the elderly waitress, my lips pursed, eyebrows raised. Is this the tale that locals tell every clueless stranger who asks how the village got its name? "You're joking," I say.

"Cross my heart," Dot swears, while crossing herself twice for good measure. "It's the holy truth."

"You mean, there's never been a waterfall or dam in Pigeon Falls. Just birds falling out of a tree?"

"Just birds falling out a tree," she says. "Pigeon Falls wasn't even a town officially until 1947."

"Okay," I tell her. "What about that odd farmhouse out at the Sandberg farm? What's that all about?"

"Oh, gracious!" Dot exclaims. She adjusts the bow on her apron. "Each generation thinks it has a better idea than the last one, right?"

Dot goes on to explain that the original section of the Sandberg farmhouse, the cream city brick part, was built in the 1800s, even before the Sizemore family owned the land, which was decades before Swede Sandberg bought it from them. During World War II, Swede and his wife put on the big Victorian wing, thinking they'd raise a lot of children. But their son, Edgerton, was their only child. When he inherited the farm, he added the smaller modern wing.

"That last part went up in the '50s," Dot says. "Burnell's never done anything to the house himself. Joyce keeps it nice on the inside, but the outside, oh my!"

The rest of the crew have come down for breakfast and are making their way to the back of the room. I thank Dot for her history lesson and find my spot at our table. Skinny is handing Eddie a plastic poncho and a pair of rain pants. "They'll be a little long, but you need some protection today," he says. "You can cuff 'em."

*Rain defense?* We have it. Ponchos, waterproof pants, rubber boots, good gloves. The one thing a construction worker finds more miserable than anything else is working in the rain, especially in a cold rain. When the front moved through, the temperature in Pigeon Falls bottomed out at 50° overnight. It isn't expected to rise much above that today. In a cold rain, there's no amount of layering or insulation that can keep your hands and feet warm and dry. Water and a chill will always find a way in.

After breakfast, Dot comes to clear our table. "Pretty nasty out there this morning," Warren says to her, as he's zipping his jacket and we're getting ready to leave.

"When it rains," she replies, cheerfully, "look for rainbows." Dot and her proverbs. I wonder how often she'll repeat this one today.

**Whitewater is** churning up and down Pigeon Creek when we turn off US 53 and cross the narrow bridge that connects to Sizemore Coulee Road. Sizemore Creek is also moving with purpose. It reaches halfway up to road level. I switch my wipers to their highest speed to better follow Skinny's taillights. When we turn at the red mailbox onto Burnell's long driveway, rainwater in the culvert along the driveway is two feet deep and streaming briskly towards Sizemore Creek. At least three or four inches of rain has fallen overnight, and it's still coming down heavy. During the normal construction season, MSP gives us the day off when a storm this severe hits, but now, every hour of downtime brings us nearer to failure. We're fighting the clock here, not rainwater. Luckily, there's no lightning this morning or we'd be forced to shut down for sure. A nest of rebar conducts electricity better than a lightning rod.

Skinny and Carson were up early today when the heavy rain started around 3:00 a.m. They drove out to the jobsite to get sump pumps running in each pit. When we park at the jobsite, rainwater is streaming across the plateau and being whipped by the wind. The long hoses that Skinny and Carson laid out from the pumps are running at full capacity and carrying water from the floor of the pits to the edge of the escarpment, where gravity pulls it downhill towards the Sandberg's farm. Thanks to our pumps, water is only an inch deep in both pits.

My boots get good traction on the concrete mud mats. Walking up and down the ramps is another story. The clay subsoil clings to my boots and is as slippery as ice. There's also danger in working up on the rebar nest. It's easy to lose footing or have a rod slip out of your hand, potentially landing on someone below. Despite these challenges, our crew works with careful confidence all morning, and though it takes us twice as long as usual to add rebar to the second nest, slowly but surely, the dome takes shape.


**For lunch,** we eat inside the foreman's trailer. Joyce has come alone today and is using Albert's old van for transport. She peels back the first sheet of aluminum foil to reveal a bread I've never seen before, round pieces of dough that have been deep fried. "Well, look at that," Skinny says, gleefully. "*Fry bread.*"

"You know it?" Joyce asks.

"Yes, ma'am," Skinny replies, "and I love it."

Next, Joyce uncovers a pork roast that's been sliced and topped with brown gravy. A third sheet of foil comes off to reveal a casserole of yellow corn, green beans, and orange squash. "Really?" Skinny says. "*Three sisters succotash?*"

"How do you know these dishes?" Joyce asks. Her voice hovers in that narrow range between wonder and disbelief.

"When I finished school," Skinny says, "my first job was in Flagstaff. They have fry bread, succotash, blue corn pancakes, a lot of Native dishes out there."

She pulls back the last piece of foil. "You know this one?"

"Blueberry pudding," Skinny says.

Joyce smiles and leans against the trailer wall. It doesn't look like she plans to leave us right away today. I think she's waiting to see if we enjoy what she's prepared, a meal close to her heart.

The electric heater in the trailer isn't very powerful, so the cold rain dripping from my clothing and running down my back chills my body as I sit down to eat, but it takes only two swallows of Joyce's tri-color vegetable dish and my body starts to warm.

"This bread is amazing," Buck says and uses an edge like a sponge to dab at the steaming juice on his plate.

"My mother made traditional dishes every meal when I was a girl," Joyce says and puts a big serving spoon in the blueberry pudding. "I don't usually fix them, unless it's the holidays, when my daughter is home with her family. Melinda loves traditional food, and her boys are good eaters." The door to the trailer pushes open.

Led by a gust of wind and a spray of cold rain, Burnell hurries inside. He's dressed in a slicker with a camouflaged pattern, and he sports matching waterproof pants and knee-high boots, all top-of-the-line brands. He closes the door and removes his cap. "You boys getting anything done today, besides eating lunch?" Burnell asks.

Warren rises out of his chair, a plate of pork roast and succotash in hand. "It's pretty slippery in spots," he says, "but we're moving forward."

"It's gonna rain until dark," Burnell informs Warren. "We were supposed to get an inch or two. Now the radio's calling this a twenty-five-year storm. We got six inches so far. In Minneapolis, they already have ten."

"We can work through it," Warren replies. "We're finishing the frame for the second platform now."

"When you pouring cement?"

"If the rain stops, we'll fill the bottom of both platforms tomorrow."

Burnell looks at the food on the table, the steaming pot of vegetables, golden-brown meat, fry bread and purple pudding. He sniffs at the aroma and then points a finger at Warren's plate. "Usually, she saves this for... *special occasions*," he mumbles, letting his lips expel the last two words in one long disgusted protest. Burnell seems disappointed that we've been treated to private family recipes.

"Burnell, would you like a plate?" Joyce asks.

"I've got Walter Schmieding out in the truck," he says.

"Mr. Sandberg, we want to thank you for your lunch idea," Skinny says. "Your wife's meals are nothing short of outstanding."

"Joyce is the best cook in Trempealeau County," Burnell says. "Second place isn't close." Burnell doesn't linger on the compliment. "I've brought a business friend up here," he says to Warren. "We're going to drive over to the holes you're working in. I want to show him whatever progress you've been making." He settles his cap back on his head. "I expect to see you back at it."

"Soon as we finish lunch," Warren says and sits again.

Burnell looks at Warren a couple of seconds longer than necessary and shakes his head. "Knock yourself out," he replies and then leaves. The friction between Burnell and Warren is obvious and growing. Warren had assumed the role of go-between for us, keeping separate our animosity for Burnell and his for us. But now, the tension we've been feeling has spilled onto Warren as well. Outside, the unsettling rumble of Burnell's truck lessens as he drives away.

I ask Joyce, "How many children do you have, ma'am?"

"Two," she says. "My son Martin lives near San Francisco and works with computers and the homeless. Melinda is a surgical nurse in Omaha." Joyce starts covering the dishes. "Melinda comes and visits every summer. Red loves her three boys. He lets them steer the tractor, and he carries them all over in the bucket." She makes a stack of containers and returns them to a cooler. "Martin, you know, he's not especially close with his father. Martin never had an interest in farms or farming."

After we finish sorting our dishes and silverware for her, Joyce puts on her raincoat and pulls the hood over her beautiful hair. "See you tomorrow," she says as she's going out the door.

"Interesting family," Carson remarks a minute later, as we're leaving the trailer. "Just as messed up as mine."

**The rainfall** never slows the rest of the afternoon. At times, raindrops are falling so thick I can see only a few feet in front of me. If someone unfamiliar with our jobsite were to walk around the plateau in this blinding weather, they'd run the risk of falling into a pit or stepping over the edge of the ridge. Warren informs us that the cold front from Canada has slid lower than expected, and a conflicting front over the Great Lakes is blocking the storm's exit.

Midafternoon, my stomach problems return, so I take an extended visit to the porta-potty. Sitting within the shadows of an outhouse during a cold rainstorm is an experience I wish for no one. My naked butt shivers on the plastic toilet seat, while various aches and pains argue across my abdomen, until my colon finally sorts things out.

**Setting the** steel fit-forms for the first pit took us only two hours to complete on Monday, but that's not the case today. Part of the reason is how slippery everything is, and part of the reason is Bud's challenges with the crane. Working the long neck is more difficult and dangerous than ever, as gusts of wind sweep across the plateau and bend the tops of pine trees along the ridge. Even though Warren knows we can't lose any more time, he tells Bud to park his machine if the risk is too great. Bud replies that we should press on, he can manage it, and Bud is right. He comes through expertly, maneuvering the crane as if its long blue neck were an extension of his own body. Flawlessly, Bud guides three dozen of the steel fit-forms over to the second pit and sets each load gently on the mud mat.

Late in the day, Buck and I are double checking the connections we've made. Despite how dismal the day has been, we're making progress, just not as much as Warren had planned. "This storm is really messing with Warren's spreadsheet," Buck says.

I've been thinking the same. If rain continues overnight, there's no chance we'll be able to pour concrete in the morning. In addition to the added water, the declining arc of the sun and the shift in wind direction are working against us, plus the ground isn't retaining heat like it did a few days ago.

"Finishing in time will be close," I reply to Buck.

**After putting** up night lights, we're past 7 p.m. by the time we return to our trucks and start stowing gear. In the distance, I notice a honking sound and turn towards it. Then, out of the darkness come the headlights of the approaching vehicle. It's Albert's old minivan cresting the ridge. I assume he's coming with our envelopes of cash, but his speed and the warning from his horn are telling me something else, that something's not right. Albert fishtails to a stop in front of the foreman's trailer. Warren pops out of the trailer to see what the disturbance is all about. We all meet at the bottom of the stairs.

"Mr. Sandberg!" Albert shouts through the downpour. "Mr. Sandberg you help!"

"What's the problem?" Warren says.

"Fast! Fast!" Albert babbles. Then, Albert's English skills abandon him completely. He says a long sentence in what I assume is Hungarian and motions frantically with his arms for us to follow. He hurries back to his van and starts honking again, as he drives away.

"Someone could be hurt," says Carson.

"Let's find out," Warren replies and locks the trailer. We take off after Albert.

The drive to the bottom of the escarpment is a challenge. Streaming water has cut crevices across the rocky dirt path, so our decline to the valley floor is slick with mud and lined with bumps. Rainfall presses hard against my windshield, creating a curtain of water and making headlights and wipers nearly useless. All I have guiding me are Carson's faint taillights. One major slip of a tire and any of us could tumble hundreds of feet to the bottom of the coulee. A few tense minutes pass before we've all made it down from the plateau.

Albert picks up his pace. With the skill of a race car driver, he navigates the route between the plowed fields. We stay close behind. At the driveway Albert turns left, towards the farmhouse. The culvert along the driveway has overflowed its rim, and rainwater is tossing and spitting as it spills across the gravel. I spot Albert's son and the three Guatemalans out in front of the farmhouse. They're shoveling mud next to where the culvert bends away from the outbuildings.

Albert parks on the gravel circle in front of the farmhouse. We slide in around him and assemble under the flagpole. The smell of pig manure seems more oppressive than usual. "It is shit tank," Albert tells us, in English again. "It break! Come! Come!"

Albert leads us on a narrow walking path around the privacy berm that shields the farmhouse from the hog confinement. I have a flashlight pointed out in front, but its narrow beam offers me little confidence as I move along the unfamiliar route. "Fast, fast!" Albert calls, over his shoulder.

On the slick ground, my boots try to find traction but are constantly frustrated. After we pass the first big curve in the berm, the manure tank looms in front of us, rising out of the murkiness like the Great Black Wall of Trempealeau County. The round tank is a menacing structure, a cylindrical shape at least 100 feet in diameter and 15 feet tall. It's made of concrete blocks and is open at the top.

The path we're following mirrors the curvature of the tank, and I notice that the wall's woven design of concrete blockwork is a technique from an earlier era. They don't make them like this one anymore, and for good reason. Most of the old blocks are chipped and deteriorating, and in the mortar lines between them, cracks have spread up the wall like the wrinkles on my father's neck. High overhead, a brisk wind is whipping down the escarpment from the plateau above and flushing rainwater across the top of the tank. The spray mixes with manure and fills the air.

We continue to trail Albert like a search party, looping around the tank towards the far side. Soon, we see Burnell and Joyce standing side by side, under cover of a shared umbrella. Their flashlight beams are nothing more than faint yellow dots nibbling at the base of the wall. Burnell calls out something, but I can't understand what it is, so I ask Carson in front of me, "What's he saying?"

"Something about the whole damn thing coming apart!" he shouts back towards me.

Our party continues to move towards Burnell and Joyce, but I'm still too far away to see what they're concerned about. Then, as we're closing in on the Sandbergs, Carson sees it first and yells,

"There's a breech in the wall!" and the emergency becomes clear. A big front-end loader with its bucket piled high with cut firewood has slid down a muddy embankment and skated head-on into the wall.

Albert turns towards us. "It is my boy drive skid steer," he says. His voice is quivering to the point of crying. The notes of regret and shame I hear from Albert are so painful they hurt my ears. No one on their side explains why a fourteen-year-old boy was hauling firewood in a rainstorm, and no one from our crew is in any position to ask.

I have a clear view now of the point of impact. The damage is catastrophic. The bottom blocks have been pushed in, creating an irregular wound that's two-by-three feet in size. Sludge darker than the darkest night gushes out the jagged opening. It's flowing past the front-end loader and mixing with rainwater on the ground that's already been fed by runoff from the plateau. Gravity is pulling the entire mixture downhill and out into Burnell's plowed field. From there, it appears headed even farther south, towards Sizemore Coulee Road.

From what I estimate, a few thousand gallons of manure have already escaped the tank. Tens of thousands more are still inside and ready to flee. I shine my flashlight up the side of the tank. A crack in the wall, one-inch-wide, rises to the top. Along its length, manure is escaping in spurts and trickles, which then bleed down the concrete blocks. Secondary fractures radiate out from the main line. The whole thing appears ready to collapse, exactly as Carson just told me, and once the rest of the manure flows away and reaches Sizemore Creek, the contamination will continue on to Pigeon Creek, and from there it'll flow downstream to the Trempealeau River. After that, it's only a few miles before the devastation reaches the Mississippi. We're looking at what will be tens of thousands of gallons of concentrated pig manure fouling the area's waterways.

The coarse smell of the pig manure will annoy everyone living along the way and sicken some, as well. Even more important, however, is the ammonia in the manure. If manure gets into the rivers and streams, the ammonia will kill uncountable fish and other wildlife. A spill like this could ruin the area's waterways for months to come, if not for years. The potential disaster is not lost on any of us. We're looking at an event that could get national attention.

"How full is the tank?" Skinny calls out.

"At top," Albert says. "Two hundred-twenty-thousands gallon." The number represents more pig manure than I can comprehend.

"I had a company coming out in two weeks to empty it," Burnell adds. "I didn't expect a storm like this. Or a tractor accident."

Surprisingly, Burnell's usual cocksure voice has left him. His tone is more contrite now. It has the wounded pitch of anyone's who's ever faced sudden ruin because of a couple of unforeseen mistakes.

The heavy rain continues to fall. I direct my flashlight again to the top of the wall and notice that the blocks alongside the major vertical crack are bowing outward. Suddenly, a chunk of block the size of a toaster pops out of the wall halfway up, and a jet-black gusher shoots from the opening. "Move back!" Warren orders.

Even though we need to do something, and as quickly as possible, the manure tank's owner is standing as stiff as a fence post, trapped in the fog of war. Burnell stares at the shiny stream of waste that barely missed Buck's head, utterly mesmerized by its dark, hissing beauty. Albert has moved next to Burnell. He, too, is as lifeless as a statue. Having already fulfilled the last order he was given, that of getting us to the spill, he awaits a new assignment from his boss.

But no new order comes. The scope of the looming devastation is only a few feet in front of Burnell, yet he's paralyzed. He's even lost his voice.

**Anyone could** step up and be the hero tonight, but it's Warren who comes alive, his voice the foghorn that warns us of the shoals, his flashlight the beacon that will lead us to safe harbor. "This is what we're going to do," Warren says with confidence and authority, absent any fear or panic.

He calmly addresses each of us by name, directing us to specific tasks, such as how high to dig a dike to hold back the spill, where the dike needs to go, and what to watch for if anything changes. In front of us, I'm watching a leader being born on the battlefield and wonder if somewhere deep inside Warren, in some quiet corner of his subconscious, he's been rehearsing for this moment his entire life.

"Work with Albert's son and the others," Warren orders Carson and Eddie. "See if you can channel the spill back our way. Just keep it from getting in the culvert."

Warren tells Albert and Burnell to get shovels and help the rest of us in the open field where we'll build the dike. Joyce will stay at the tank and let us know when the breach opens more. Skinny, Buck, Warren, and I get our own shovels and hustle fifty yards across the muddy field. For the first thirty, we're slogging through a slurry of manure and rainwater that's pooling in furrows two and three inches deep. Warren stops and points uphill behind us, back towards the manure tank. "See how rainwater is flowing the way we came?" he says. "Most of the spill will take that path to the river."

We retreat another thirty yards closer to Sizemore Creek. Albert and Burnell have joined us. "We need bobcats, skid steers," Skinny says. "Shovels aren't going to cut it. Once the whole tank breaks, the wave will be too much to stop."

Through the scattering noise of wind and heavy rain, Burnell answers, "I called around already. No one would come out."

Skinny turns to Warren. "You gotta drive to town, boss," he says. "Mike will know who to call. We'll do what we can, 'til you get back."

"No one's coming," Burnell persists.

"Go, boss," Skinny insists. "You can convince them."

Warren agrees with Skinny and hurries to his truck and drives away. I set up the one portable light stand I had in my truck, only to discover its brilliance in the downpour doesn't even reach the ground.

"I've got a lightbar on my truck," Burnell says and scurries away.

We've set up our defensive position nearly a hundred yards south of the breach. From here, I can barely see the yellow light escaping the windows of the hog confinement. The manure tank itself is nothing more than a dusky cylinder highlighted in amber silhouette. Joyce is somewhere out there too, with her flashlight, but I can't see her or her light. Albert looks over at me and nods, which seems like a sort of thank you, I guess. It's my only moment of connection with him.

With each shovelful of mud we lift, we add a fraction of an inch to the earthen dike we're making on our downhill side. We're working as fast as we can, but the undertaking already seems like a losing battle. A shovel of muddy manure weighs as much as a shovel of concrete. My arms, already drained of energy from a long day of work, soon grow numb to the heaviness of each new load. So far, our wall is half-a-foot tall and 30 feet wide, not nearly the size it needs to be.

Burnell returns with his truck. The LED lightbar on the roof is powerful. It and the truck's headlights brighten the ground around us with the power of a couple dozen light stands. Burnell starts shoveling next to me. Off the top of my head, I say to him, "Once you get the wind farm running, are you getting rid of the hogs?" My question is only intended as a distraction from my shoulder and back pain. I don't expect Burnell to give the answer that he does.

"I think about selling every year," he says. "But there's still profit in pork. I can't get rich on four hundred head, but if I sell the operation now, there's nothing for Albert and the others to do. They'll be out of a job. I've got to think about their families." Burnell's reply is a stunner, the first time he's shown concern about anyone other than himself. I don't know what to make of it.

Carter runs into our field of truck light. "We can't keep the shit out of the creek! We need help!" With Warren gone, Skinny has taken over as leader. He tells Buck and Albert to go to the ditch with Carson. Skinny, Burnell, and I will keep shoveling where we are.

Then, I hear Joyce's voice piercing the darkness. "It's opened all the way to the top!" She runs towards us and says that manure is pouring out so fast that the tank will be empty in minutes.

From where we stand, light from Burnell's truck helps us see some of the ground between us and the manure tank. A wave of sludge that's four or five inches higher than anything we've seen so far is already moving our way. Warren correctly determined which ruts the runoff would follow, and he was right at first about where in the field we needed to build our dike. What he hadn't foreseen was where a larger breach would cause the flow to follow different creases in the land.

"We have to shift over there!" Skinny shouts. Burnell, Joyce, and I follow him 100 feet away, where the surge is already starting to arrive.

**The rain** continues to pound against my head, and I reach my lowest point. Pig manure touches every corner of my clothing. All of us have slipped to the ground a few times, so the slime has made its way into our boots and down the back of our pants. My socks and gloves are soaked with it. The filth is in my hair and trickles across my forehead. It slides down my cheeks and across the back of my neck. Oddly enough, I barely smell it anymore.

We've continued to pile mud and manure as fast as possible, but our efforts are hopeless. The crest of the wave is upon us, and our dike is not yet tall enough to do much of anything. Each shovelful now is as much manure as mud. At best, we're slowing the flow. At worst, we've already lost the war.

With my hands on my knees, I stop for a moment to catch my breath. That's when I hear a horn in the distance, the muffled sound coming from out near Sizemore Coulee Road. Burnell and Skinny relax their shovels and turn towards the noise the same moment I look up. A pair of faint yellow headlights is approaching. Then, a second set flickers behind them. And then another set, and then one more.

The lights grow brighter. It's Warren returning with three vehicles trailing him. They're pulling trailers with front-end loaders strapped on. Warren leads two onto the path dividing Burnell's property. One trailer continues past the turn-off, on towards the farmhouse. Skinny runs over to explain to Warren our revised strategy for stemming the spill. The helpers park fifty yards downhill from us and get to work.

In less than two hours, the big machines have dug and pushed together enough mud to make a curved seawall that's three feet high and nearly a quarter the width of Burnell's valley. The rainy sludge is already rising in the earthen tub they've built, forming a shiny black lagoon between us and the ruptured tank. None of the spill will make it to the county's waterways.

Carson rejoins us as the two pieces of heavy equipment are being reloaded onto their trailers. "They saved us up at the house," he says with a smile, his clothing and face stained dark with manure and mud. "The driveway is clear."

**While we're** standing behind the dike, enjoying our victory, the storm begins to weaken. Soon, the sky has transitioned from torrent to drizzle. Under cover of their umbrella, Burnell and Joyce quietly drift away from the rest of us. As they disappear into the night, their small bodies seem weak and battered. Burnell holds his arm around his wife's waist, and she is leaning into him. The Sandberg family has once more knocked elbows with failure and recovered just enough to survive.

Albert reaches inside Burnell's truck. He shuts off the lights and then the ignition, leaving us in darkness again. We trudge back to our trucks near the farmhouse and add our shovels to those already leaning against the flagpole, the blades and handles caked in mud and manure. Carson calls over to Warren, "The townies weren't gonna come, were they?"

"They came, once they realized what would happen if the spill made it off this property."

"Yeah. They wouldn't come just for him."

**The rain** has stopped completely now. Because we had been shivering in our encampment around the flagpole, Albert built a bonfire for us, on the edge of the gravel circle, using fuel oil and dry wood his son fetched from the pole barn. The flames tower over us now, filling the empty sky with yellow light and breathing warmth into the air around us.

"No way I'm putting these clothes in my truck," Skinny says. He's dripping manure and rainwater from every corner. He tugs his long arms out of his jacket sleeves. "I'm going home buck naked, boys."

Skinny's declaration doesn't surprise me. Maybe I'm too tired to think straight. Or maybe it's because Skinny says unexpected things from time to time. But I get what he's saying. Eddie on the other hand isn't so sure. "You're going to the hotel with no clothes on?" he asks.

"Everything's covered in shit, son," Skinny replies. "I'll never get the smell out of my truck if I drive like this."

"I'll full Monty with you," says Carson, spitting filth as he speaks.

Skinny points towards the side of the farmhouse. "We can wash off in that hose over there."

Warren's too tired to come up with an alternate idea, so he signs onto Skinny's plan too. "I'll see if Joyce has some towels."

"What if someone sees us in town?" asks Buck.

"Hell," Skinny says. "You think the good folks of Pigeon Falls can't take a joke?"

Warren returns with a stack of bath towels in various shades of pink and light blue, along with a plastic sack that's the large size people fill with leaves or grass clippings. "Joyce said to put our dirty clothes in this bag, and she'll wash them for us," Warren says.

"That's kind of her," replies Skinny, "but we gotta burn it all. Everything's useless. And even if it wasn't, Joyce shouldn't have to do our laundry." We look at each other and agree, the clothes will go in the fire.

I remove my gloves first and then my coat. Next off are my boots, pants, and top. Finally, my socks and underwear are added to the clothes pile that's forming at my feet. Nothing is salvageable. Manure has soaked through every item. I carry my things to the bonfire and throw them in. The powerful flames consume my offering. Even though the night air away from the fire is cool, I've been sweating so much that my body hardly pays attention to the chill. My thoughts have turned instead to the odd situation we're in.

I've never seen a coworker naked before, not at MSP and not at any other place I've worked. It's a bizarre notion, having a crew get naked together and wash off in a communal garden hose. In fact, *it's unheard of.* I'm only able to reconcile the idea by taking it as a spur of the moment initiation, a once-in-a-lifetime rite of passage with friends, like cutting the palm of your hand with a pocketknife and becoming blood brothers.

Skinny is first at the hose. As he directs the nozzle from head to toe, I'm amazed by the number of tattoos inked across Skinny's body. I've seen the arm tats before, but ink covers the rest of him too. Though I'm not inclined to watch him, it's hard not to.

Geometrical patterns surround Skinny's left arm like a patchwork quilt, and rainbow stripes wrap his right arm like a sleeve. Cherub faces appear in a bank of puffy clouds across his back. Above them, the wings of an eagle span the distance between his shoulder blades. A morning sun that's washed in pink and blue cotton candy highlights rises on his abdomen, and a burnt orange late-in-the-day orb sets at his lower back. Already, I'm feeling embarrassed staring at Skinny, until I realize the rest of our crew is equally entranced in the elaborate artwork.

Skinny picks up on our curiosity. "I'm getting a pigeon right here when I get home," he says and points to the top of his left shoulder. "That way I'll never forget Pigeon Falls. Or maybe a pigeon on one side and a pig on the other."

Several minutes earlier, Albert and his son departed in Albert's old van, taking the three Guatemalans with them. Albert had heard us talking about getting naked and may have wanted to spare his son the awkwardness of such a scene.

When Skinny finishes at the hose, he goes over and stands in front of the warm glow of the flames. Warren is next in line to wash off, and then it's my turn. For Skinny, Warren, and me, everything at the hose is pure business. No time to waste, just get the manure off your body and dry yourself. But when it's Buck's turn, he takes the hose and squirts Eddie, who lets loose with a childish scream. Carson snatches the hose and squirts Buck. Buck tries to regain the nozzle but gets squirted again. When it comes to his turn, Eddie squirts both Carson and Buck. Then, the hose makes its way around a second time. For a few minutes, our youngest teammates have become a trio of naked adolescents clowning around at summer camp after lights out.

Finished with the hose, our crew stands around the bonfire, basking in its warmth and enjoying the comfort of Joyce's soft towels. An upstairs light in the farmhouse goes out, and I wonder if someone inside has been watching. Warren walks over to his truck, and when he returns, he hands a familiar white envelope to each of us.

"Burnell wanted to make sure we got these," he says. I have no pocket to put the cash in, so I clutch the envelope between my teeth. The others do the same.

**By the** time we get back to town, it's after midnight. The streets of Pigeon Falls are moist with memories of the epic rainstorm, but no cars remain in the Shoe's parking lot or on the street out front. The restaurant and bar have been closed for hours. The interior is a sad dark void, like the feeling I used to get when I'd come home to an empty house late at night after my divorce. For a moment, I'm reminded how lonely it can be to live like that, with no one to see at the end of the day. Fortunately, the feeling doesn't linger, as it did on the jobsite yesterday afternoon, and I push on towards the staircase leading up to our rooms. Although we've missed dinner, I have no hunger, no unfilled space in my stomach at all. I'm just glad we're finally back at the Shoe. Eddie is first up the stairs. Warren and I are the last to climb to the second floor.

Standing on the landing before going inside, I ask him, "How'd you get the townies to help?"

Warren smiles. "It was Mike," he says. "He made some calls."

Warren opens the door to the second floor, then stops. He holds up his white envelope. "And I paid each driver two-hundred-and-fifty bucks."

"Of course," I say, my disappointment showing.

"Heck, it's only money, Tom. If that much manure had gotten into Pigeon Creek, imagine the people from state government out here tomorrow. The wind farm would be on hold, and we'd be trying to explain what went wrong. We prevented more than one disaster tonight." He goes inside.

I take another glance across the slanted rooftops of Pigeon Falls. They shimmer in a somber wet radiance that's reflecting the soft salmon light coming from a handful of village streetlamps. Off in the distance, caution tape still binds Mercy House's wounds. A blue tarp has been stretched over one corner of the roof. It's low enough to cover broken windows on the second floor but not nearly large enough to cover all the building's broken pieces. I then wonder about the people sheltering in the high school gym tonight.

When I get to my room, it's too late to call Rockford. Instead, I stand for several minutes under a warm shower and search for places I missed with the hose. I soap myself everywhere, and then apply several dabs of shampoo. I cover and recover every inch of my body, lathering and scrubbing, but no matter how thick I lather and no matter how hard I scrub, the smell of Burnell's pigs refuses to go away completely.

# Part Four

# Another Man Down

## Friday, November 8

The morning after the spill, the once-in-twenty-five-year storm has moved on, and our crew is as hungry as ever, having missed dinner last night. Everyone orders a hearty breakfast. Four eggs instead of three, bacon plus ham and sausages, hash browns with a side stack of pancakes. I get caught up in the crew's optimism and order more food than usual, though in the end I only finish a third of my plate.

I've never seen Candace at this hour of the morning, but there she is now, entering the Shoe. She's wearing blue jeans and a red and black high school letter jacket. Her blonde hair is tucked under a black stocking cap with a red hawk logo stitched on front. She's make-up free, and the absence of eye liner and lipstick makes her look even younger than she usually does. She comes straight to our table.

"You're up early," Skinny says.

"I heard about last night," says Candace. "Thought I better check on you boys." She assumes a casual pose behind Eddie. Her hands lean on the back of his chair. "You guys are heroes, you know."

"All's well that ends well," Warren says.

"Really, you are. You saved the river. It's all on Facebook," she informs us.

Carson scrolls through his phone. "She's right," he says. "We got 32 likes already."

"The people who came out from town are the real heroes," Warren says.

"Well, I'm proud of you," she says.

"Just don't get too close," Skinny warns her. "We smell like shit."

Candace laughs. "That can stay with you," she says. "My uncle had pigs." She zips her jacket and readjusts her hat. "Well, just wanted to check in. I'll catch you later." As she leaves, she drags one hand across the top of Eddie's chair, touching his shoulders. Not even noticeable, unless you were watching for it

**After breakfast,** we make a shopping run before getting back to the jobsite. All our gear from last night, everything from our ponchos and hoodies to our gloves, hats, underwear, socks, and boots, it's all a pile of ash now. Everything must be replaced. With us pouring concrete the rest of the week, we need to be dressed right.

Carson searches his phone and finds a big box store in Eau Claire, about 35 minutes north. They don't open until eight, so we finish our breakfast without rushing. I ask our waitress, an older woman I haven't seen before, for a second glass of milk. Warren phones the Sandberg farm to tell Burnell we'll be arriving late, but no one answers. He leaves a voice message.

To save on gas, we take only two trucks to Eau Claire. The first few miles there's little traffic. The old county highway follows a circuitous route around the ridges and valleys that define the Driftless Area. Thick and swirling clouds, remnants of yesterday's storm, keep trying to kiss the damp pavement in front of us, but without success.

On the drive to Eau Claire, we learn that Warren phoned the concrete company after breakfast and pushed back deliveries until one o'clock this afternoon. His call wasn't unexpected, he tells us. Although flooding overnight was general throughout the county, according to the dispatcher at the concrete company, the record rainfall wasn't what everyone between Interstate 94 and the Mississippi River was talking about this morning. What everyone was talking about was the near disaster last night out on Red Sandberg's farm, how his busted manure tank nearly killed the Trempealeau River.

We pass through Harrison, where the Mercy House residents are in temporary Red Cross shelter. I keep an eye out for the high school where they're staying but never see it. We connect to the Interstate and abruptly transition to a landscape of gently rolling farmland and a freeway teaming with traffic. Shopping in Eau Claire goes quickly. I've been in all-purpose stores like this a hundred times. The store names and layouts differ, yet once you find the right department, getting the things you need is easy.

Outside again, the overcast sky that brought so much rain to Trempealeau County is already thinning. It's quarter to nine when we're back at our trucks in Pigeon Falls, and bright sunlight is breaking through weaker spots in the cloud cover. Pigeon Creek and Sizemore Creek are moving with pace as we pass them on our way back to the jobsite, though they're not nearly as swollen as they were last night. The Sandbergs' long driveway is littered with puddles and clumps of leaves and branches. We turn onto the muddy path crossing Burnell's fields and then Warren, who's in the lead, brakes to a stop, halfway to the far side of the valley. I pull in close behind and the others fall in behind me.

The dike the townies built is holding firm and looking larger in daylight than it did in the dark. The new pond is a sickly purple-brown color that stretches all the way back to the manure tank and the tractor that caused the spill. In the daylight, I can clearly see the wide breach in the tank's wall. It's the kind of nasty wound that won't heal without leaving an ugly scar.

Warren starts up again and guides us along the slippery west face of the escarpment. Halfway to the top, I switch into 4-wheel drive. When we crest the ridgeline, I see Burnell's red truck parked next to the foreman's trailer, though Burnell is nowhere in sight. Warren pulls in next to the red truck, my truck lines up next to Warren's. Buck, Skinny, and Carson are right behind us and park just as Burnell and Albert approach by foot from around the corner of the trailer.

"You boys are two hours late," Burnell yaps.

"We had to replace our clothes," Warren explains. "Everything got ruined last night."

Burnell takes out a cigarette and lights it. "We're another two hours behind schedule."

"I left you a message," Warren says.

Burnell stares at us, as if we're missing another point he's making. Then, he turns and continues walking to his truck. Albert keeps one measured stride behind his boss. They get in and drive away. Nothing was mentioned about the spill or the major catastrophe we averted.

If Burnell is at all grateful for our help with saving the county's rivers and keeping his project on track, he said nothing about that. I wasn't expecting the manure spill to change Burnell completely, yet I'm wondering where did the gentler man from last night go, the one who was humbled by near ruin and spoke compassionately about his farm workers and their families? Wherever that side of Burnell is today is anyone's guess.

There's only a trace of rainwater on the mud mat in the first pit. Its pump worked well overnight. Unfortunately, that's not the case in the second pit, where water stands six inches deep. We move the first pump to the second pit, and two hours later it too is dry.


**By noon,** sunlight has regained control of the sky, and I'm on my way back to the trailer for lunch. Eddie is walking beside me and telling me that something is wrong with his nose, that all he can smell is pig manure. Then, he stops unexpectedly and says, "What's that?"

Out ahead of us is what looks like a big black heart that's moving across the sky and shifting direction on every throbbing pulse. "Do you see it?" Eddie asks. There's a tinge of fright in his voice, as if he thinks he might be hallucinating.

"I see it," I assure him. "It's called a *murmuration*."

The dark shape moving across the sky is a flock of starlings, thousands of the sleek black birds. They're moving together in a strange aerobatic dance that seems choreographed by either a genius or a madman. For years, I've known about starlings and their shape-shifting phenomena. I tell Eddie that murmurations occur in autumn, when colonies of the birds gather before migrating south in search of warmer weather. Some say the birds assemble for protection from predators, the way fish gather in schools. Others claim their wild flight patterns generate warmth for the flock, as colder temperatures settle in.

Above us, the starlings have changed from a heart shape into the shape of a wave, and then just as rapidly they reform into a dragon, with a long tail heaving behind its head and body. Eddie and I continue to watch the birds change direction and transform into a dozen unique figures. The shifts happen so fast that I can't keep track of what each one reminds me of. For their final act, the starlings cascade towards the ground like an inky waterfall and then pull up at the last second and veer southeast towards Pigeon Falls, re-forming into of what looks like a fat black spear. We lose them to the horizon.

"Now I've seen everything," Eddie says, shaking his head. "We don't have a lot of birds by my house, just seagulls that land in the parking lot at school."

"We were lucky to see one. It's my first in a couple of years."

"Why do they call it a murmuration?" Eddie asks, as we continue towards the foreman's trailer.

"If the birds come close enough, you can hear the sound their wings make. It's a low humming sound, a 'murmur.'"

**We gather** for lunch on the southside of the trailer, out of the north wind. Before we start eating, Candace picks up Eddie to take him to the bank. Joyce has come alone again today. Even after all that happened last night, Joyce has found time to prepare another amazing meal, a mouth-watering feast that includes a double-decker chocolate cake. The cake is without candles, yet its size and shape get Carson thinking. "You guys remember when we bought that DQ birthday cake for Jimmy, and what's-his-name left it in his car all day?"

"Randall," I say. "His name was Randall."

"Yeah, Randall," says Carson. "Middle of July. Melted ice cream all over the back seat. What a mess."

"Whatever happened to Randall?" Buck asks. No one knows.

Joyce is holding a serving spoon in one hand and a blue oven mitt covers the other. "Thanks for helping us last night," she says and turns a heaping portion of vegetables onto Warren's plate. "Burnell was going to replace that tank ages ago. It must be fifty years old."

"What will happen now?" Warren asks.

"Someone started pumping the field this morning," Joyce says. "They said it'll take a few days. I'm just thankful Albert's son didn't get hurt."

*Workplace mishaps.* It isn't always easy to explain why they happen. Sometimes, there's a mistake made, a problem that can be corrected. Other times, it's just best to call it fate and move on. A guy slips and breaks a leg. A cage unexpectedly moves, and a finger is lost. On a jobsite, I've seen everything from cuts and bruises to food poisoning and lightning strikes. Every now and then, something spectacular happens, like the day I saw a cement truck topple into a pit and land on its side on top of a nest. And, of course, there's the night a middle-schooler drove a tractor loaded with firewood into an ancient manure tank.

In Pigeon Falls, our crew's biggest challenge hasn't been overcoming mistakes or bad luck. It's been staying the course. We could have quit several times already, like when we lost two experienced co-workers and replaced them with a teenager who'd never worked construction. We also could have gone home when our workload doubled, and our client turned out to be the most disagreeable person we've ever worked for. But again, we stayed the course. Then, when we were asked to work eleven-and-a-half-hour days and give up music, we could have said this was beyond our limit. Instead, we ate faster and embraced silence. And what about when we shoveled so much pig manure that we had to burn our clothes? Well, we're still here.

*This job's tougher than usual… but look at the wages we're making.* That was the refrain we heard every time another obstacle presented itself in Pigeon Falls, and for a while it was the money that was keeping us here. That's changed. Now, what keeps me going out to the plateau each morning is no longer related to my bank account. Why I'm still here and why, I think, the rest of our crew is still here has more to do with *pride* than with money now. There's the pride we feel in our ability to overcome challenges. The pride we share in the quality of work we do. And most of all, there's the pride we have in our ability as a crew to keep our word, to finish a project that we've promised we would.

**Rotating drums** of fresh concrete queue up after lunch, in a long line stretching out to the far end of the plateau. The drivers empty their wet mix into the bottom quarter of our nests, what we call a platform's *basement*. It's a space that's 56 feet in diameter and 36 inches high, all of it contained by the ring of fit-forms.

Concrete for a nest isn't carried in hand-held wheelbarrows or slid down a long metal chute, like we did for the mud mat. Filling a platform requires a lot of mix flowing at a fast pace. For this we use a heavy-duty pump attached to a long hose. With a hose that's six inches in diameter, we can shoot the mix like a water cannon, deep into the nest, and at a good rate of fill. Hoses that size when filled with mix are too heavy for even an entire crew to lift. It takes the strength of two men just to point the nozzle where the mix needs to go. So, we use Bud's crane to move the hose around the pit.

At 1:00 p.m., we start filling the fit-forms for the first basement and finish filling the second basement six hours later. Albert drives up as we're putting away tools. He gets out and hands each of us a white envelope.

Buck is first to count his money, and he's not happy. "What the fuck?" Buck squawks. "There's only a hundred bucks in here!"

"Mr. Sandberg says you miss two hours today," declares Albert. He stands stiffly beside his minivan, alert to danger, the loyal soldier out on a risky mission behind enemy lines, while his commanding officer waits for his report back at headquarters.

The rest of us open our envelopes and find the same lonely $100 bill, not the $180 we've been promised.

"Is that what he says?" Carson replies and holds up his bill to the stars, as if to check if it's real. "*We missed two hours?*"

Carson advances a couple steps towards Albert. They're close enough that if they touched it'd be forehead to chin. "We saved his sorry ass last night!" Carson shouts with much more volume than needed for as close as he is to Albert, yet Albert doesn't flinch.

"Ah, let it go." Warren says. "I can get Davenport to pay the overtime."

"That's not the point," Carson continues. He's reached his breaking point and isn't backing down. He stares at Albert. "You know, Mr. Sandberg could cut us some slack, show some gratitude for what we did for him. I still smell like shit."

"Me too," Eddie says nasally, while holding his money in one hand and pinching his nose with the other.

Carson continues his stare down with Albert but only a beat longer, because Eddie's timing couldn't have been better. Carson starts laughing and the tension between him and Albert is released.

"Your boss is a fucking loser!" Carson shouts, as Albert is getting back into his van. "A hundred doesn't even pay for the clothes we lost!"

**Candace is** standing behind the bar when we trudge into the Shoe. She's filling a pitcher with draught beer and seems in her usual good spirit, smiling at customers, joking with Mike. The more difficult our days have become, the more I find myself relying on Candace's cheerfulness to keep my head above water.

"Hometown heroes!" she calls to us over the noise of the room. "There's buckets of fresh perch and walleye in back. I hope you're hungry." She starts filling a second pitcher. "Don't forget the special tomorrow night. I reserved your table for 7:30."

Customers throughout the Shoe are happy and louder than usual, what with the end of the work week. When I finally sit at our table, my shoulders feel heavy, but my appetite is the strongest it's been in months, though I order only half a plate of fish and skip the fries.

Halfway through the meal, Skinny turns to Eddie and asks, "You feelin' any homesickness, Ed?"

Eddie contemplates Skinny's question for a moment. "I miss my brother," he says. "I text him every day, but it's not the same."

"I get it," Skinny replies. "I miss my pals in Florida." Turning towards Warren, Skinny asks, "How's your family doing, Warren? They're not used to having you out on the road like this."

Warren nods. "I FaceTime them at night. I like to see Gloria and the girls before they go to bed. But it's not the same as being there."

"Well, the good thing is, you'll be back with them in no time," says Skinny.

Buck puts down his knife and fork. He squares his shoulders. "Don't get me wrong," he announces. "This is not a complaint."

Carson points out the obvious. "That's, like, the definition of complaining, Buck."

"Hear me through," Buck continues. "I just want everyone to know that I'm tired of all this bullshit. I'm tired of Burnell shorting us the money he owes. I'm tired of the long days with no extra help. I'm tired of having to burn my clothes." Buck does look tired, so tired that he can't sit straight on his chair.

"You are *complaining*, man," says Carson. "Suck it up and stop with the video games before bed."

"I thought you had your sights set on buying a new truck," Skinny says. "You're getting rich here, man. You forgot that?"

"I've just had enough with all the hassles, Skinny. I'm worn out."

"I parked next to a beautiful new Silverado in the lot tonight," Skinny says, dreamily. "Pearl white. Chrome wheels. Had a camper shell. You should take a look."

Skinny's information is like a syringe of Red Bull injected into Buck's tired body. Buck's new-truck imagination returns to life, and in no time, he's sitting upright again and smiling. "I'm gonna go outside and take a look," he says.

When the rest of us get up after dinner, Eddie hangs back. We stop at the bar and talk with Mike for a minute, and then I'm the last of us out the front door. I look back and see Candace sitting down at our table and then sliding in next to Eddie. For a moment, I watch from the sidewalk, the two of them side by side and backs against the wall, their eyes keen on a small book Eddie is holding.

**Room 5** is located at the middle of the upstairs hallway. On one side of me is Buck. On the other and closer to the exit is Eddie. Carson's room is directly across the hall from me, and Warren is next to Carson on one side. Skinny is at the end of the hall across from Eddie and opposite the door leading outside to the stairs.

Back in the day, century-old structures like the Horseshoe Inn were built to last several generations. A lot of plaster, hardwood, and brick was used. Even so, the sound proofing they did in 1900 wasn't any more effective than it is today.

Half an hour after returning to my room, I'm brushing my teeth when I hear on the other side of my wall what sounds like Candace's voice. I stop brushing and listen. I can make out Eddie's voice as well. I can't hear the exact words the two of them are saying, nor do I try to, but Candace is definitely next door, in Eddie's room. The tone of their conversation sounds normal, no crying or anger, nothing loud or frantic, just the usual sounds of two people who know one another, talking together... *in a hotel room.*

I ask myself if I should be wondering what's going on in there, because I am wondering what's going on in there. The two of them together, it's not a moment in isolation. Already, there was the delicate touch of a shoulder at dinner, the evening spent reading to children after the fire, the help with a bank account, sitting together at the back of the dining room while lost on the Internet, the exchange of gifts.

**Eddie and** Candace are still talking in Eddie's room ten minutes later. Should I remind them she's married, that her husband is a maniac, that they're together... *in a hotel room?* I decide to call my father, instead. I haven't spoken to him in a couple of days.

My sister answers and says, "Dad's feeling great. The tumble is behind him." She reports that his stitches will be out in a few days, and for dinner they had beef roast and mashed potatoes, the way he likes them. She puts my father on the line.

"You got to stay off ladders, Dad," I tell him.

"It was only a step ladder, Tommy," he says. "It's not like I was on the roof cleaning gutters. Hey, I've got a joke for you."

Outside my window, a vehicle in the street lets loose with one long blast of its horn. I step to the glass with my phone in hand and see Jared Vreelander's black pickup idling below.

"Okay, Dad, I'm ready. What's the joke?" I listen to my father, while keeping an eye on the truck outside. I'm not sure if Candace is still next door with Eddie.

My father asks, "What can furniture always find in a dark room?"

Jared honks again. Out in the hallway, a door opens and closes, followed by footsteps hurrying away.

Setting my father up for the punchline, I reply, "I'm not sure, Dad. What can furniture always find in a dark room?"

I'm watching the street, as Jared exits his truck. My father starts laughing before he's delivered the punchline, just as Jared is approaching the front steps of the Shoe.

"Your shinbone," my father says, finally, and then repeats himself. "Your shinbone."

Jared gets to the Shoe's front door, and directly under me, before he notices his wife coming from around the corner of the building. His shoulders stiffen when he sees her. He never expected her from that direction.

"You get it, Tommy? Furniture finds your shinbone in a dark room."

Jared and Candace come face to face and exchange words. I know by his arm movement that Jared is angry. Candace continues talking and resisting her husband's temper. Jared glances up towards the second floor and then shouts at her. I don't dare open my window, even though I'd be able to hear them better. Jared looks up at the second floor again.

"I said, did you get it, Tommy?" My father's question summons me back to my phone. "You know, your shinbone bumps into furniture," he says. "That's what it finds in the dark."

"Classic, Dad. Your jokes are the best."

Jared's posture forces Candace to retreat two steps. He grabs her by the coat sleeve, and she pulls away. I lose sight of them as he follows her  back around the building. Seconds later, Jared returns to his truck and gets inside.

"I'm looking forward to you coming home," my father says.

"Can't wait, Dad."

My sister is back on the line. "We practiced that joke a hundred times," she says, "Dad couldn't get the ending right, so I had him write it out."

"He hit it perfectly," I say to my sister.

Candace, in her small silver sedan, pulls out of the parking lot and onto the street. She switches on her headlights. I watch her ease onto US 53 and accelerate towards the west, with Jared following close behind in his big truck.

## Saturday, November 9

Before breakfast, I stand on the landing outside the second floor and gaze to the east, across the rooftops of Pigeon Falls. The first pink edge of dawn is only minutes away. A few stars are still visible in the lingering twilight, quivering as rare and as delicate as fine crystal. Arriving on a northerly breeze this morning, the air is cool and fresh. Everything points to a fine day ahead.

I've convinced myself that if we can stick to Warren's schedule, we can beat the coming freeze and complete the project on time, but I also know my body is much less willing now to haul equipment and trowel concrete than it was when we first got to town. This morning the feelings of wear and tear are the strongest they've been in a long while.

I enter the dining room and see that Warren and Carson are already at our table and staring like zombies at menus they memorized days ago. Dot is off this morning, so we have Betty to take care of us. Betty looks even older than Dot and moves a bit slower. She comes over and pours coffee. Betty doesn't know me yet, so I have to ask for a glass of milk.

"I heard you're the men building windmills out at the Sandberg place," she says and sets the milk glass in front of me.

"Guilty as charged," Warren replies with a welcoming smile, while adding a second packet of sugar to his steaming cup.

"Terrible thing, that spill," Betty says. "Poor Joyce. She never catches a break."

"It's good the manure didn't get in the rivers," I say, trying to put a positive spin on the near disaster.

"You know, Joyce and I go way back," Betty says. "I used to sit for her kids when she was working at the bank." Betty takes our order. "Such a nice pair of kids she has. They take after their mother, don't you know."

Betty's no slouch. She notices Warren, Carson, and me exchanging curious glances. "Come on now, I'm not talking out of church," Betty continues. "Red Sandberg can be a real son-of-a-gun."

Buck and Eddie arrive and sit at the table, with Skinny not far behind. Betty pours more coffee and says, "A couple days back, I drove up on the county road, you know, up behind the farm. I never saw any windmills there. How's that going?"

"We'll be done here in a few days," Warren tells her. "But we're only the beginning. All our work is below ground. Then, another group comes and puts up the towers."

"People are saying, Red's getting a bunch of them." There's a disgruntled wrinkle in Betty's voice.

"The first two before Christmas, we hope. The rest in spring," says Warren.

Betty shakes her head and leaves.

**Out on** the plateau, we check the hardness of the concrete basements we poured yesterday. Both are solid. Overnight, the temperature dropped to 45°, the coldest reading we've seen since arriving in Pigeon Falls. A low of 45° at night is still warm enough for concrete to fully cure, as long as the daytime highs reach into the 50s. So far, we're doing okay. But just to stay on the safe side, we'll need to start covering our platforms with thermal blankets overnight.

At breakfast, Betty told us that a hard freeze last night had brushed along the north shore of Lake Superior, 200 miles away, and the temperature in some inland places up there had dipped into the low 20s. She said this new front isn't close to us yet, but it's expected to move south eventually and cover half of Wisconsin by late Monday or early Tuesday. It's a wide area that will include Pigeon Falls.

To stick to Warren's latest plan, we need to pour the middle third of each nest today, adding concrete above the basements that we poured yesterday, and complete pouring the top thirds on Sunday. Normally, it takes us two 8-hour days to pour and finish a single nest, but with our extended hours and some extra effort, we're hoping to be done with Burnell's pair of nests by the end of three long days. At least, that's the idea.

Before we can we add any more concrete to the platforms, we have to remove the fit-forms from around the basements. Bud's crane lifts the steel walls out of each pit and over to the flatbed trailer, where we're waiting to sort them out.

Filling a nest with concrete above the basement is a tricky undertaking and requires a lot of teamwork. Warren and I will control the nozzle end of the hose, working from the top of the nest and shooting fresh mix down into the rebar frame. Eddie has been assigned to the back end of the hose. He'll feed the pump with concrete from the trucks. Skinny's job will be to show Bud where to move the hose around the pit. Buck and Carson will push long rakes into the mix, first, to make sure any air bubbles have been coaxed to the top, and second, to make sure every inch of the nest is filled with concrete.

Once we get started, all is going smoothly, until Burnell shows up at 9:30 a.m. and parks above the first pit. He stands, with his toes to the edge, gazing down at us. Even though he remains silent, his non-stop pacing is a distraction. Then, he begins shouting.

"What does that fool want now?" Carson says.

Noise from the waiting trucks and the sound of the pumping machine prevent us from hearing what Burnell is ranting about. Warren gestures at Burnell, trying to make him understand that we're in the middle of a truck load of mix and can't stop what we're doing.

Warren's hand signals appear to make sense, because Burnell stops shouting, even though he continues pacing along the rim. I watch his small body moving in short quick steps, shoulders hunched over, both hands in his coat pockets, head pointed at the ground. It's body language even a fourth grader could read. *Impatience and disgust.* Burnell lights a cigarette.

After the current drum of mix has been emptied, it takes a few minutes for the driver to clean his chute and pull away, before the next truck in line can take his place at the pump. Warren climbs off the nest and hustles up top to meet with Burnell. They talk for a few minutes and then Burnell gets in his truck and drives away. Warren returns to the nest.

"What now?" Carson asks.

"Burnell doesn't like the weather forecast," Warren reports, and we laugh uneasily. "He's serious. He said the temperature is dropping too fast, and there's snow coming in a few days. He sounded… I don't know… *desperate.*"

"Then he shouldn't have asked for a second tower," Carson says. "That's *his* fucking problem."

"That's right," says Buck. "It was his idea for two."

"It's failure," I say. "That's Burnell's real problem. More Sandberg failure, it's all he's thinking about."

"You're probably right," Carson remarks. "But I can't feel sorry for an asshole."

"I feel sorry for Joyce," says Buck.

"And don't forget the pigs," Eddie adds in deadpan. He's come down into the pit to find out what was going on. We share a laugh and then get back to work.

The last of the morning's twenty trucks leaves just after noon. Joyce is waiting at the folding table when we assemble for lunch in front of the trailer. She apologizes for not making a bigger lunch today. "I figured you'll be ordering the special at the Shoe tonight," she says.

Considering how my stomach felt at breakfast, I take only two brownies and three slices of warm bread. Joyce notices my meager plate, and I vaguely explain my issues with digestion.

Joyce takes out her cell phone. She wants to show us photos of her family. "This is Melinda and her husband," she says, swiping through the gallery on her phone. "And these are the boys, Michael, Matthew, and Mark."

The last photo she shares is of her son, Martin. In the background is the Golden Gate bridge. Joyce is standing next to him. Martin is short like his father, but he has his mother and sister's rich dark hair.

We're halfway through the meal when Skinny asks, "How did Albert end up in Wisconsin?"

Joyce is excited as she to tells us about a special federal program with work visas for foreign farmers, and how she and Burnell sponsored Albert to come to the U.S. She adds that unlike the two Europeans who came to supervise the hog operation before Albert, only Albert knew the best ways to manage a struggling pig farm.

"Albert saved us," Joyce says. "He knows pigs inside and out."

She goes on to tell us that Albert's wife works part-time as a checker at the IGA in Templeton and the family's dream is to become American citizens. "That's all they want. To live here for good," she declares.

And now something starts to make sense. Albert behaves like a servant because Burnell has him over a barrel. Albert's whole deal is for him and his family to stay in this country. Pleasing Burnell is the key to attaining that dream. Screw around with Burnell, and Albert and his family are back in Budapest.

**Throughout the** afternoon, another twenty trucks bring us more mix. We fill in the middle third of the second nest just like we did the first, and near the end of our workday, we've finished smoothing over both surfaces with our hand trowels. It's time to cover each platform.

While Carson is carrying a too-tall stack of thermal blankets to the first pit, a gust of wind rips them out of his hands and scatters the blankets across the ground. Carson kicks weakly at the fallen items and shouts, "I hate this fucking place!"

Carson's anger is barely noticed by the rest of us. His fatigue and frustration are simply added symptoms of the tension that we're all feeling. We're ready to break. We've been pushing ourselves for eleven hours today and working for more than a week without a day off. Fatigue and frustration live in all of us. We should be on vacation. We should be relaxing. Instead, we're in Pigeon Falls.

Eddie runs over and helps Carson gather the scattered blankets and bring them into the pit.

After we've covered both nests with blankets, Albert pulls up in Burnell's truck. He gets out but keeps the door open and engine running, as if he's preparing for a quick getaway, which he probably is. Albert hands each of us a white envelope and leaves.

Buck counts his bills twice: $180. "That's more like it," he says and stuffs the money into his pants pocket. I'm too tired to count anything. I just put the envelope in my glove compartment and take off for town.


**The Shoe's** parking lot is full when I arrive and so is the street out front. I find an open spot a block away and then head upstairs to shower. There's no rush getting to dinner, thanks to Candace reserving us a table. I turn the shower faucet to its highest setting. The water is soothing enough to put me to sleep, but a new bar of lilac-scented soap, left by the housekeepers, perks up my senses.

A few minutes later, I run into Carson in the hallway on my

way down to dinner, and we take the stairs together. Carson says tonight he's just as upset with the Sandberg project as Buck was last night. He's had enough of the added hours, the manure smell that won't go away, Burnell shorting us on money, and of course the unyielding wind.

"I hope they don't ask me to come back here in spring," Carson says, "because I won't do it. Forget about the money. Life's too short."

We're the first of our crew to get to the dining room. Every stool along the bar is taken and every table throughout the room is crowded with fun-loving customers. Food, music, laughter, drink: the perfect recipe for relaxation with close friends and family. A familiar country ear worm is playing on the jukebox. The room smells of Italian seasoning, barbecue sauce, and beer, a combination that seems to sweeten Carson's sour mood, a little. "I plan on getting my money's worth tonight," he says.

I notice Dot across the room. Looks like she's picked up an evening shift. And Mike is behind the bar. He's mixing an Old Fashioned and sees us come in. He floats a cocktail cherry over the ice and hands the drink to a customer. Then, he motions for us to meet him at the end of the bar, where a closed door leads to the kitchen. Mike's expression doesn't match the gaiety in the room, and that worries me.

"She's been here since noon," Mike whispers to us and opens the door to the kitchen a crack.

Seated on a stool in the short hallway is Candace. She's wearing her white uniform with burgundy piping. Her nametag is pinned to her blouse. She looks up when Mike opens the door, but her eyes look away as soon as she sees Carson and me. It takes me a few seconds to make sense of what's in front of us.

"I wouldn't let her work tonight," Mike says. "I couldn't let her go home either."

Candace's face is a mess. One cheek is swollen, and her jawline is red and raw. Those youthful lips of hers, which normally form such a hopeful smile, are deeply cut at one corner. A bloated purple halo encircles her eye. My first thought would be she's been in a car accident, but I know that's not it. "Did you call the police?" I say to Mike, as Carson squeezes past me. He's not gotten a good look at Candace until now.

"Oh, shit," he gasps and steps back.

"She won't let me call anyone," says Mike. "Says she'll leave if I do."

We return to the dining room. Mike closes the door behind us, and the three of us huddle at the end of the bar. "She's been waiting for you guys to get off work," Mike tells us. "She wants to see Eddie."

"I don't know what Eddie can do. She needs a doctor."

"Her husband?" Carson asks, even though he already knows the answer. Mike nods. "Where's he now?"

"Jared called a couple hours ago," says Mike. "I told him she never came to work."

Carson reopens the door to the kitchen and steps into the small hallway. I slip in next to Carson and kneel in front of Candace. "We need to call the police," I tell her.

She shakes her head. Candace isn't crying, though she refuses to look at us directly. "I just want to see Eddie," she mumbles.

"Candace, you need to see a doctor," Carson says. "You gotta get fixed up."

"I had her put ice on her face," Mike says, as he hovers above us. "Dot cleaned the worst of it."

"You need x-rays," I tell her. "Maybe stitches."

The rest of our crew has entered the Shoe while we've been talking with Candace. Now, they're crowding behind us at the door. Skinny pokes his head in first. "Oh, Jesus," he moans. Warren and Buck see enough to understand. They move back.

Carson remains with Candace in the hallway, while Mike

gathers the rest of us outside the door and explains what he knows. "Jared knocked her around last night and again this morning," he says. Why is still unclear.

After Jared left for work this morning, Candace put on her uniform and drove herself to the Shoe. Mike and Dot took care of her the rest of the day. "She's still in shock," Mike says. He glances around at us. "Where's Eddie?" I realize that Eddie hasn't come in with the others.

"He forgot something in his room," Warren says. "He'll be down any second."

"Candace wants to see him," Mike says again. "That's all she wants."

A moment later, Eddie walks into the Shoe and sees us at the end of bar. The look on our faces tells him something isn't right. He hurries over. "What's going on?" Eddie asks. In his hand he's carrying the book Candace wanted him to read, *The Prophet.*

"She wants you," Mike says and nods towards the kitchen.

We make room for Eddie to get through. Even though for the last week he's been hanging around men twice his age, Eddie is still an innocent kid. He moves warily towards the kitchen door, unsure what's waiting for him on the other side. Skinny stops Eddie before he opens the door.

"I don't know if you've seen something like this before," Skinny says, "just try not to let her know how upset you are. She needs you to be the strong one."

"Let's get our table," Warren tells the rest of us.

Eddie slips in through the half-opened door and replaces Carson at Candace's side. I'm already around the corner and on my way to the back, so I don't know how Eddie reacts when he first sees her, but my own perception of the Shoe tonight has changed in a matter of minutes. While others in the dining room are engrossed in lively conversation and enjoying the evening, my stomach is churning, and my head is spinning. I resist a sudden urge to throw up. Warren notices my distress.

"You okay?" he says to me, as we take seats around our table. "You're pale."

"She told me he never hit her."

Carson is fidgeting in his chair, not sure if he should sit or stand. "This has gone on too long," he says. "The guy's gotta be stopped."

"She needs to let someone call the police," Warren says.

"The girl's scared and hurting," Skinny says. "She doesn't know where to turn. Maybe Eddie can convince her to call them."

"Eddie won't be able to convince her," Carson says. "We should call them."

Dot comes to take our food order. All she says is, "I'm so sorry."

Everyone but me wants the special. I take a strawberry shake and some soup. Despite how hungry we are, no one's heart is in the meal tonight.

Ten minutes later, while I'm still feeling the warmth of adrenaline pumping through my body, Buck motions towards the front door. Eddie and Candace are leaving the Shoe. She's pulled a coat over her shoulders with the hood up. Eddie has his arm around Candace's back, in a protective pose.

"Leaving here is risky," Carson says. He gets up from the table and heads after them. A few minutes later, he returns. "They took off in her car," he says.

While we're eating, we consider the kind of man who does violence to his wife and contemplate what we'd do if someone close to us was beaten like Candace was. We do our best to talk away the anger and helplessness we're feeling, but it's not easy. The more we describe Candace's injured face, the crazier our options become for solving the Jared problem.

Because I can't watch Candace anymore without being reminded of Paige, I'm wondering how I would have reacted, so many years ago, if someone had harmed Paige like Candace was. Would I have called the police or gotten a gun and gone looking for justice on my own?

"I begged her to let us call the cops," Carson says, "but she said no."

"Why don't we call them anyway?" I say. "Right now. Let them take it from here."

"If she won't cooperate with law enforcement," Skinny points out, "they'll let Jared go. Who knows what he'll do to her after that?"

Before we finish eating, Eddie returns to the Shoe. He's alone and takes the empty seat at the head of the table. His arms and shoulders are trembling.

"Look, we can find him ourselves," Carson is saying. "Settle this once and for all. We don't have to kill him, just hurt him some."

"Where is she?" Skinny asks Eddie. The teenager is wearing a glassy stare that sees no one clearly. Skinny asks again.

"She's in a safe place," Eddie whispers.

"She needs to see a doctor," I say. "She might have internal injuries."

"She will," Eddie replies, his voice a little louder. "She's trying to figure it out."

"What about the cops?" asks Carson.

"I told her we have to call them."

"Well?"

"She said she will, just not yet."

Dot sets a glass of orange soda in front of Eddie, a drink he hasn't ordered, yet Dot knows. When Eddie sees the glass, it's as if his entire week in Pigeon Falls just flashed before his eyes. He slumps deeper into his chair, and his shoulders nearly melt into the table. Eddie doesn't want us to see him cry. He rests his face in his hands and stays like that for some time. Skinny places an arm over Eddie's shoulder. "She's gonna be all right, partner," he says. "You are too."

When Eddie looks up again, his eyes are red and wet. "I don't know what to do," he says.

"You don't have to do anything," Skinny says. "Right now, we're your family, and we're gonna look out for you."

"Eddie, what about Candace?" Warren asks. "Is she with her family?"

"She doesn't want them to know what happened."

"How long has Jared been hitting her?" Carson asks.

"I'm not sure," Eddie says. "She showed me some old bruises on her stomach."

Carson stands. "I'm done waiting," he says and looks across the table. "You with me, Buck? I know his truck." Buck pushes back from the table and gets up. Carson then looks at Skinny. "You want a piece of this?"

Skinny remains silent, as his eyes roam the room, moving from wall to wall and front to back. He's trying to decide, I think, if it's best to get up or remain seated.

"I can't go," Skinny says, finally. "Not now. I'm too angry."

"We're all angry," says Carson. "That's the point."

"I'm afraid of what I'll do if we find him."

"If we don't put an end to this now, who will?"

"Brother, I know what you're saying, but we've got to let it be," Skinny says. "If she doesn't go to the police in the morning, then we'll go ourselves. I promise."

Warren picks up his knife and fork and resumes eating. "I agree with Skinny," he says. "Finding Jared on our own is a bad idea. It isn't how this should work."

"What if he finds her first?" Carson asks, even though we all know the answer to that.

"Is she really somewhere he won't get to her?" Warren says. Eddie nods.

"Damn, she's only a kid," says Buck. "We have to do something."

"This is not our town," says Warren. "We don't know everything that's going on."

"We know what he did," Carson argues. "That's enough for me."

"Me too," echoes Buck.

"You're absolutely sure she's safe, Eddie?" I ask.

"He won't find her," Eddie assures us.

"I wouldn't bet on it," Carson says.

"As much as I want to see him get what he deserves," I say, "we'll end up in jail if we go after him now."

We've come to an impasse. Carson and Buck are desperate to seek justice on their own, but now they're weighing the risks. They're angry, but no one wants to end up in jail. Warren calmly motions them to sit, and reluctantly they do. As we continue eating, no one speaks for several minutes.

To stabilize my thinking, my thoughts shift to the jobsite and a review of today's progress. The two nests are more than half-done. We have all of Sunday to complete what's left. Then, we can tackle the crowns on Monday. MSP has never poured two nests and two crowns in four days, and with only a six-man crew. Even so, if everything holds to plan, our team will be the first to accomplish such a feat. Then, if freezing temperatures arrive on Tuesday, as the forecasters predict, it won't matter. We'll have finished all the concrete work for the platforms. What we will have accomplished won't be a miracle, exactly, but it'll be close.

I finish my soup and milk shake, though moments later I'm not able to recall anything about how either one tasted. Skinny stops to talk with Mike at the bar as the rest of us continue upstairs. I notice that Candace's little sedan isn't in the Shoe's parking lot, which I take as a sign that she's somewhere safe. In my room, as I undress, my body reminds me of the extra-long day we just completed. My lower back is hurting worse than ever. My shoulders and knees ache too, and my hands are swollen and throbbing. I've never been one for taking pills, but I carry ibuprofen and acetaminophen with me on the road. I pop some before settling into bed.

I have no energy left to worry about anything more tonight, not about Candace or Burnell, not about the changing weather, not even about my stomach problems. I'm asleep as soon as my head hits the pillow.

*Raw, raw violence.* That's what wakes me. The sound of shouting and pounding on a door. Was I dreaming? Is it morning? Several seconds pass before I clear my head of sleep and coax my feet to the floor and stand up. My phone on the nightstand surprises me. I've been asleep *only an hour.*

More shouting in the hall, a man's voice that I've heard before but can't place. "Where's my wife!" he barks.

The racket isn't right outside my door but down the hall. A second man's voice speaks with less anger, but I can't make out his words. Then the first man bellows again: "I found her car, asshole! You hid it behind the fire station."

"Fuck off!" says the second man, raising his voice now. I recognize that second voice. It's Skinny Martin's.

"I want my wife!" Now, I recognize that first voice too. "Candy! Get your ass out here! I know you're up here."

A moment of silence and then it's Skinny again. "Take your fucking hands off me."

"Don't push me, freak."

"You're not coming in my room, asshole!" Followed by another silence.

Then, there's the thud of something heavy hitting the floor, the sound a ten-pound bag of potatoes would make if dropped from a step ladder. Footsteps are trailing off now, escaping by the back stairs. Instead of sending me out into the hall, instinct summons me to my window, where I watch Jared Vreelander dash across the street and jump into his black pickup. After a sharp U-turn, the truck speeds out of town, heading east towards the Interstate.

When I get out into the hall, Carson is already kneeling beside Skinny, whose legs stretch across the floor like two long twigs dressed in flannel pajamas. A red stain has spread across Skinny's white tank top and is getting larger. Carson says, "He's been stabbed, Tom." Carson's hands are applying pressure.

The 9-1-1 operator tells me to stay on the line until help arrives. A deputy is only four minutes out, she says. Skinny struggles to take in air and stares blankly into space. Buck is kneeling next to Carson now, his turn to apply pressure. I'm standing beside Warren, off to the side, along the wall. Eddie's door opens a crack and Eddie peers out.

"Keep her in there and keep the door closed until the police get here," I tell him. He shuts the door.

"Candace is in there?" Warren asks. "Did you know?"

"I just figured it out."

Heavy footsteps rush up the outside stairs, the first responders arriving. My legs get shaky as I watch the medics work. Compression bandages, an IV-line, oxygen in a mask.

The deputy arrives, and Warren introduces himself and tells him what we know. "The young lady is in the room right there," I say and point to Eddie's closed door.

When the Shoe's owner arrives, he squeezes over to where we're standing. "I've got someone coming to clean the floor and wall," he assures us.

A collapsible stretcher appears and Skinny is strapped to it, but before he's carried away, we all step closer and tell him to hang in there, even though his eyes are closed. Warren orders Carson to follow the ambulance to the hospital. He then returns to his room to call MSP's owner.

Buck and I are outside Eddie's door and listening to the fading ambulance siren when a man with silver hair and a gold badge clipped on his suit coat pocket ambles in from outside. Senior Inspector Bill Jamieson, Trempealeau County Sheriff's Department. Buck and I shake his hand. "What can you tell me?" he asks.

Inspector Jamieson scribbles in a notebook while we repeat everything we know about the attack on Skinny and what happened earlier in the day. Next, the inspector knocks on the door to Eddie's room. The door unlocks and he goes in. Soon after, a woman with a bucket and sponge comes to clean the wall and floor.

"We were only supposed to be here a week," Buck says to me. "Now, shit like this is going down. Fuck this place."

There's nothing for us to do in the hall, but Buck and I are still standing here when the inspector leaves Eddie's room. "She was roughed up pretty bad," he says to us. "I told her we can take her to see a doctor tonight, but she wants to wait until morning. That's fine by me."

The inspector writes down our names. "Tomorrow, we need her at our office in Waterford, and she wants the young man in there to go with her."

"Eddie can take my truck," Buck says. "Jared knows her car."

"Everyone who was up here when the assault happened needs to stop at our office and give an official statement. Can you spread that message?"

"We can," I tell the detective.

"Since she's staying here tonight, I'll leave a deputy outside." The inspector folds his notebook and returns it to the inside pocket of his suitcoat. "How do the two of them in there know each other?" he asks.

"Eddie works with us, and Candace was our waitress," I say. "Same age. I guess they became friends." The inspector nods.

"We're building a wind farm outside of town," Buck adds.

"Red Sandberg's windmills. There's always something with that family." The inspector walks away, but before crossing to the outside stairway, he turns back towards us. "To be fair, I gotta give Red credit for trying something new. Around here, times have never been worse for small farms."

Buck and I return to our rooms. It's nearly midnight. I go to my window and look out. A small crowd of locals across the street is breaking up, singles and couples walking off in different directions. A few minutes pass and the street is empty again, except for the deputy's car that will be out there until morning.

## Sunday, November 10

It's 5:45 a.m., and I'm at my window, gazing down at the deputy's cruiser parked on the street below. Silent gray exhaust escapes the car's tailpipe. Wake-up has come too soon. If I had any dreams during the night, I don't recall them. I only remember getting up to pee and struggling with visions of Skinny's body draining blood against the wall outside his room.

Above Pigeon Falls, a dark failing sky seems unable to roust itself from sadness, while streetlamps also try without success to push their luster through this low ceiling of nothingness. In the aftermath of the assaults on Candace and Skinny, it's like the village has become trapped between guilt and despair. This sinking mood is contagious and has corrupted my heart as well. I sluggishly put on my jacket and head down to breakfast, wondering if Skinny is alive or dead.

Warren and Buck are already in place at our table, and Buck is saying to Warren, "If that bastard hadn't insisted on putting up a second tower, none of this would've happened. We'd be home by now, and Skinny would be okay."

"We can't change last night," Warren says and gently peppers his scrambled eggs. "What's done is done. Skinny's stable now. That's all that matters."

"Maybe we can't change what happened, but I'm the one who insisted we stay and take Burnell's money," Buck insists. "Take the money. *Take the money*. It's my fault Skinny got stabbed."

"Knock it off, Buck," Warren says and puts down the pepper shaker. "It's not your fault. What Jared did is on him."

"Skinny's okay?" I ask.

"Carson called around three," Warren says. "Skinny was going into surgery, but he was stable."

I order three eggs over easy and a large milk. I also have an appetite for bacon but think twice about that choice. I'm sure that some of the nausea I'm experiencing is because of my undiagnosed illness, but I also feel remorse over Skinny's attack.

"It's not just the money, Buck," I say, "or how long we've been here. The problem is, we didn't stop Jared before it was too late. I should've let the police know he was mistreating her. For days, I thought about doing something, but I didn't do a thing. I saw the bruises. I even talked to Candace about it. But I told myself it wasn't our place to get involved. That's on me."

"Guys, enough already," Warren demands. "There's one person who's guilty here... *Jared Vreelander*. Have you stopped to think what might've happened next week or next month if we hadn't been in town?"

Warren's phone rings. "It's Carson," Warren says and puts the phone on speaker. "I'm at breakfast with Buck and Tom. What's the latest?"

Carson tells us Skinny made it through the first surgery. They stopped the bleeding and gave him four pints of blood. But he needs more extensive treatments than they can do in Eau Claire, so he'll be transferred to Minneapolis later today. "I'm in my truck now," Carson says. "I'll be back soon." The call ends.

"We can put the blame on Jared, but I still could've done more to protect her," I say.

"And Skinny too," says Buck.

Warren ignores us and keeps eating. His phone dings. He reads the text message. "Good news," he says. "Davenport is sending two people to help finish the project."

"Well, it's about fucking time," says Buck, sounding relieved.

Warren keeps scrolling. "They're on the road already and should be here sometime this morning."

"The more, the merrier," I say. It's a long message, and as Warren continues reading, he puts down his fork and begins to look concerned. "What's wrong?" I ask.

"The two people they're sending are Rhonda from Payroll and Rick from IT."

Buck starts chuckling. "That's funny, boss."

Indeed, the idea of sending Rhonda and Rick is ridiculous. How are two middle-aged office workers who've never lifted anything at work that's heavier than a stapler supposed to help us pour and finish tons of concrete? Buck can read Warren's uneasy look as well as I can, and he says, "You're kidding, right?"

"I'm not."

Warren phones the person in Davenport who's messaging him. They talk, while Buck and I eat. After Warren ends the call, he says, "I think they did all they could to find helpers. Out of everyone at MSP, only Rhonda and Rick could get here this morning."

*Timing.* That's the problem, of course. Given the short-term weather forecast, anyone arriving in Pigeon Falls after today would be arriving too late to do us any good. If we don't finish the nests today and let them cure overnight, then our Monday window for pouring the crowns will be closed. And without a crown, no tower can be attached to a platform, which means there will be no wind turbines up and running around here until spring.

"It's nice of Rhonda and Rick to offer to help," I say, "but…."

"But they're not construction workers," Buck finishes my thought. "Even together, they can't do what Skinny did alone. Rick's even smaller than Burnell, and Rhonda hates working outdoors."

"We're missing Eddie too," I say.

Like it's no big deal, Warren asks, "What do we have left? The top of two nests and a couple of crowns? That's it, and then we're done. *We've got two days*, guys."

The skepticism showing on my face and Buck's is considerable. The concrete work we have in front of us would typically take a full crew three or even four days to complete. "Okay, it's a lot to get done," Warren admits. "I'll see if Burnell will give us Albert today. It's Sunday."

**Our table** in the dining room seemed crowded only a week ago, but this morning it has as many empty chairs as what remains of our crew. Jimmy Gilligan is sitting in jail, and Manny is in Texas. Skinny is hanging by a thread in an ICU bed. And Eddie has Candace to tend to. Carson will get here, though he's still in transit. Rhonda and Rick? We'll have to wait to see how that works out.

Warren, Buck, and I sit in a small knot at one end of the table. "Look around," I say. "Only three of us left."

Warren's not the type of office manager to let his coworkers feel sorry for themselves. He takes out the yellow legal pad he's been carrying everywhere he goes and starts scratching on a fresh page. Apparently, our pessimism has sparked in him a new idea.

It takes a few minutes before Warren finishes, but then he shows us a new flow chart he's created, one of his classic mind maps of circles and arrows and wavy lines that's meant to crack the maze of any challenge facing him.

"I've readjusted everyone's responsibilities, made two teams for finishing. And I added Rhonda, Rick, and Albert." Warren pushes the pad towards us. Buck and I follow every pathway on the page to its logical conclusion.

"This might work," Buck says politely, though he's not thoroughly convinced it actually will. Neither am I.

"Come on, it has to work," Warren answers. He sets the yellow pad aside and resumes eating. "Look, if we shut down now, Burnell will have his lawyers suing us before we're back in Davenport."

Carson arrives as we're finishing our meal. His eyes are droopy, and his feet barely rise off the floor. "You should get some sleep,"

Warren tells him.

"Too much to do," Carson replies. "All hands, on deck."

We wait for Carson to finish breakfast. He tells us he was up most of the night in the ICU. "Skinny looked so old, not like we're used to seeing him."

Our waitress brings more coffee and a plate of donuts. I get another chocolate milk. "Where's Eddie?" Carson asks us.

"He's with Candace," I say. "My guess is they're still in his room."

Buck says, "The deputy was parked outside when I came down."

"He's still out there," says Carson.

**Buck rides** with Warren to the jobsite because Eddie needs Buck's truck today. At the farm, Warren continues straight ahead to the Sandberg farmhouse, while Carson follows me across the fields and up to the top of the ridge. Despite what Warren said about whose fault it is, the guilt I'm feeling about Skinny's stabbing is still festering inside me and feeding my unsettled stomach. I make a quick stop at the porta-potty while we wait for Warren and Buck to rejoin us.

**"We get** Albert and his son all day," Warren tells us. "They'll be here in thirty minutes."

"Did Burnell know what happened last night?" Carson asks him.

"I'm not sure, but he didn't seem surprised when I talked about it."

"Did he ask how Skinny was doing?"

"All he said was, very cold weather is coming and we're out of time."

**This early** in the morning the sky is still a riddle, hovering between departing darkness and approaching light. It's a time when you have to remind yourself if you're coming or going. Out on the plateau, two white auras mark where we set up our spotlights last night, just enough glow to lead us to the pits. For an hour, we remove the thermal blankets draped over each nest. Albert and his son arrive and pitch in. As pinkish-blue daylight washes over Sizemore Coulee, a parade of concrete trucks begins to arrive on the plateau.

Rhonda and Rick pull in at 9:30 a.m., all excited and ready to go. Warren thanks them for coming and sends them with me for orientation. We labor the rest of the morning without a break. It's 12:45 p.m. when we're done pouring and finishing the top of the first dome. Warren phones the ready-mix company and asks if the afternoon loads can be delayed 30 minutes to give us time to eat lunch. The dispatcher apologizes and tells him that the first truck is already on its way. So, while Albert and his son eat bag lunches in their van, we hustle over to the foreman's trailer for our meal. Joyce is already gone when we get there, but she's laid out another nice spread for us.

Rhonda and Rick ask all the expected questions during our quick break. What exactly happened to Skinny? What are the police doing about it? Are we still in danger? And then there's the question they finally realize is staring them full in the plate. *Why is there such a fancy lunch on a jobsite?*

Rick puts down his fork. "This is really good."

Rhonda asks, "Where's the young man from Chicago?"

Rhonda knows about Eddie because she helped fill out his payroll paperwork over the phone. The rest of us leave all the answering to Warren, who gives streamlined responses to every question: the attack, our lunches, Eddie's absence. But he never mentions the $180 cash payments, or Candace's blossoming friendship with Eddie. Warren's explanations come way too fast and are sprinkled with plenty of missing details, but Rhonda and Rick appear satisfied. As we head back to the pits, their voices are focused more on the fine food they just ate than the events that brought them to Pigeon Falls.

**More concrete** is delivered throughout the afternoon. I watch the metal barrels on the trucks slow-spin their drums, the constant motion that prevents fresh mix from hardening in transit. That endless spinning now reminds me of past times when I'd be driving on a highway and see a concrete truck's barrel turning like these are. I knew back then that somewhere nearby, someone was building something. Even though I couldn't tell if the truck was delivering mix for a driveway or a skyscraper, I was certain of one thing. If the work was done right, the end product would be terrifically strong and last a long time.

Throughout the afternoon, the trucks bring us load after load, several tons of mix. By 3:15, sunlight has broken through the cloud layer, and by 3:30 we're working under a ceiling that's bright blue again. You'd think a cloudless sky like this one would mean that the sun was roasting us, but that's not the case up on the plateau now. The north wind is too cold for the soil to hold much heat anymore, and the angle of the sun is too low to generate enough radiant warmth to overcome the wind. Fortunately for us, everyone is working so fast and sweating so much that the cool air actually feels refreshing.

By now, I've started to recognize individual truck drivers bringing their loads, though I don't know any of their names. Oftentimes, a driver will get out of his truck while waiting in line and walk over and stand above the pit, curiously watching what we're doing below. One old driver is up there now. He calls to us. "I feel for you boys," he says. "That's a back-breaking job, moving shit by hand all day. I'll stick to driving it."

When Eddie gets back to the jobsite, it's almost 4:00 p.m., a much later return than I expected. I'm anxious to hear about Candace, but now's not the right time. There's still too much work to do.

As dusk invades the plateau, the second nest is full of concrete, so we can start troweling the dome. Finishing concrete with a hand trowel might seem like the easiest part of our job. There's no heavy lifting, no shoveling, and nothing dangerous to worry about. But moving a trowel back and forth is hard on the wrists and a drain on your arm muscles.

Even worse is what troweling does to your hands. Constant finger cramps require you to keep switching the tool from one hand to the other. And even with rubber gloves protecting the skin from chemical burns, your fingertips grow numb in the cold. With my hands aching and my knees pressed against the surface of the dome on only a small square of plywood, I stretch again for the umpteenth time, trying to coax warmth and circulation back into my hands and joints.

**Burnell drives** up after sunset, with a man his age sitting next to him in the red truck. They talk for a while, and then Burnell gets out and walks down the earthen ramp to the mud mat, while the other man remains inside the truck. Most of our crew are on our knees, troweling the vast top half of the second dome. We don't have time now for more of Burnell's nonsense, yet here he comes again.

Burnell positions himself on the lip of the mud mat, in the full shine of our work lights, and calls up to Warren, "It's been bothering me all day, Mr. Foreman."

"What's that?" Warren responds.

"Why'd you let your man mix it up with that worthless Vreelander kid?"

Warren continues troweling but calls back to Burnell, "We were asleep. None of us went looking for trouble."

"Well, you're down another man and running out of time."

"We got some help from our main office." Warren points to

Rhonda and Rick, who raise their trowels in greeting.

Burnell glares at the pair and says, "Are you kidding me?" He takes out a cigarette and lights up. "Have you heard a hard freeze is coming tomorrow night?"

"I heard."

"Hell, it might snow on Tuesday."

"We should be fine. Though we'd be even better, if you wanted to give us Albert again tomorrow."

"My friend in the truck, he knows cement work. He says you'll never get done in one day, all that you got left here to do. Not even with Albert." Burnell exhales a suffocating cloud of white smoke that swirls around at the bottom of the pit. "So, then what?"

It's hardly a comfort seeing Burnell as his overly-confident self again and talking like a concrete expert now. He and his friend must have noticed the two empty crowns that poke above the domes we're troweling, those four-foot-tall cylinders of rebar that still need to be filled. I'm not about to give Burnell the satisfaction of agreeing with him, but his friend is partly correct. Finishing two crowns in one day is about as easy as putting two gallons of mix into a one-gallon pail.

"We'll start on the crowns first thing in the morning," Warren says, "after this part has cured overnight." Warren's voice is listless. He seems tired of interacting with Burnell. For sure, he's no longer trying to please him. Most telling, there's no obvious indication in Warren's voice that he's willing to do anything to get the project finished on time. Not like before. I think Warren just wishes the man would leave us alone.

Burnell says nothing for three or four minutes. He paces along the mud mat while we continue smoothing the dome's surface. I almost forget he's there.

Finally, Burnell stamps out his cigarette and sputters, "You let me down, Mr. Foreman. You all did."

Burnell's voice is sounding surprisingly weak all of a sudden. It's lost its cocky whine. Gone too are the sharp inflections he makes when he berates us or brags about something. I'm reminded of how he sounded the night of the spill, when he talked remorsefully about how he had waited too long to get his manure tank emptied.

"Everything will get done," Warren promises, but in a monotone. "But I agree with you, we've got one big day ahead of us tomorrow."

"*One big day*...." Burnell's faint words disperse into the chilled air like the final breath of a lost soul.

In the glare of the bright lights, Burnell gazes up at us from the mud mat with his cold cheeks glowing red. "You boys have no idea how important this wind farm was going to be to me and my family."

Burnell's eyes are heavy. His lips barely move. I can only guess what he's thinking, but I'd bet it's something like this: All that stands between me right now and my family's most colossal failure is this foreman's preposterous belief that in one day his crew can accomplish something that my friend in the truck has already told me is impossible to do.

"This will kill my family," Burnell says.

I stop troweling. Burnell is moving in a circle now and he can't stop shaking his head. I'm not sure what's happening or why it's happening, but something is not right.

Then, I wonder, am I watching a dying animal? A creature so disoriented and wounded that it's lost all faith in being rescued and doesn't even know where to turn to save itself? Burnell's fatalistic thinking is sinking him deeper and deeper into a despair that's all his own making. His thoughts, of course, are illogical. His wind farm isn't mortally wounded, no more than he is. No matter what happens with the weather or how much we get done tomorrow, if not before Christmas, then Burnell's six towers will go up in spring. But right now, it looks like our client can't see that far ahead. All that Burnell can visualize is ice and snow and another family failure that will come with this year's wintry mix.

Carson shouts, "If your wind farm is so important, why couldn't you wait until April, when the weather's better?" Burnell hears the question but looks even more confused as he tries to figure out where the words are coming from.

Carson continues. "I said, 'Why put everyone through all this bullshit before winter? Why not just wait until spring?'"

Burnell stops circling, as his eyes search for the critic.

"What's a few months anyway?" Carson shouts. "The government isn't going to take your money back!" At this moment, Burnell seems to have fallen to his weakest point, and Carson isn't letting up. "You couldn't even settle for one-fucking-tower, you had to have *two!*" Burnell shields his eyes from the lights, and his gaze finally find Carson's voice at the top of the dome, next to me. "I hope you realize *you're* the reason our friend is laying in a hospital tonight!"

One thing I'd forgotten about Burnell was how he thrives on confrontation, how conflict is what feeds his inner fire. He's probably been like that all his life. Within seconds, a transformation takes place, as Burnell's spine stiffens and his shoulders flare. Burnell has had enough of Carson's verbal abuse, thank you very much. He finds a cigarette in his coat pocket and lights up. Burnell will no longer play the dying man. As he exhales, he steps forward, taking center stage.

"Don't you morons get it?" Burnell bellows, as those familiar highlights of bluster and arrogance return to his voice. He points up at Carson. "Only a fool waits when he gets the opportunity to do something important! You might never get another chance!" Burnell takes a fresh drag on his smoke. "Nothing about tomorrow is guaranteed! Don't ever forget that!"

In equal measure, Carson has had enough of our client and won't back down. "Whatever!" Carson yells at him. "Just so we're clear. Because you couldn't wait until spring, our friend is fighting for his life!"

"Carson," Warren says, "That's enough."

Carson sidebars with Warren. "I'm just giving him what he deserves, boss. All he cares about is *his-fucking-self*. I hope he has a heart attack."

"If your friend makes it," Burnell shouts towards the top of the dome, "ask him why he picked a fight with an idiot!"

"He didn't pick a fight with anyone!" Carson shouts back.

"If you say so!"

"Yeah, I say so!"

"Well, I don't give a goddamn what you losers say!"

This argument has become a playground squabble, grade schoolers out for recess, and Warren wants none of it. "Ignore him Carson," Warren says. His words are spoken as a command, not a suggestion, but Carson isn't listening. He gets up off his knees.

"You're the loser!" Carson shouts at Burnell. "You don't know jack-shit about anything!" Carson hands me his trowel.

"Stay here," Warren orders, but Carson has already started climbing down the platform on one of the extension ladders we set up next to the dome.

"You need to trust me, Mr. Sandberg," Warren calls down to Burnell, once again the diplomat. "We're gonna be okay. We're gonna be okay."

"Trust you? Shit!"

The rest of us are watching Carson descend and doing our nervous best to hold on to the dome, clinging to the platform like excited finches on a bird feeder.

Burnell starts in on a soliloquy that's aimed at no one in particular. "Seventy-five percent of the pork in this country comes from only three companies," Burnell thunders. "What farmer can get anywhere when three companies control everything? These towers were supposed to be my way around a rigged system. But ever since you crybabies got here, it's been one excuse after another. You don't have this. You can't do that. I need a coffee break. Where's my music? *Waah, waah, waah.* You're all a bunch of losers, and so is your loser company."

Albert had been up on the rim, cleaning the area where the trucks unload, but now he's walking with pace down the earthen ramp and looking worried.

"What don't you understand?" Burnell calls to the top of the dome. "The future of my family is not pigs! *It's wind power!*" Burnell shields his eyes from the bright lights again in order to see us better. "This is my chance to do something special," he says, "and you people are not going to fuck it up!"

Albert approaches Burnell from behind and parks himself an arm's length off his boss's left shoulder.

"If you *don't* finish on time," Burnell continues, "I'll sue your goddamn company for incompetence... breach of contract... and lost revenue.  And I'll sue every one of you for pain and suffering!" Burnell has assumed the role of misunderstood hero in the tragedy that's playing out in his confused mind, though to us he's acting more the part of lunatic-jester.

Then, Burnell notices Carson's purposeful descent on the ladder and realizes the imminent danger. And not a moment too soon. A blind man walking towards a tornado would be at less risk than Burnell is now.

Burnell shucks his cigarette to the ground and as he slides backwards into a retreating shuffle, he balances himself with open hands and arms stretching out to the side. After a couple of steps, Burnell bumps into Albert behind him.

Carson has reached the bottom of the ladder. Warren has seen what's coming too and calls to Carson to come back to work, but Carson keeps moving forward. Albert has also been watching Carson and knows that nothing can stop the peril that's about to be let loose upon his boss. This time, Albert holds no illusion of protecting Burnell, he must *save him.*

Albert grabs Burnell by the arm and leads him up the ramp and out of the pit, quickly putting distance between them and Carson.

"Now, I see what they were talking about in Davenport," Rhonda says to me. "That guy is nuts."

A minute later, Burnell and his friend are driving away. Albert returns to his clean-up station above the pit. Carson climbs back up the ladder. I hand Carson his tool. In no time we're back at it, troweling and more troweling. Burnell has fled, no one is speaking, and all of us are once again focused only on one thing: *getting to the finish line.*

On my section of the dome, my flat tool continues into the night, coaxing roughness out of the moist concrete, the sharp metal edge shaping and re-shaping the flawed surface that's around me. In order to work the dome to a perfect shine, my labor becomes so meticulous that I'm also starting to believe the very future of everything that's yet to come in Pigeon Falls might largely depend on whatever imperfections my weak hand can remove.

**Dusk has** been a faded memory for more than an hour. It's past 7:00 p.m. My phone app tells me the current temperature is 43°, just within our curing margin. The app's short-term forecast says it'll hold steady at 43° for the next two hours. After that, the temp will gradually drop to a low of 35° overnight. There's no cloud cover above us to hold in what little heat is lingering in the air, so the plateau tonight will get very cold before morning.

It's 7:45 p.m. before we finish troweling the second dome. It takes another hour to lay thermal blankets over both platforms. Warren takes a phone call from Mike at the Shoe. The kitchen is still open, and they have our table ready, but Mike is wondering if we're still coming.

"It's been a tough day," Warren says to him over the phone. "We'll be there in a few minutes. But we need seven chairs tonight."

Warren has invited Rhonda and Rick for dinner. They've booked motel rooms in Eau Claire, but they're happy to eat with us in Pigeon Falls. Warren also invited Albert and his son to join the crew, but Albert declined. He said his son has school in the morning, though I'm guessing Albert's loyalty to his boss also figured into his decision.

**Driving into** Pigeon Falls, I notice only a few cars parked in front of the two taverns on US 53, at the edge of town. The rest of the village appears dead. No one is on the street. Nothing is moving. But quiet here is not unexpected. It's Sunday night in a very small town in rural Wisconsin. For almost everyone, it's past bedtime. A new workweek begins in the morning.

When we walk into the Shoe, the big room is nearly empty. Sitting on stools along the bar, two middle-aged couples are playing four-handed cribbage, and a booth against the wall holds a family of five finishing ice cream sundaes. Mike is restocking bottles of spirits on shelves behind the bar.

"Any word on Skinny?" Mike asks as we shuffle past. We tell him about the plan to transfer Skinny to the Twin Cities.

Two tables in back have been pushed together with seven chairs and set with nifty linen placemats. Someone has taken the time to line up silverware and fold cotton napkins into white pyramids for us, making the table look like a formal dinner party. We take turns washing hands and faces in the restrooms.

Dot comes to our table and says, "You boys look worse than what the cat drug in."

"I'd have gone straight to bed," Carson says, "but an engine won't run without fuel."

"I like that," Dot says. "I might steal that one from you."

"Be my guest," Carson tells her.

"Thanks for such a nice table," Warren tells her.

"My pleasure," Dot says. "You boys hear anything about our girl?"

"The police took her to a shelter," Eddie says. "I'm not supposed to say where."

"Understood," Dot replies and hands out menus, stopping at Rhonda and Rick. "Newbies?" Warren makes the proper introductions.

"I'm sorry about Daniel," Dot says. "He's such a nice man. I've been praying for him." Dot's use of Skinny's given name is unexpected. No one calls Skinny that. How she knows the name is a mystery.

"When I see him, I'll tell him," Warren answers.

"You know, I watched Jared Vreelander grow up," Dot shares with us. "People are blaming what happened on Iraq, saying that's what made Jared mean, but he was already like that in middle school. The war just made it worse."

Dot takes our orders and before leaving says, "You know, the more time we take each day to appreciate what we've been provided, the fuller our life is."

While we're eating, no one mentions Candace or the stabbing. We whine about our aches and pains and praise Rhonda and Rick for the help they've given. Buck says he's looking forward to hunting in Montana next week with his brother. There's been snow in the foothills, which is good for tracking.

"I'm beat," I say. "I just want to do nothing until spring. But you know how that goes. After the holidays, I'll start getting restless. Come February, I'm missing everyone. By March, I'm anxious to build stuff."

Warren raises his glass. "A toast to building stuff," he says, and we clink glasses.

Carson hasn't said anything since his confrontation with Burnell, and I haven't noticed him texting since the attack on Skinny. His phone isn't even on the table now. "What about you, Carson," Warren asks, "will you be ready to get back at it by April?"

"I can tell you one thing," Carson says. "I don't plan on coming up here in spring and building anymore platforms for Red Sandberg.

I'll quit MSP before I do that."

"Me too. Let another crew suffer his bullshit," says Buck.

"That won't be a problem," Warren says. "I'll talk with the front office."


**After Rhonda** and Rick finish eating, they thank us for dinner and leave for their hotel. Then, I say to Eddie, "So, tell us about Candace. Is she okay?" Eddie has been quiet throughout dinner, but once he starts talking about Candace, the emotions pour out.

First, he apologizes for what happened. He thought she would be safe in his room. They hid her car behind the firehouse, not realizing how easy it would be for Jared to find.

"When we heard him arguing with Skinny, we knew we were in trouble," Eddie says. "We thought about going out the window, but it was straight down to the street. We pushed a dresser in front of the door."

"So, you came out when you heard us talking?" I ask him.

"We figured it was safe."

"But you didn't know then what had happened to Skinny?" Eddie shakes his head. "Did Candace get a look at him?"

"I saw more," Eddie says, "but she saw enough for her to cry all night. She says everything's her fault."

"When you see her again," Warren says, "tell her Skinny will be okay."

"You think he will?"

"I don't know. But tell her he will."

"And let her know what happened isn't her fault," Carson adds.

"They took her for x-rays," Eddie says. "She has a broken rib." The teenager is speaking now with a voice that reflects a maturity I haven't heard from him before; it's a composed sound and shows a wisdom that grows out of experience. Eddie even sounds older than he did a week ago, and he articulates his words as if each syllable is a vital detail in the story of what happened.

"Have you told your mother what's going on?" Warren asks.

"I called her. I didn't tell her everything, but I said a worker got hurt. And that we're almost done with the platforms."

"Does she want you to come home?"

"She would've said, *come home now*, if I'd told her someone got knifed, but I didn't want her to worry."

"You mind if I call her tonight?" Warren asks. "I think it'd be good if she heard from me again. I won't mention the stabbing."

"Sure, you can call. She's always up late."

As we're getting up to leave, Buck remarks, "You know, Burnell never paid us tonight." Warren's face appears too drained to handle another problem, and Buck notices. "Just saying," Buck adds, as an apology.

"No, you're right, Buck," Warren replies. "We'll get our money. Burnell's just reminding us who's in charge."

"I'm sorry for what happened with Burnell this afternoon," Carson blurts out. He speaks so eagerly, it's as if he's been holding the words inside himself since we sat down. "I'm to blame for that. I should've kept my mouth shut. I'm just so tired I wasn't thinking straight. And he's such a prick."

Warren's phone dings as we're leaving the dining room. A new text. Warren is in the lead, so when he stops to read the message, we stop behind him. "Rita and Manny have a baby girl. Six pounds, ten ounces. Her name is Valentina."

Our collective cheer is a weak gathering of tired voices. It's everything we've got left in us tonight, but not the celebration deserved for the best news we've heard in a while.

Another text dings.

"Ten fingers. Ten toes. Three smiley faces." Warren shows us the emojis. We take out our phones and send Manny our best wishes.

**It's late** when I get to my room, too late to call my father. Although I felt okay at dinner, I'm suddenly feeling miserable. It's not my stomach this time, it's my head. The pain is targeting my temples and the center of my forehead. I should be feeling great. Manny's first child was just born. Skinny made it through surgery. And Candace is safe. Yet, something feels off.

I wish I could talk to my father before bed. Even when a problem is nothing major, his voice still helps me stabilize myself when I'm feeling unsettled. This is one of those times I need to hear that voice, but it's very late now. I decide not to call.

## Monday November 11

Today, I'm awake two hours earlier than usual. I try the usual ruses to trick my brain into sliding back into the deep sleep my body still craves. I try slow breathing, adjusting my pillow, repositioning my arms and legs. I turn to a more comfortable side. Nothing works. A purple soup is swirling behind my eye lids, a constant rotation that I can't stop from moving. If my brain is worried or afraid about something, I can't figure out what it is.

I get up and get dressed.

I sit in the chair at my writing desk and read yesterday's news off my phone, flipping through sports scores and Hollywood gossip. I do my mandatory weather check to confirm that, yes, just as Burnell said, a hard freeze is forecast for tonight. The temps tomorrow won't climb out of the thirties, which means today is indeed our final chance to pour concrete. That's what I'm worried about.

The Shoe opens an hour early this morning to give us extra time on the plateau today. At the breakfast table, Carson and Warren are already there when I arrive. Carson is playing with a pair of salt and pepper shakers. Two horses, one a golden palomino, the other, a black appaloosa. In Carson's large hands, the two ceramic miniatures are head butting each other. I have never seen Carson looking so glum.

"What's the matter?" I ask him.

Carson puts down the horses. "Maybe, what we're trying to get done just isn't possible," he says. "Warren, I know you thought we could finish this thing. But man, I'm wasted. We all are. Putting up two crowns in one day? Never been done."

"Look what we already accomplished," Warren says. "Two nests in three days. That's never been done either. Finishing two crowns in one day… it's doable."

Carson is trying to accept Warren's optimism, but he can't. "We gave it a good fight, boss," he says with an energy level that's so deflated he's barely able to sip his coffee. "So, so close," he mutters.

I'm hesitant to add anything to the discussion. I want to believe Warren, but I've learned that in Pigeon Falls, optimism comes with a warning label: *Expect the Unexpected.* The problems we could face today are daunting. Jared Vreelander is on the loose. Burnell could muck things up again. Our fatigue is the perfect catalyst for making costly mistakes. And worst of all, we don't even know if the concrete we poured yesterday got the heat it needed overnight to set strong enough for us to add the two crowns today.

**Rick and** Rhonda are parked near the foreman's trailer and waiting for us when we get to the jobsite. They're sitting in Rick's car and holding extra-large *Kwik Trip* take-out coffee cups. They get out as we're parking.

"You been over to look at anything?" Carson asks them, directing his flashlight towards the first pit.

They shake their heads. The plateau is blanketed in darkness, except where security lights outline the two pits and Carson's flashlight skips across the ground. "You think something might've happened over night?" Rick asks.

Peering through the darkness, Carson quips, "Around here, anything's possible."

Enough said. We set off walking to check on the first pit.

Our journey is a group shamble, all slouched shoulders and foot dragging, not a good omen for the start of such an important day. It's obvious the long hours have finally caught up with us. There's not even enough energy among us for conversation. The only sound I pay attention to is my boots scraping the hard ground under me. To make matters worse, a cold wind blows out of the north with a sharpness I've not felt up here before. I remove my hardhat and pull my hoodie over my head.

Halfway to the first pit, we're passing the shipping container when Warren orders us to stop. "Gather around," he says, waving us together. I'm certain he's concerned about the dreary slope to our backs and the hopeless dragging of feet. We form a circle with Warren at the center. His face is side lit by the white glow in the distance, from the lights encircling the first pit.

Warren starts. "I'm not telling you anything you don't already know. But I'll say it anyway. Today is the big one. Game day. If we're going to finish this job, like we promised, well, it's now or never."

Everyone admires Warren. No one is fidgeting out of disrespect. No one is looking down at the ground. We're all looking at him. And then Warren gets it. The uninspired looks on our faces are telling him we have no appetite for clichés so early in the morning.

"Okay, let me start again," he says. "We've got two crowns to finish and one day to do it. Simple as that. We won't have Albert today. We won't have Skinny or Manny. We won't have Jimmy Gilligan or any other helpers."

Warren pauses. If he's intending to inspire us with his list of what we don't have, it's not working. It only makes our shoulders droop more. I look away. So do Carson and Buck. Warren knows he's almost lost us for good. He takes a deep breath and starts his speech a third time.

"Let me tell you a secret only my wife knows," he says.

I'm thinking, okay, telling a secret is always a good way to start.

"I never wanted to come to Pigeon Falls and join your crew. I never wanted to be here at all."

Warren has our attention again, but I'm not sure this approach is going to be any better than the others.

Warren continues. "I pretty much hated the idea of coming up here. I'm happy with the job I have back home. I don't like leaving my family, not even for a day. I like seeing my girls after work. I like sleeping in my own bed."

Every one of us, we're looking at Warren with full concentration now, still giving him the benefit of the doubt, but wondering where this speech is going. He's looking straight at us, as well. He takes in another big breath, followed by a long exhale. "I only came to Pigeon Falls because I had no choice. The company needed me, so that's what I did. I came up here to be your foreman.

"We've been together for eleven days now. A lot's happened. One thing I noticed is how skilled you all are, you know, the high-quality work you do. I also saw how you take care of one another. How you look out for other people too, some you hardly know, some you don't even like."

Warren pauses to refocus his thoughts.

"What I'm trying to say is... *I wouldn't trade the last eleven days for anything.*"

Warren pauses again.

"You're the hardest working crew I've ever known. And even more than all that, you're the best people I've ever worked with." Warren wants to say more, I can tell, yet he's starting to choke up.

"I'm proud to be one of you," he says and zips his jacket and readjusts his gloves. "Let's do whatever it takes today... to finish up... and then get the hell out of here."

As halftime speeches go, Warren's isn't bad, a five out of ten I'd say, maybe a six because it was unexpected and had a pastor's kid using the word *hell*. Though to Buck, the speech must have been a perfect ten, perhaps a flashback to some locker room he sat in years ago, because Warren's words have lit a fuse in Buck. We haven't gone five more steps before he discovers a reservoir of energy hidden deep inside him, and he breaks into a jog towards the first pit.

Not to be outdone, Carson takes off after Buck. Eddie joins them as well, and their jog quickly turns into a dash. Seconds later, Warren and I are galloping side by side. Rhonda and Rick are not far behind.

Then it hits me. We're in a race, but not to check on the hardness of the dome, or to see if something happened to our jobsite overnight. Sure, the finish line is the first pit that's 50 yards ahead, but we're not in a competition to see who can get there first, with one winner and the rest losers. We're racing as a team, a team that needs to build two crowns in one day. And the prize at the end of the race is that we all get to go home.

Buck is out ahead, though he's only as fast as a small university linebacker. Carson is not much quicker. Eddie has the real speed, much more than I imagined. He passes Buck and then Carson and arrives at the pit first. The rest of us dribble in behind them and assemble along the rim. Everyone is huffing and puffing, hands-on-knees tired. We form into a crooked line of irregular figures and stare down at a mound of blue quilts that's 10 feet tall and 56 feet in diameter.

Someone unfamiliar with what we build would only see us, a hole in the ground, and a pile of blankets. We know how much more there is down there than what meets the eye. We know there's two-million-pounds of concrete and steel hidden under those blankets. And we know what it took from all of us working together to shape it into a platform that's strong enough to support a wind turbine tower that will stand as tall as a football field is long, and last for decades to come. Warren straightens his back and starts clapping.

"What a beautiful sight," he says.

**A crown** is the top 4 feet of a cage. And only half of it is visible above ground. That might not seem very significant, considering the much more massive dome below it, but the crown is more important than any other part of a platform.

Before we can fill our two crowns with concrete, we first need to surround them with a plywood outer wall to hold the mix in place. That's our goal for this morning. While the rest of the crew removes the thermal blankets, I go around to the tops of both domes and test the hardness of the concrete we poured yesterday. Having been helped by the warmth of the thick blankets, the mix has cured well overnight. Both crowns are ready to be worked on.

Around 9:30 a.m., I'm on my ritual mid-morning trek to the porta-potty. The sun is floating like a small yellow balloon, not too high up in a baby blue sky. I gaze south across Sizemore Coulee towards US 53. Not far in the distance, an enormous flock of geese is flying in V formation towards the southwest, above what's left of the shimmering pond of pig manure. They call, *He-whew. He-whew. He-whew.* In my chest, I can feel their powerful presence.

Out on the open land below the birds, I spot a speck of blaze orange far off in the field. It's Burnell in his hunting coat, walking alone. He's following the curve of the hillside at the bottom of the escarpment and traveling at a leisurely pace, not needing the stride of a traveler who has to be somewhere soon, just taking the slow smaller steps of someone out strolling. Between him and Sizemore Coulee Road, there's only empty space, nothing but fallow land and that sparse line of outpost oaks.

I pause a moment to watch Burnell and wonder what he's doing out there in the middle of nowhere. Is he plotting another get-rich scheme? Did he and Joyce have an argument? Maybe he's sulking about yesterday's confrontation with Carson? Or perhaps, he's just enjoying the morning sunshine. I could stand here forever and speculate about Burnell, venture why he's walking alone or why he behaves as he does. But I know I'll never figure him out. I turn back towards the porta-potty and pick up my pace. I've got more important things on my mind right now than Burnell Sandberg, and little time to get to them.

**Joyce is** gone again when we arrive at the trailer for lunch. She's left us a big sliced pork tenderloin with a white peppercorn sauce. To the side, she's laid out a neat line of long white vegetables no one recognizes. Though we all agree, if Skinny were here, he'd be sure to know what they are and recall where he's had them before.

There's also a new batch of frybread on a tray and a couple dozen sugar cookies. It's our last meal from Joyce. We planned to thank her for all she's done, and compliment here again for her tasty meals, but she didn't stick around to give us that opportunity. "I bet he told her not to talk to us," Carson says.

"Or she heard how dangerous you are," quips Buck.

We eat quickly and stack our dishes. After lunch, we split into two crews, each one tasked with filling and finishing a crown. All afternoon, we work at a fast pace and without a break.

Pouring and finishing a crown is not a tiring job, compared to building a nest, but it's time consuming. Although each crown needs only four loads of concrete, the tricky part comes when setting the large bolts and other hardware that need to go into the wet concrete. After the final concrete truck leaves and the plywood frames are full of mix, we smooth over the tops. My responsibility now is to get the measurements and placements correct for where the anchoring bolts go.

Bud's crane lifts a 10-foot diameter disk of half-inch-thick steel from our flatbed trailer and places it atop the first crown. The heavy circle nestles on the setting concrete, leaving only a few inches of white PVC pipes sticking up through a hole at the center. Bud's crane then rolls over to the other pit and repeats the process. Before the concrete sets too firm, we insert 36 long bolts into the mix, pushing them in through pre-drilled holes within the steel disk. I use my 2-foot hand level and my measuring tape to make sure the bolts are perfectly upright and positioned at the depth we want. This is why the crown is so important. These heavy-duty bolts are all that keeps a 300-foot tower from falling over.

After we've said our goodbyes to Bud and his crane, we start cleaning threads on the bolts and fine-troweling edges. Buck, Carson, and I are finishing up at the first crown, when Buck calls out, "I saw a snowflake!" We stop and search the air around us, looking for more.

"It's clear sky," Carson says.

"I saw one, I really did," Buck assures us. We spot nothing.

By the time all the bolts are clean and every edge has been finely troweled, it's been night for more than an hour. We're re-covering the platforms with thermal blankets when MSP's owner phones Warren. He's in Minneapolis. Skinny had another surgery this afternoon, and his condition was upgraded from critical to serious.

Our final hour is spent inventorying supplies and cleaning the jobsite, making it ready for the tower crew that will arrive a couple of weeks from now. We're so spent as we're returning tools to the shipping container that our voices have gone silent again. Then, from the access road, a deputy sheriff car approaches and parks near our trucks. The deputy gets out, and we go over to see him.

"Thought you'd like to know," the deputy says. "They arrested Jared Vreelander in Beloit, near the state line. They'll transfer him back up here in a day or two."

"Can I let Candace know?" Eddie asks.

"Not a problem," the deputy says. "But tell her something else, too. Even if a judge sets a high bail, Jared's family can pay it. And he'll be free until trial. There'll be a restraining order, but she needs to stay alert." The deputy gets back in his cruiser.

Before pulling away, he says through his open window, "I've known Jared all his life. He's never been anything more than bad news held together by skin and bones. But honestly, I don't think he intended to kill your friend when he stabbed him. Jared is ex-military. If he wanted to kill someone with a knife, he knew how." The deputy drives off, and his taillights are quickly swallowed by the night.

We're standing near our trucks and watching the car disappear when Buck steps up on his truck's footrail and raises clenched fists above his head in a victory stance. "We did it!" He shouts again and pounds a fist against the roof of his truck on each word.

"*We… did… it!*"

I'm so tired that it takes me a second to understand what he's talking about. But the others have caught on, and Buck's celebration begins a chain reaction. Carson raises both arms to the sky. "Yes!" he says, and Eddie follows. Warren is smiling and starts clapping. I join in, as do Rhonda and Rick.

What seemed impossible two weeks ago has actually happened: two platforms finished in record time and under the most difficult of circumstances. And all before the start of winter. Adrenaline is surging warmth throughout my body again, but this time it's a good feeling. I say to myself, *this is what a miracle must feel like.*

Buck calls to Warren, "We're all done up here, boss, am I right?"

"What do you mean?"

"You know, can we say this job's over, officially?"

"There's Dry Day tomorrow. And we need to backfill the pits the day after," Warren says, "but Tom and I will be here for that. The rest of you get to go home in the morning. So, yeah, you're done now, officially."

Buck takes his boombox from inside his truck and sets it on the roof of his truck. We watch him pair the box to a song on his phone. Starship's "Nothing's Gonna Stop Us Now" begins to play. The song's drum and bass lines open deep and rich, and for the first time in days, enough music is reaching out across the plateau to make Carson smile again.

The electric piano enters high and puts a bounce in my step that

I'm not expecting. Buck turns up the volume and starts to dance on the hood of his old truck. Rick and Rhonda do the same but keep their feet on the ground.

When the chorus comes in, Buck inches the volume up another couple of clicks and rotates the speakers. The sound rolls down the escarpment and into the valley below. It carries out past Sizemore Coulee Road to US 53, and for all I know, people can hear the concert all the way back to Pigeon Falls.

If Burnell is home, then he's hearing the song too, of course. And if he's hearing it, I'm certain we'll not be receiving anymore white envelopes of cash. For tonight, though, I'm more than satisfied with the tradeoff. It's the price of having music again.

**Driving to** town, I gaze back towards the ridge over Sizemore Coulee. From inside my truck, I can't discern any separation up there, no line between land and sky. I also can't pick out any stars shining overhead. Everything to the north appears cloaked in darkness, though that won't always be the case. At this time next year, someone passing in daytime on US 53 will see a wind farm standing up on that ridge, six sleek towers rising hundreds of feet into the air. I can picture them already.

And after sunset next year, the turbines' red night-beacons will float in that darkness along the ridge like six shiny gemstones, blinking out a nocturnal code only few understand. Maybe, those towers will be gossiping over the comings and goings along US 53. Maybe they'll be communicating with the fierce wind up on Sandberg Ridge, reminding the wind to never let up, that the people in Pigeon Falls and dozens of other towns in Trempealeau County are counting on that breeze to keep them alive. Or maybe they'll just be celebrating the night.

**Eating together** one last time, our crew thank Rhonda and Rick for their work on the two platforms. Our helpers from Payroll and

IT will be leaving in the morning and returning to Iowa. Warren hands Rhonda the keys to Skinny's truck. Rhonda will drive it to Davenport, where the truck will stay until Skinny's situation becomes clearer.

Finished with dinner, Rhonda and Rick say goodbye and depart. Warren then removes from his jacket pocket a sheaf of white envelopes, bound with a rubber band. He hands one envelope to each of us. "It's what Burnell owed us," Warren says. "He left them with Mike."

"Burnell actually paid us?" I say, shaking my head. "Hard to believe."

"Don't be so surprised," Carson remarks. "He still needs people to put up more towers next spring. He's just playing us, again."

**Back in** my room, I call my father. "I'll be home in a couple days," I tell him.

"That's good news, Tommy," he says. "I'm looking forward to it. This year has been a long one."

I don't mention my appointment at the clinic tomorrow or what happened to Skinny. Those things can wait. My father has no joke for me tonight, so I wish him goodnight. Hearing his voice was all I really needed.

Lying in bed, I'm thinking about Skinny, and I realize that with him in the hospital, I've become the senior member of our crew. So far, no one has asked me how I thought our last meal tasted. Or for that matter, my opinion about anything, as they regularly did with Skinny. No one has come to me for advice, another of Skinny's specialties. My new seniority status has only reminded me that time passes faster than we realize, or as my father once put it, "You get old, Tommy, long before you notice."

I'm not even fifty yet, but tonight I'm feeling ancient.

# Part Five

# Backfill

## Tuesday, November 12

The day after a crown has been poured, we call *Dry Day*. No real work is done on Dry Day. Instead, we let all the concrete we've poured cure a little longer before we backfill the pit. Dry Day is a travel day for most of the crew, a time to stop at home and see family, a time to take care of personal business or head to the next project and wait for it to start. Typically, the foreman and one other worker stick around for Dry Day and the day after that, when the pit is filled in with dirt. Because of my follow up appointment at the clinic, I volunteered to stay these two days with Warren.

Cold air from Canada has snuck into town overnight and is waiting for me when I come down for breakfast. It's 15 degrees colder outside this morning than it was yesterday, only 27° now, five below freezing. A thin white veil of frost covers rooftops and tree branches.

During breakfast, Buck tells Eddie, "You're gonna need a heavier coat," and offers to take him as far west as his brother's place in Missoula, if Eddie wants the ride. Eddie accepts the coat advice but declines the ride. He says he has other things to take care of before he can leave, which we all know means Candace.

Carson and Buck plan to stop in Waterford to give statements to the Sheriff's Office before hitting the road. Then, Buck is off to Montana, and Carson is headed for the Quad Cities, 250 miles south from Pigeon Falls. The woman Carson was texting this week, an ER nurse in Rock Island, has invited him to visit.

"I feel good about his one," Warren assures Carson, while crossing fingers on both hands.

"We can only hope," Carson replies.

He and Buck say goodbye to Eddie, and the moment is more emotional than I saw coming. They fist bump and exchange phone numbers. Then, Carson opens his arms wide to Eddie and says,

"Bring it in, man."

Eddie heads out right after Carson and Buck. With Jared behind bars, Eddie will get Candace's car at the firehouse and then drive her from the women's shelter to her sister's home, twenty miles away along the Mississippi. Eddie has reserved his room in Pigeon Falls for one more night and then tomorrow he'll take off for California. He hasn't said how he'll get there.

Having been through so much together, I'm sad seeing our crew split up, and I feel a little of that same emptiness in my heart again, the dread of going forward alone. So many powerful emotions are swirling within me because of what we experienced here. The tough work, the attacks on Skinny and Candace, our interactions with Burnell and Joyce, Mike, Dot, and all the others. Even though I expect most of our crew to be together on future projects, nothing will ever match the time we shared in Pigeon Falls. Just thinking the town's name is enough to choke me up.

**My return** medical appointment is an hour away. When I leave the Shoe, Warren is sipping coffee and talking with the excavating company on his phone. Buck was right about Eddie needing a warmer coat today. I have to scrape a laminate of ice off my windshield before I can hit the road.

There's no traffic on the county highway heading away from Pigeon Falls, not until I fall in behind a school bus a mile out of town. After another mile, the bus turns off and I have the road to myself. Soon, I cross into the high plain of central Wisconsin, and the valleys and ridges of the Driftless Area withdraw behind me. As I head towards the town of Fairview, I'm going in reverse of the route I took from the clinic nearly two weeks ago.

Past Apple Grove, I enter the same long stretch of pine forest I passed through earlier, the same shifting green shadows and clingy claustrophobia. It's like driving through a dim, mossy canyon. With my windows protecting me from the outside chill, I smell none of the redeeming scent of pine needles that I enjoyed during the previous trip.

At the far end of the pine canyon, I notice hundreds of grackles high on a telephone wire beside the highway, balancing wing-to-wing like glossy black pearls strung out along a thin dark chain. Ever alert to intruders, the birds with their pointed beaks and empty eyes suspiciously monitor my passing.

Since my first night in Pigeon Falls, I haven't thought much about my medical tests, but I do now. I wonder what secrets the doctors have discovered inside me. Will they order changes to my diet? Start me on a new treatment? Give me some special pills to take? For sure, they'll advise more rest, but what about exercise?

Of course, it could be the tests found nothing too serious at all inside me, simply my body getting older and my bones and muscles less able to handle concrete work like they used to. Up ahead, a dozen Holsteins idle along a fence line near the road, pressing tightly against one another for warmth, or conversation. A quarter horse grazes far out in a pasture.

A short while later, I spot a glistening stream peeking from behind a hedge of bushes that borders a marsh, and just beyond a grove of cattails lies the muddy bank of the White Claw River. Behind the dense thicket of cattails, two birders are crouched with binoculars. They're the only humans I've seen for miles. Twenty minutes later, I arrive at the clinic.

**Other patients** and family members sit around me in the waiting area. It's a full house today. A nurse calls my name, and I follow him down a long hallway. It's not the same corridor from my previous visit. This time our walk ends at a large sunlit office, not the examination room I'm expecting. "Dr. Welton will be in shortly. You can have a seat," the nurse says and then leaves.

The airy room has floor-to-ceiling windows that look out onto a square of wooded parkland. As offices go, this space seems more like the realm of a senior professor on a university campus than the workstation of a physician in a clinic. It contains no stainless-steel counters, no jars of gauze pads, no boxes of latex gloves. Every doctor's office I've seen before this one has had maps of human body parts displayed on its walls, those colorful dissections of organs, muscles, and skin, along with other posters about a host of diseases you want to avoid at all costs. This clean and well-lighted place is nothing like those rooms. This is a sanctuary.

I select one of two burgundy leather armchairs positioned in front of a desk whose expansive top is glossy and uncluttered. The armchair is sturdy yet disarmingly comfortable, especially the padded arm rests. A flock of diplomas and other awards with fancy lettering and shiny seals gaze at me from the wall behind the desk. On the wall that's opposite the tall windows hang two original oil paintings of bright yellow sunflowers, nearly identical bouquets, though one bunch is in a blue vase and the other vase is red. Between the two paintings is mounted the only clue reminding me I'm in a medical facility, an old white metal light box once used for looking at x-ray film.

Dr. Welton enters. He's the doctor who did a lot of the talking when I met with the GI specialists last time, though this time he's alone. Dr. Welton wears a white lab coat with his name and title stitched in navy blue thread above the chest pocket. A narrow band of hair resembling a white collar encircles the back of his head, though on top he's shiny bald.

Dr. Welton greets me with a warm handshake and wastes no time getting down to business. He settles in at his desk and adjusts a computer monitor so we both can see the screen. "This is what we found, Tom," he says and flips through a series of colorful imaging slides. He stops on a front view of my stomach, small intestines, and colon. "Look here," he says and points to where a string of orange dots circle around my intestines, the way someone would trim a Christmas tree with holiday lights.

"So, the problem's not coming from my stomach?"

"No, the problem started in your small intestines. There's a lot of inflammation in that area. That's why you have difficulty with digestion. But if you look at the shaded part here, you can see that the disease has spread into the peritoneal lining of your abdomen. Each spot of orange you see is a tumor."

"All of them are *tumors*?"

Dr. Welton pushes his chair away from the monitor and takes a folder from his desk drawer. On the cover is the logo for the clinic. He slides the folder across the desktop towards me. "You'll only remember half of what I tell you today, Tom, so this folder contains everything we'll talk about. It's yours to take with you."

What follows next is a whirlwind of medical terms and information, starting with the word *mesothelioma*. I've heard of the disease before today. It's what filled my mother's lungs and led to her death. I look at the color monitor again. None of the orange dots are located in my chest area, all are lower than that.

"I thought mesothelioma was what people got in their lungs."

"Your case is different, Tom. You probably know that it most likely comes from asbestos dust. People breathe it in, so the disease usually shows up in the lungs. But not always. Sometimes the fibers get into the digestive system and work their way into the abdomen. That would have happened to you many years ago."

"I've never worked with asbestos. My parents worked with it, at an insulation plant, but I was just a kid."

"Probably your parents brought the dust home on their clothes. If you sat on their lap, it could have gotten on your hands and then into your mouth. It's rare to pick it up that way, but it happens. Like a non-smoker breathing secondhand smoke."

My thoughts are racing now and not in a straight line, more like spirals and backflips. These muddled thoughts return me to my childhood, to the time when we lived in New Jersey, when my mother and father worked together at the same plant. I remember them coming home with dusty clothes after work. I can see their shirts and pants on a clothesline in our backyard. My mother beating out the dust with a broom.

Or did she? I was only a kid. Is my memory playing tricks?

Dr. Welton puts up a new slide. "This image reveals some scarring along your left side and tells us the disease has been developing for a long time," he says.

I want to believe what the doctor is telling me but feel compelled to resist. "My father worked the same job as my mother, and he's *fine*."

"Why some people get the disease and others don't, I can't say. It's one of those mysteries we don't understand. Hopefully, someday we figure it out." He clicks to another image. "I want you to look at this, Tom."

It's a side view from my ribs to my thighs. All along that distance the orange dots are visible, but they're brighter the closer they get to my pelvis, away from the wrap of intestines. Dr. Welton points and says, "This is your liver and here is the base of your spine." He clicks to an even closer view, where I can clearly see that there's a lot of orange right up against my pelvis. "Have you been experiencing back pain?"

I nod and tell him, "I thought it was the extra lifting we've been doing at work."

"It could be both. Even so, the tumors have moved into your lymph nodes." He turns off his monitor and sits back. "Once something like this spreads around the body, Tom, everything else happens pretty fast."

I know what he's saying, the ultimate bad news, yet my brain won't let me go there. "Will the pain get worse?" I ask.

"That might not happen for a while, but slowly you will get weaker."

Out of the same desk drawer he lifts another booklet and hands it to me. It's a nice-looking publication that's printed in color and several pages long. It reminds me of brochures for cruises I planned with Paige, the ones we never took.

"I want you to start thinking about chemotherapy," Dr. Welton says and begins a monologue so long it has my head spinning when he's done.

"You'll have to decide if you want chemo or not. If you decide that you do, then we should start as soon as possible. I know you have family in Rockford. I can recommend treatment options there. Or we can do the chemo here. It's up to you. You should understand that your cancer is well along. The treatments might not help a lot. But until you do them, it's impossible to know for sure if they will or won't. The medicine we give to kill cancer cells is powerful and will make you feel lousy. That medicine can even lead to some very bad days for you, time you won't get back. You need to keep that in mind, Tom, when you decide what you want to do."

"What about surgery?" I ask.

"No," Dr. Welton says, kindly shaking his head. "In your case, surgery isn't possible. The cancer has spread too far. I'm sorry."

"I figured that from the pictures," I say. "Too much orange."

"Yeah, too much orange."

Dr. Welton waits for me to say something, but my brain is stuck in a maze that I can't escape. "You have a lot to think about, Tom," he continues. "Like I said, it'll take a few days for this news to sink in. That's normal. When you have questions, I'm here to answer them. Just call our office. We also have counselors at the clinic. You can talk with them anytime, day or night. They're very helpful."

I slide the travel brochure into the folder I'm holding.

"I'd also like you to get a second opinion," he says. "I'm confident in everything I told you, still it's good to hear what another specialist has to say. I made a list of some very good doctors in the Rockford area." Dr. Welton hands me a sheet of white paper. I didn't see where he got the paper, it's like it materialized out of thin air. I glance blankly at the half dozen names of doctors and their contact information.

"If you decide to do your treatment here, then my staff and I will care for you throughout the course of the disease. We'll be with you every step of the way."

"So, to make a long story short," I say, "this is it, right?"

Dr. Welton looks at me for a moment and then he nods. "Yes, it is. What you have and how it's developed, it's a terminal illness."

"How much time are we talking about?"

Dr. Welton shifts in his chair. How many times has he been asked this question? "There's no exact amount of time," he says. "But from my experience, I estimate you have around eight to ten months."

"What could I have done different?" I ask.

"Nothing," says the doctor. "You had no control over this, Tom. It's not your fault."

I exit the building and walk to my truck. My thoughts are a jumble of medical terms and orange dots, yet I try to focus on anything other than that, like getting out my car keys, taking deep breaths, making sure my shoelaces are tied. Warren is waiting for my return, I know. His plan is to go to the jobsite when I get back. We have to make sure everything is ready for the earth movers when they arrive tomorrow. We have work to finish, but Pigeon Falls seems so far away right now. I start up my truck but can't convince myself to put the shifter into gear. I remain in the parking lot with the motor idling, my body numb and my thoughts in a daze.

More than ever before, I realize how fate enjoys irony. I've never been a risk taker. I've never smoked or been overweight. My heart is strong and I eat smartly. I've never worked with asbestos. Yet a terminal disease like mesothelioma finds me, even though I've done nothing in my life to lead it my way.

My diagnosis and Dr. Welton's timeline keep trying to sink in, even as my brain keeps resisting. I didn't expect to hear the word "cancer" at my appointment. Of course, in the back of my mind, I knew cancer was a possibility, but the word still came as a surprise. As much as I want to talk to someone now, I know that breaking bad news over the phone is not a good idea. I'll have to wait a couple of days, until I'm back in Rockford, to tell my father and my sister what's going on.

Then, a new idea starts to evolve in my head. It's a crazy idea, in fact, but a possibility no less, and it has me thinking forward.

I say to myself, if I had Paige's phone number I could call her now, even after all these years. I know she'd listen to my predicament and talk me through it. That's the kind of person she is. If I can find her phone number somewhere, maybe on the internet, then she can be the steady hand I need to see me through this. She'll know what I should do. She might even agree to come up from wherever she is and see me again.

I full stop on that last thought, having realized I've drawn out the fantasy too far. Now, I feel ashamed. I don't know Paige's number and even if I did, the idea of calling her is wrong. She's not a part of this.

So, instead of searching for a phone number to make a call that I shouldn't, I sit in my truck and hold onto the only silver lining I have at the moment. Now that my disease has a name, I know what symptoms to pay attention to.

**During my** return drive from the Fairview Clinic to Pigeon Falls, my understanding of time changes. I've always been a clocks and calendars person, someone who boxes his life into predictable units that make sense, time parcels the brain can deliver. Like Thursday follows Wednesday, breakfast at six, taxes due April 15, be there in a minute. But now, as the rural Wisconsin landscape rolls by, time makes no sense to me. I don't care what time my dashboard clock is showing. And it doesn't matter anyway, because I can no longer discern any meaningful difference between minutes and months.

Don't tell me about tomorrow or next year, I'm thinking. I don't want to hear it. Don't tell me if I'm early or late. It's meaningless now. If I'm going to be connected to anything, it's only to this moment, to right now. Though even *now* is feeling unsteady, because I've already forgotten what day of the week it is.

My hands grip the steering wheel as I merge onto the highway again, though my hold has already grown weaker since leaving the clinic. My eyes are also failing me. I can no longer see clearly. Everything beside the road is a blur. The sky and birds and farms and trees, they're all covered in a watery haze. Only the blacktop in front of me appears clear, along with its broken yellow stripes that for years now have become a life rhythm all my own.

My brain ignores whatever danger awaits around the next curve. My ears hear nothing beyond the wind passing over my windshield. Yet, it's a surprisingly consoling sound, the wind, something soothing to listen to, endless and even. And after some miles more it kindly coaxes me towards sleep. It's okay, the wind whispers, just close your eyes and relax. That's right, take your hands off the wheel. Everything will be okay.

I pull sharply off the highway and park along the gravel shoulder, where the White Claw River again comes in close to the road. I'm *not* ready for sleep, I remind myself. I still have things to do in my life.

My engine purrs as it holds energy in reserve. A list starts to form in my head. To me, that's a good sign. Meet with Warren. Return the land to how it was before. Drive home. Get a second opinion. Decide about chemo.


**Clusters of** white boulders to my left stand midstream on the White Claw and stick out from the riverbed's dreary backdrop of scrub trees bordering the shore. Farther downstream, I spot a big blue heron along the bank. In a stretch of river grass, it's posing as stiff as a lawn ornament. Its gaze is focused on something obscured in a muddle of cattails between the bird and me. It takes me a moment, but then I spot them, the two birders from earlier this morning. The pair are crouched now among the reeds with their binoculars pointed towards the elegant heron. Neither side moves, each spying the other, no secrets left between them.

While I'm watching the standoff, my brain flirts again with thoughts about Paige and chemo, and chemo and cancer, and then cancer and dying, but my thoughts go nowhere useful. Then, I think about the unpredictability of fate. Fate leads me to *Amor Fati*, which leads me to Candace, and soon I'm trying to recall everything she told me about her so-far short life.

**Jared proposed** when Candace was a junior in high school. She said no, she was too young. He proposed again at graduation. She said yes. A wedding for the following June was planned. During that fall after high school, Candace lived at home and commuted to the university in Eau Claire. She couldn't decide on a major because she was interested in everything. In January, she and Jared moved into an apartment together. In February, he asked her to quit school. He said the university was too far away, she was gone too much. She refused his several requests to drop out. By March, Candace was having second thoughts about getting married. Things went downhill from there.

One spring night, Candace came home late from school, and Jared's reaction was to throw a bottle against a wall. The next week, he dented the bathroom door with his elbow. Soon after, she got her first bruise. Candace wanted to stop the wedding but had no idea how to make that happen. She had no one to talk to and nowhere to turn. They were married at the end of June, and not long after that, Jared told her he wouldn't allow her to return to the university. She started working at the Shoe in July.

Searching my memory for these many details, which Candace

shared with me, is proving to be a helpful diversion from my thoughts about cancer and death, so I continue.

Candace said that what finally helped her cope with Jared's anger, and her own mistakes, was what she had learned in her college philosophy class, particularly something the German philosopher Friedrich Nietzsche wrote about. That night in the Shoe, Candace had asked me if I had heard about Nietzsche's idea of *loving one's fate*. I told her that I hadn't. "Well, our fate is like riding a roller coaster," she said. The high points in life are the good things that happen to us, and the low points are the bad. "Life has its ups and downs, just like a roller coaster."

According to Candace, Nietzsche believed that we shouldn't just accept our fate in life, we should *love it*, especially the bad things that happen. "It's what we learn from the low points," Candace said. "That's what will lead us to the best life we can live."

**I've been** sitting in my truck beside the White Claw for twenty minutes, trying to remember every detail from my conversations with Candace. The big blue heron and the two birders along the river are nowhere to be seen. As I pull back onto the county highway, the tiniest snowflakes begin to fall, but their crystalline dance is too light and dry for any of them to stick to the asphalt. During the rest of my return to Pigeon Falls, I think about Candace and fate.

It's while I'm passing through Apple Grove a third time that I realize she was right. I can't change what's already happened, but I can have a say in what happens next.

**I arrive** at the Shoe and find the last open spot in the parking lot. Warren is waiting at a table near the window of the busy room, savoring the grilled cheese and bowl of tomato soup in front of him. As I settle in the chair across from Warren, he asks, "Good news?"

I summarize for him my morning in Fairview. Warren looks

more and more somber as I lead him to my prognosis and treatment options, though I tip toe around the worst of it.

"I'm sorry, Tom," he says, deflated. "I never expected that. If you want to head home now, go for it. I can handle the backfill."

"I'd rather stay," I tell him. "Finishing here will help me clear my head."

"You want me to say anything to the front office?"

"Yeah, tell them I'd like to work in spring, if I can." Dot sets a bowl of chicken noodle soup and a strawberry shake in front of me and leaves. "What have you heard about Skinny?" I ask.

"They still have him in ICU," Warren says. "He's stable."

"Is that good news or bad?"

"I don't know. Tomorrow afternoon, I'll drive over to see him."

During the last few miles of the drive back to Pigeon Falls, my stomach became so nauseous I almost pulled over. Now, the chicken soup has settled that uneasiness, along with my nerves. "Were you out to the jobsite already?" I ask.

"I waited for you," Warren says. "I called Burnell this morning and told him to meet us at the trailer tomorrow, after we backfill. He needs to sign some paperwork."

"He's okay with that? I think he's been avoiding us."

"He grumbled a little, so I had to explain that we need to go over everything we did and that his signature officially ends our work. I don't think he's ever done a contract like this before."

After lunch, Warren and I ride out to Sizemore Coulee. A septic tanker is parked on the path between Burnell's two largest fields. The long hose that connects the truck to the manure pond has sucked up most of what's left of the spill, yet even with our windows up, the bitter stench infiltrates the cab.

Warren doesn't slow down enough to give the smell enough time to stay with us. He climbs the escarpment and drives to the first pit and then the second. Thermal blankets cover the crowns and the rest of the domes. Everything looks perfect. Warren and I refill the generators and leave them running so there's no need to return again at night. We then drive to Waterford to give statements at the Sheriff's Office.

**Tonight, it's** the first time in two weeks where Warren and I can sit down to dinner at a reasonable hour. Now that I'm no longer focused on our race to finish Burnell's platforms, the troubles in my stomach and lower back have regained my attention. Doctor Welton wrote me a prescription for pain medication, but I'm reluctant to start down that path.

When Warren and I walk into the Shoe, Mike greets us with a smile and then a friendly nod that is pointed towards Eddie, who is sitting at a table halfway into the room. We join Eddie at his table, and the first thing he says is that tomorrow he's driving to California... *with Candace.*

"The two of you, together," I say. "In her car?"

"She wants to get away from here, before Jared is out on bail."

"Good idea," says Warren.

"You know, it's a long way out there?"

Eddie pulls his chin closer to the table. "I told her we could go to my house in Chicago if she wanted. I know she'd be safe there. I even asked my mom. But Candace wants to go to California. She says that's been my dream all along."

Sounding like the father he is, Warren asks, "What do *her* parents say?"

"They think she'll be safer out there, than back here."

"Knowing what Jared's capable of, I think they're right," Warren says.

"I met her parents yesterday. They're happy she's done with him."

"What about a trial?" I ask.

"We'll come back. She's talking to a divorce lawyer tomorrow."

"Man, Eddie," I sigh, "a lot's happened since Warren picked you up on that freeway ramp in Chicago."

"You can say that again."

"You sure you don't want to take a break for a while, get yourself organized again?"

Eddie doesn't answer immediately. He's facing the front of the room and looking serious. As he stares in that direction, I'm fearing he's noticed someone through the windows. I turn to see what he's looking at, but there's no one outside. Eddie's just thinking.

"It's been crazy, right?" he says, finally. "But I still want to see California."

Warren and I have never been to California. We open our phones and, like two worried uncles, consult road maps and calculate distances. While also trying to figure out the best routes for avoiding snow when crossing the mountains, and where to stop overnight along the way. I search Trip Advisor for the top sights, and Warren checks an app on his phone for the lowest gas prices. We're having a hard time letting Eddie go and doing our best to delay the inevitable.

I say, "Candace told me you speak Spanish."

"Yeah, since sixth grade. Spanish helped at the dollar store."

"You know, a lot of people speak Spanish in California," Warren says. "That's a good skill to have out there."

Eddie answers with a thumbs up.

*Saying good-bye.* We're standing in the parking lot now, Eddie about to get into Candace's small sedan. In a minute, he'll be on his way to Waterford to fill up with gas and then to Candace's sister's home to see how she's doing. We'll say our goodbyes now.

There's so much of a chill descending on Pigeon Falls tonight that the air out here feels brittle. Eddie zips his jacket. I give him a hug. Warren does the same.

Eddie thanks us for showing him how to build platforms for wind turbines. "Now, I can tell people there's a bunch more to them than what we see above ground," he says and gets into the car.

"You take care," Warren tells him.

"And Candace too," I say. "She's special."

Sitting behind the steering wheel, Eddie rolls down his window. "You know, she's really glad everything didn't turn out worse," he says. "It sure could have."

Warren and I wave as Eddie leaves the parking lot.

On the Shoe's outside staircase, going up to our rooms, I say to Warren, "You ever ask him if he has a driver's license?" Warren stops and thinks for a long moment.

"Nope," he says, shaking his head. "Never thought of it."

**Back in** my room, I phone my father. My sister is there when I call, and she answers. I let her know I'll be in Rockford by dinnertime tomorrow. Shannon says she'll cook something special. "How was your visit to the clinic?" she asks.

"You know… doctors, tests, hospital stuff. I haven't had more than a second to think about it. The last two weeks have been really strange. I have a ton of stories." I ask her to put my father on the phone.

"Sorry, I don't have a joke tonight," he says.

"That's fine, Dad. I wanted to ask you something."

"Okay, shoot."

"I've seen some colorful sunsets up here in Wisconsin. Do you remember what you once told us were your favorite colors at sunset?"

There's a long pause on his end of the line. "I don't know," my father says, sounding a little stumped.

"You said the ones between summer and fall had the best colors."

"I don't remember that."

"Well, your favorite colors were *blood orange* and *lavender*. That's how you described them."

"Oh, sure, I remember that. But those weren't my favorite colors,

Tommy. Those were your mother's. Blood orange and lavender, that's what she liked best. Did you see some where you are?"

"No," I say, surprised that I'd forgotten it was my mother who liked those colors. "It's too late this time of year, Dad. I was just thinking about it."

## Wednesday, November 13

For a change, my final breakfast in Pigeon Falls starts after the sun has come up. I order two toasted English muffins, honey, and a cup of hot chocolate. Warren's hungrier and has a scrambler with Canadian bacon.

The temperature overnight dropped to 24°, four degrees lower than expected, and the near-term forecast is trending the same. It would have been impossible to pour concrete yesterday, today, or tomorrow, so in the end we lucked out on the weather. That constant worry we had about not completing the project before the first freeze is already feeling distant to me, so less important than it was only a couple of days ago.

The only major task Warren and I have left to do this morning is to remove the blankets from the pits, so the excavators can backfill them. We'll be finished by noon and can leave Pigeon Falls after lunch. I ride with Warren out to the jobsite.

The sun is well above the ridge when we get to the foreman's trailer,  though a veneer of pearly white frost still coats the roof. Warren goes inside, while I walk over to the first pit. Ice crystals crackle like broken glass under my footsteps. I shut off the generator and wheel it back to the shipping container. Then, I gather the portable lights and stow them away.

Looking south, I see layers of autumn fog hovering over Sizemore Coulee, like the folds in a silver shroud. Heavy mist like this often forms in the mornings late in our work season, when colder night air squeezes against whatever warmth is left on land.

Today's blanket of autumn fog also covers an array of other coulees out in the distance, and it's a beautiful sight to see with so many wrinkles of glossy fabric glistening in the sunlight. Below me, I cannot make out the Sandberg house through the fog, or their outbuildings, only the top of the silo is poking through the mist, its white cap clear above a ring of navy blue.

Warren exits the trailer, and together we remove and then fold the thermal blankets from the pits. It takes us several trips to the shipping container, but we have everything stored by the time the excavators arrive with their heavy equipment.

Two heavy flatbed trailers approach on the access road and send clouds of gray dust drifting southward. One trailer hauls a big diesel shovel strapped to its bed. The other trailer lugs a yellow Cat earth grader. Warren shows the drivers where to park.

We watch as giant mouthfuls of earth are returned to the first pit, starting with the rocks and brown subsoil, and then adding the darker topsoil, until only a few white PVC pipe ends, some dark steel bolts, and the gray lip of the concrete crown are visible above ground. The big shovel lumbers to the second platform as the Cat begins smoothing the soil over the first pit, one careful pass after another.

By 10:45 a.m., the sky is mostly blue with a few wispy white clouds drifting in. The valley has cleared itself of the autumn fog. We've reached 38°, without the windchill. Where the wind darts across the vast openness of the plateau, the temperature still feels frigid, a few degrees below freezing. Warren returns to the trailer.

Turning away from the heavy equipment, I notice movement in the valley below. Four bodies are installing a green liner in the old manure tank. Two other workers are mortaring in new concrete blocks where the old ones gave way. Burnell, it appears, has decided to repair the ruptured tank, not replace it.

The shovel and the earth grader finish restoring the land and are loaded back onto their trailers. As the excavators are driving away,

Burnell pulls up and parks. He remains in his truck, talking on his phone. He hasn't noticed me standing along the ridge. When he finishes his call, he goes inside the foreman's trailer.

Low pillowy clouds that resemble bolts of gray cotton have begun to roll over the plateau. In the few spots where sunlight squeezes through the fabric, it paints the valley with streaks of golden brightness, as if the direction of each light beam has been individually chosen from somewhere hidden above. After ten minutes inside the trailer, Burnell comes out and returns to his truck. He's talking on the phone again as he drives away.

I'm watching the red truck descend into the valley, when I realize something that will be essential to understanding whatever lasting perspective I take with me regarding my two weeks in Pigeon Falls.

What hits me is this: Burnell Sandberg has won. He's beaten the odds. He's finally acquired the one prize that eluded his family for generations: *wealth*.

As it turns out, Burnell didn't need cash crops, hogs, boats, or sketchy schemes to obtain a family fortune. A treasure chest was hiding on the Sandberg property all along, all he had to do was open it. Sadly though, Burnell's victory with wind power hasn't come about from anything remarkable he did himself, not from hard work or genius, not from perseverance or penance. It's mostly come about because fifteen-thousand years ago, a wall of moving ice decided to stop where it did and create a random geological phenomenon unlike anything else in the area, maybe unlike anything else anywhere.

I doubt Burnell will hold onto his wind farm for more than a few years. Then he'll cash in when the market is right, and he'll move on. It's not in his DNA to stick to a plan for long, even a successful one. He'll sell the farm to a power company or a co-op, at a profit that's more than generous, even after his board of directors receive their shares. Burnell's most valuable inheritance was not a passel of pigs or several hundred acres of farmland, but a breeze that never stops blowing.

Some could argue that MSP won too. I won't disagree. We finished the project on time, as we promised, and every one of us got paid a boatload of money.

**Warren exits** the trailer carrying a folder of papers. He locks the door and goes around back to shut off the generator and lift it into his truck. He then comes over to where I'm standing. "Everything work out?" I ask.

"He signed what he had to sign. And I explained what will happen when the tower crew gets here. I thought he'd ask more questions, but he just shook my hand and told me MSP is a great company." I stare at Warren in disbelief. "He also said our crew does fantastic work."

"*Fantastic*," I repeat, and Warren smiles.

Before getting into Warren's truck, we pause to look out across the plateau at where the two pits had been. The earth movers have done a fine job. It's hard to pick out the first crown around the freshly groomed topsoil, but it's there if you know where to look. The second crown is too far away to see anything at all. In spring, when groundcover sprouts again, no one passing by will know that there's tons of concrete and steel under this tilled field. All they'll see are two enormous white turbine towers rising above Sizemore Coulee, with their thin long blades moving as gracefully as a pair of swans in flight.

Descending the ridge with Warren, I notice a plume of smoke rising from one of the chimneys atop the Sandberg farmhouse. "Someone has built a fire," I say to Warren.

The white smoke barely escapes the brickwork before the wind whips it like a kite tail in flight. The rippling reminds me of a medieval pennant, flying at the tip of a battle lance and carried by a knight who is galloping towards a foe. Burnell Sandberg is not that shining knight, of course, though his family's long battle with failure was almost as epic. That said, I doubt he will ever be content with his victory. Burnell's like a lot of people who want to have it all. Even after they get everything they'd ever dreamed of, it's never enough.

**Warren decides** against a late lunch and checks out of his room. He wants to get a jump start on his drive to Minneapolis. We say our goodbyes at his truck in front of the Shoe. "I'm taking the stuff from Skinny's room with me," Warren says, as he lifts a suitcase into the backseat.

"Safe travels and give Skinny my best wishes," I tell him.

We shake hands. Warren opens his door and climbs inside. "You take care of yourself, Tom. All of us in Davenport will be hoping to see you in spring."

A minute later Warren is out of sight and headed towards the Interstate. It's approaching 1:00 p.m., and I still have to finish packing. But I also need to eat something before starting my return to Rockford. I go inside the Shoe and find a table under the old-time photos along the side wall.

The dining room is a third full. Two men with their backs to me are sitting at the bar. I recognize that one of them is Burnell. He's wearing a wool Scandinavian sweater, the expensive kind with an elaborate knit pattern. His emblematic blaze orange parka is draped over the back of his stool. The man with Burnell is about my age and dressed in a light gray business suit. Both men have sandwich baskets and green bottles of imported beer in front of them.

Resting on the stool next to the man in the suit is a black briefcase. The man is paging through a sheaf of papers scattered on top of the bar, between him and Burnell. Burnell is watching with interest, and occasionally he points at something on a page. Theirs is a serious business conversation. When I've finished my bowl of soup and vanilla shake, I go to the bar.

I'm standing out of Burnell's line of sight but close enough to hear his familiar voice. I have my money and check in hand, and while I wait for my waitress to come out of the kitchen, I listen to Burnell and his lunch partner talking. It takes me only a couple of sentences to realize that the man with Burnell is a representative of the wind turbine company that follows us, the one that's coming to Pigeon Falls in a few weeks to erect the two towers atop our platforms.

"They have to go up now," Burnell is saying with that imperial voice I've heard so often, his inflated grumble of demand and urgency that he's so good at using to his advantage. "It's all I'm asking. Get them up now."

The other man gathers his documents and slides them into his briefcase. He's packing to leave, even though his sandwich and bottle of beer are only half finished. "We're good at what we do, Mr. Sandberg. We've put up a lot of these towers."

"I know. I know. I'm just saying, the sooner the better." Burnell swivels his stool so he can keep an eye on the tower rep. "So, are we agreed on the overtime hours and the Thanksgiving pay? You know, around here I'm known as a very generous person."

"Yes, I'll put those changes into the contract and send it back for you to look over, Mr. Sandberg."

"Please, call me, Red."

Burnell hasn't noticed me waiting behind him, so I could listen to more of this conversation if I wanted, but I've heard it all before. My waitress comes out of the kitchen, a high school girl who's younger than Candace and shorter and stockier. She has black eye liner and matching lip gloss. Her hair is also dark, a kind of rough dye-job, like freshly mined coal. A wild display of gold rings and silver studs decorate her nose and ears. She seems like a diligent worker, but beyond that work ethic there's no resemblance to Candace whatsoever. I hand the waitress the money for my meal and tip. She thanks me kindly and wishes me a good day.

As I'm leaving the dining room for the last time, my muscles feel overly tired, my body terribly worn out. I recall how Dot incorrectly called Burnell's towers *windmills* and not wind towers or wind turbines. But now, I'm thinking, maybe Dot had it right all along. The Sandberg project has yet to produce any electricity, but it did a pretty good job of grinding my body down to almost nothing.

**Back in** my room, I pack my bag of toiletries, while thinking about Burnell and the guy from the tower company. I wonder if the tower crew will have as strange and difficult an experience with Burnell as we did. Unfortunately, I decide, it's likely.

The second floor of the Horseshoe Inn seems dead quiet. No one is up here but me. I've kept all the cash I received from Albert in a room safe that's tucked away in the armoire. I retrieve the money and slip the bills into my suitcase, under tee shirts and pajamas. It's a thick stack of mostly tens and twenties, nearly $2,000, all of it tax free.

While closing my laundry bag, I'm surprised to hear the door next to my room, as it opens and closes. Then, two pairs of light footsteps walk away down the hall. At first, I figure it's the ladies who clean our rooms. Maybe they've come to prepare the rooms for the next boarders, though that's only a guess. After a minute and still feeling curious, I go to my window.

Candace's small sedan is parked at the curb across from the Shoe. The trunk is open and inside rest a pink suitcase and a black backpack. A light snow is falling, nothing measurable, just tiny flakes disappearing as they hit the pavement. Eddie comes around the car and puts a cardboard box inside the trunk. Sticking out of the box is a pair of yellow boots that I recognize. Eddie purchased them in Eau Claire the morning after the spill, and I helped him try on several pairs as he searched for the right size.

Eddie readjusts the boot box and then closes the trunk. He opens the back door and looks inside. On the rear seat lies the camouflage-print duffle he also bought in Eau Claire and on top of it is a similar bag, though in drab green. I can just make out the top edge of another pink suitcase wedged between the two duffels and the far door. Seemingly satisfied with the full back seat, Eddie closes the door and stands beside the car.

A young woman emerges from the Shoe.

If not for the familiar slope of her shoulders and the unique curve of her hips, it would have taken me longer to realize that the woman crossing the street is Candace, because her hair isn't the puffy bleached blond look that I'm accustomed to. Her hair is straight now and light brown. Her shoulder-length strands are tied in a ponytail that sticks out the back of a blue baseball cap. I figure Candace has been talking to co-workers inside the Shoe, maybe telling them of her plan to go to a safer place, somewhere far away, but I don't actually know why she was inside the Shoe. Maybe she was just picking up her last paycheck.

When Candace gets to her car, she and Eddie talk in the street for a moment and then start laughing. The tiny snowflakes falling over Pigeon Falls are turning wet and heavy. The flakes drift down around the couple in a slow-motion descent, like a scene from a child's snow globe.

Then, Candace raises her right arm and Eddie does the same. Their hands high-five each other. It's an action done not as an oath or a pledge, but more as something of a promise,  an exchange between comrades embarking on a great campaign. They laugh again and Candace slides into the driver's seat and closes her door, and Eddie gets in on the passenger side.

Like a sigh of relief, a spurt of blue smoke escapes the car's tailpipe, and the sedan's skinny wiper arms make a valiant attempt to clear away the fat flakes that have clouded the windshield. I watch as the car completes a slow U-turn in front of the Shoe, its small tires drawing a sharp semi-circle track on the whitening pavement. Here is the moment the real trek to California begins. Two birds of a feather taking flight together for the first time, guided only by fate and a prevailing wind. From my window, the last I see of their car is its slight silver shape gathering speed as it heads towards the Interstate.

# Epilogue

"Out of suffering have emerged the strongest souls.
The most massive characters are seared with scars."

Kahlil Gibran, *The Prophet*

Between Thanksgiving and the end of January, I undergo two rounds of chemo. My sister and father have convinced me to give it a try, arguing that any chance for success is better than none. But I stop the treatments in February. Not only do my scans show no improvement, but there wasn't a day since Christmas when I felt anything like my old self. I also didn't enjoy the dry mouth and foul body odor I got from the drugs. In stopping the treatments, I remember something Dr. Welton said at the clinic back in November: *If you decide to start chemo, be ready for what comes next.* Dr. Welton was so right. Chemo knocks people down, and no one gets that down time back. I'm no longer fighting cancer, I'm fighting time.

It's early March and I've moved in with my father. Skinny Martin is on the phone today. He's three months out of the hospital and back in Key West. He heard from Warren about my illness. "How you feeling?" he asks.

I tell him I'm hanging in there and add, "I didn't want to go down that road, Skinny, but I've started taking pain pills."

"I hear you, man," Skinny replies. Then, he tells me he won't be returning to MSP, not ever. "My body can't take the grind anymore. Time to hang it up."

I say it's the same for me.

"I'm going to miss everyone," he admits, and that leads into news we share about the rest of our crew. Manny and Rita have returned to Iowa, along with their baby daughter. The company gave Jimmy Gilligan another chance at redemption, so long as he keeps attending AA meetings. Buck built houses in Biloxi over the winter and earned enough to pay cash for a new truck. Carson's romance with the ER nurse fizzled, but he's talking to someone in Iowa City and things look promising. As for Warren, he's back in Davenport, managing the office and seeing his family every night after work. And he assured Skinny that no one from our team would have to go back to finish Burnell's wind farm. Another MSP crew has been tasked with that nightmare.

"Have you heard anything from Eddie or Candace?" I ask.

Skinny says he talked with them recently. They made it out to Hollywood and swam in the ocean, but now they were living in Utah and going to school there.

"When they passed through Salt Lake," Skinny says, "they liked the mountains, so they went back. Funny how plans change, right?" Then he adds, "Candace told me to tell you something. She wants you to know that she's *loving her fate*. But I'm not sure what that means."

"It means she's learning from her mistakes," I tell him.

Near the end of our conversation, Skinny asks, "Tom, has this new virus got you worried?"

"A little, I guess. The President says it'll be gone by April."

Skinny says, "You know, they're calling us *essential workers…*," followed by a long pause on his end. I know he hasn't hung up. I wait and wait and then, with his voice sounding bluer than ever, he says, "I gotta tell you, Tom, what's happening to you is really hard to get my head around. You're still a young man. I'm really sorry for you."

Then he adds, "You know, sitting in the Shoe that night, sitting in my own blood, I was really, really scared. I thought I was going to die."

Maybe I should be scared too, but I'm not. Not sure why that is, but maybe it's because I have no worries about what comes next. What is difficult for me is imagining what it means to never see the people I care about again, all my family and friends, everyone who's given meaning to my life. I don't want to leave this world. I love it just like it is. Yet, every morning now, I wonder if this will be the day the pain is so bad that I can't get out of bed, the day they come and take me somewhere to wait out the end.

I try to tell myself I'm ready for whenever that day comes. I'll have lived my life as I wanted, just not as long as I wanted. And most days, I believe myself.


A week later, my father and I have just finished dinner. I'm filling the dishwasher when he says, "Let's drive to Jersey."

"Now?" I laugh. "It's almost dark."

"We'll go in an hour. Get our things together and go."

My father has been talking about a trip back East since I stopped chemo. We still have relatives there, though it's been years since we visited. I say, "I'm not sure driving somewhere so far away is a good idea, Dad. The lockdown starts tomorrow."

"It'll be okay. We'll be there by morning."

"I think the doctors want us to stay put."

"The President says it's not a big deal."

"It's a *lockdown*, Dad. To me, that sounds like a big deal."

"Well then, that's my point, Tommy. If we want to see family again, we should go now, before it starts. You and me can switch driving. What do you say?"

It's a crazy idea. A terminally ill patient and his eighty-year-old father. Both depleted in body and mind. Out driving on an Interstate highway for thirteen hours. And during what they're calling a *pandemic*. Even so, I agree to think about it.


"Okay," I tell him, a few minutes later. "Let's pack up." My father is thrilled. We call to let them know we're on our way. I brew some tea and fill a sack with snacks and then put our suitcases in my truck.

Masters of fate, we end up leaving at 6:15 p.m. and miss the Chicago congestion on I-90 and 294. After Gary, the traffic on I-80 thins out, and we pass South Bend around 10 p.m., losing an hour between time zones. When we stop for gas in Fremont, my father insists on filling the tank himself but then refuses to use the hand sanitizer I keep in my truck. He's unconvinced there's any danger from something he cannot see.

My father dozes beside me until we're deep into Ohio, and then it's well after midnight when we stop again for gas around Cleveland. The first oasis I try is closed, with a sign on the door mentioning the pandemic. The next rest stop is open for credit cards only. Although its truck lot is crowded with sleeping semi-trailers, there are only two cars dozing out front where I park. I tell my father we should think about resting here too, but he insists we press on.

A few months ago, my father stopped smoking because of his worries over my health. One day, he went cold turkey, just like that, and he was done with cigarettes. Since then, I've noticed he has moments of added stress that the absence of nicotine causes. This is one of those moments. "I need to drive, Tommy," he proclaims and gets in on the driver's side. "You can sleep," he tells me. "We're more than halfway there." I can't sleep, of course, unsure how he'll manage behind the wheel.

Interstate 80 is a wasteland by the time we get into Pennsylvania, no taillights, no headlights, nothing on the road but us. We go ten minutes before seeing another vehicle. The lockdown has begun.

My father has been driving more than two hours now. "We should probably switch," I tell him.

"I'm good," he assures me, "just catching my second wind."

The hills are unending when you cut across Pennsylvania, one up and down after another, and tonight at the center of the state there's nothing but pitch-black on all sides.

I finished my tea back in Ohio, yet I can still feel the caffeine. I open a bag of pretzels and realize how much taller I sit now in the seat beside my father, how much his body has shrunk over the years while I've been on the road.

"I'm glad you're with me on this trip, Dad," I tell him. He doesn't say anything for a minute.

Then he says, "It makes me so sad you got sick, Tommy. You're still so young. Just like your mother."

Now is my time to say nothing. Because I don't know what to say. We've talked about cancer a lot since Christmas. But we haven't been able to talk much about the endgame. My father has already lost a wife, and soon he'll lose his only son. How he managed to carry on after my mother was gone is something I'll never fully understand. His loss and mine, when Paige left me, are not the same.

We travel a few more miles before either of us says anything. Then, my father asks, "You know why I wanted to go back East, don't you?"

It seems like an obvious answer. He's talked about this trip for weeks, but I'm curious what he's getting at. "I guess you wanted me to see everyone again."

He shakes his head. "Maybe, but not really," he says. "Seeing everyone again is a good reason to go back, but it wasn't what I was thinking."

Now, I'm intrigued. "Well, if it's not to see family again, then… *why did you want to drive all the way to New Jersey?*"

My father glances over at me and smiles. "Well, I'm doing it *for you*, Tommy."

"You're doing it for me, but not to see family?"

He hesitates with an answer, or maybe he's just drawing out my anticipation, because in the orange glow of the dashboard light I can see my father now smiling with confidence, the big toothy grin he makes when he's about to tell the punchline of a joke.

I say it again. "What do you mean, you're doing it *for me?*"

"With everything going on, son, I wanted to get you out there for at least a week, before anything else happens."

Now I'm confused. "What's so important about a week?" I ask.

He waits a perfect beat, measuring his delivery. And then he says, "Because, Tommy, a week in Jersey can seem like… *a lifetime*."

It takes me a second, but I get it and start smiling too. "Keep your eyes on the road, Dad."

He looks ahead and then back at me, still grinning. "There's nothing to see," he says.

And he's right. Outside our truck, the vast rolling hills and endless forests of Pennsylvania remain undetectable without moonlight or stars or anyone else on the highway. Only the short gray path in the shine of our headlights lies ahead of us, and it keeps vanishing under our truck as quickly as we move eastward.

Then through the darkness, I spot something else. There's a line of red gemstones out ahead of us, distant lights that are flickering like votive candles laid out on a black velvet pall.

"Look, Dad," I say and point, "there *is* something out there."

As my father continues driving, with me riding at his side, I explain that it's the night lights of a wind farm I see in the distance, a string of red dots spread out across an invisible horizon, markers for a mighty congregation of wind turbines generating power.

But my father's not so sure. With his eyesight as it is, he can't see the lights through the darkness, let alone pick out the tall towers or their ever-tumbling blades. Nor can he hear the woosh those blades make as they slice through the night air. To him, there's only the road in front of us.

So, I tell him, "Trust me, Dad, they're out there."

He is looking ahead again, concentrating in the glow of his dashboard light. "You know," I add, "once upon a time, workers like me came through this part of the country and built those things."

My father reaches between us and takes some pretzels from the snack bag.

"Well, son," he replies, "it's nice to know we're not alone."

*Amor Fati*

# Acknowledgements

Like anyone who writes fiction, I know it's those friends and family who read our early drafts and offer their heartfelt comments, both large and small, that immeasurably help our later drafts become the best storytelling they can be. For me, that has never been truer than with *Pigeon Falls*. I have several important people to thank for their comments, critiques, suggestions, and encouragement.

To Meg Albrinck and Kevin Fitchett, your comprehensive and thought-filled reading of the novel and your unvarnished comments kept me on track early on and elevated the final product more than I would have imagined possible. Thank you, again.

To Wendy Varish and Dana Boyer, thank you for sharing your helpful impressions and edits. To JD Botana, someone who has lived the life of nomad worker, thank you for supplying me with pointers about the traveling life and giving the story a feeling of authenticity. To Reece Colberg, thank you for taking a simple concept and artistically turning it into a remarkable front cover that readers won't forget.

A special thank you to Dawn Hogue for believing that *Pigeon Falls* was a novel that mattered. In Dawn's five years as publisher of Water's Edge Press, she has brought the poetry and fiction of nearly twenty writers to audiences throughout the country, and I'm proud to be counted among them. During those years, Dawn's professionalism and support for writers and their work have been unsurpassed.

And most of all, I want to thank Valérie. From typing the first rough pages of yellow pad to proofreading galley pages, and from wondering if someone would say or do this or that to telling me when you especially liked a turn of phrase, you always helped me keep my eye on the big picture.

# Also by Jeff Elzinga

**The Distance Between Stars** is the story of two Americans divided by history and skin color. Joe Kellerman, white, is an accomplished diplomat who has spent his career solving difficult problems in sub-Saharan countries. Maurice Hightower, black, is a prize-winning but controversial journalist who has spent his life exposing injustice in the United States. During a fact-finding trip to an African country that is sliding towards civil war, and where the U.S. government is accused of supporting the increasingly violent opposition, Hightower travels alone into the bush and then disappears. The dangerous assignment of finding the missing man and bringing him to safety falls to the U.S. Consul, Joe Kellerman. The Distance between Stars follows Kellerman's hunt for a man he does not admire, traces Hightower's pursuit of a truth that ever eludes him, and balances the costs each man must pay to find redemption for a life lived imperfectly. While the novel takes place in Africa, it is a uniquely American story.

## Reviews

"...a thoroughly authentic novel of Africa whose themes of race, privilege and what it means to be American ring true to anyone who has spent time on the continent. ...characters, descriptions and scenes are so believable, and the story so engaging, I felt like this book came directly from the newspaper front pages."
—Keith Richburg, former Africa bureau chief, *Washington Post*, and author of OUT OF AMERICA

"A finely-crafted, thoughtful, and timely novel. Authentic and compassionate in its story-telling, THE DISTANCE BETWEEN STARS marks Elzinga's debut as a writer to watch."
—Nickolas Butler, author of SHOTGUN LOVESONGS and LITTLE FAITH

# About the Author

**Jeff Elzinga** is the author of the novel *The Distance Between Stars*, which was a finalist for the Midwest Book Award. Elzinga has had the good fortune of enjoying two rewarding careers, one as an American diplomat in Africa, and the second as a university professor in Wisconsin. *Pigeon Falls* is his second novel.

Learn more at jeffelzinga.com

9 781952 526213